SORROW

AND

BLISS

SORROW
AND
BLISS

A Novel

MEG
MASON

HARPER

An Imprint of HarperCollinsPublishers

SORROW AND BLISS. Copyright © 2021 by Meg Manson. All rights reserved. Printed in the United States of America. No part of this book may be used or reproduced in any manner whatsoever without written permission except in the case of brief quotations embodied in critical articles and reviews. For information, address HarperCollins Publishers, 195 Broadway, New York, NY 10007.

HarperCollins books may be purchased for educational, business, or sales promotional use. For information, please email the Special Markets Department at SPsales@harpercollins.com. Originally published in Australia in 2020 by Fourth Estate.

FIRST U.S. EDITION

Library of Congress Cataloging-in-Publication Data has been applied for.

ISBN 978-0-06-304958-1

21 22 23 24 25 LSC 10 9 8 7 6 5 4 3 2 1

To my parents, and my husband

AT A WEDDING shortly after our own, I followed Patrick through the dense crowd at the reception to a woman who was standing by herself.

He said that instead of looking at her every five minutes and feeling sad I should just go over and compliment her hat.

"Even if I don't like it?"

He said obviously, Martha. "You don't like anything. Come on."

The woman had accepted a canapé from a waiter and was putting it in her mouth when she noticed us, realizing in the same instant that it could not be managed in one bite. As we approached, she lowered her chin and tried to shield her effort to get it all the way in, then all the way out, with the empty glass and supply of cocktail napkins in her other hand. Although Patrick drew out his introduction, she responded with something neither of us could make out. Because she looked so embarrassed, I began speaking as though somebody had given me one minute on the topic of ladies' hats.

The woman gave a series of little nods and then as soon as she could, asked us where we lived and what we did with ourselves and, if she was correct in thinking we were married, how long had we been and how was it we'd come to know each other in the first place, the quantity and velocity of her questions meant to divert attention from the half-eaten thing now sitting on an oily napkin in her upturned palm. While I was answering, she looked furtively past me for somewhere to put it; when I had finished, she said she might have missed my meaning, in saying Patrick and I had never actually met, he was "always just there."

I turned to consider my husband, at that moment trying to fish an invisible object out of his glass with one finger, then looked back at the woman and said Patrick's sort of like the sofa that was in your house growing up. "Its existence was just a fact. You never wondered where it came from because you can't remember it not being there."

"Although I suppose," I went on because the woman didn't move to say anything, "if pressed, you would be able to list every single one of its imperfections. And the causes thereof."

Patrick said it was unfortunately true. "Martha could definitely give you an inventory of my flaws."

The woman laughed, then glanced briefly at the handbag hanging from her forearm by its little strap, as if weighing its merits as a receptacle.

"Right, who needs a top-up?" Patrick pointed both index fingers at me and pumped invisible triggers with his thumbs. "Martha, I know you won't say no." He gestured at the woman's glass and she let him take it. Then he said, "Would you like me to take that too?" She smiled and looked like she was about to cry as he relieved her of the canapé.

Once he had gone she said, "You must feel so lucky, being married to a man like that." I said yes and thought about explaining the drawbacks of being married to somebody who everybody thinks is nice, but instead I asked her where she got her amazing hat and waited for Patrick to come back.

The sofa became our stock answer to the question of how we met. We did it for eight years, with few variations. People always laughed.

*

There is a GIF called "Prince William asking Kate if she wants another drink." My sister texted it to me once. She said "I am crying!!!!" They are at some kind of reception. William is wearing a tuxedo. He waves at Kate across the room, mimes the up-ending of a glass, then points at her with one finger.

"The pointing thing," my sister said. "Literally Patrick tho."

I wrote back, "Figuratively Patrick tho."

She sent me the eye-roll emoji, the champagne flute, and the pointing finger.

The day I moved back in with my parents, I found it again. I have watched it 5,000 times.

*

My sister's name is Ingrid. She is fifteen months younger than me and married to a man she met by falling over in front of his house while he was putting his recycling bins out. She is pregnant with her fourth child; when she texted to say it was another boy, she sent the eggplant emoji, the cherries, and the open scissors. She said "Hamish is non-figuratively getting the snip."

Growing up, people thought we were twins. We were desperate to dress alike, but our mother said no. Ingrid said, "Why can't we?"

"Because people will think it's my idea." She looked around the room we were in at the time. "None of this was my idea."

Later, when we were both in the grip of puberty, our mother said that since Ingrid was evidently getting all the bust, we could only hope I'd end up with the brains. We asked her which was better. She said it was better to have both or neither; one without the other was invariably lethal.

My sister and I still look alike. Our jaws are similarly too square but according to our mother we somehow get away with it. Our hair has the same tendency towards stragglyness, has generally always been long, and was the same blondish color until I turned thirty-nine and realized in the morning that I could not stop forty from coming. In the afternoon, I got it cut to too-square jaw-length, then went home and bleached it with supermarket dye. Ingrid came over while I was doing it and used the rest. Both of us struggled with its upkeep. Ingrid said it would have been less work just to have another baby.

I have known since I was young that, although we are so similar, people think Ingrid is more beautiful than I am. I told my father once. He said, "They might look at her first. But they'll want to look at you for longer."

*

In the car on the way home from the last party Patrick and I went to, I said, "When you do that pointing thing it makes me want to shoot you with an actual gun." My voice was dry and mean and I hated it—and Patrick when he said, "Great, thanks" with no emotion at all.

"I don't mean in the face. More like a warning shot in the knee or somewhere that you could still go to work."

He said good to know and put our address into Google Maps.

We had lived in the same house in Oxford for seven years. I pointed that out. He didn't say anything and I looked across at him in the driver's seat, waiting calmly for a break in the traffic. "Now you're doing the jaw thing."

"I know what, Martha. How about we don't talk until we get home." He took his phone out of the bracket and closed it silently into the glove box.

I said something else, then leaned forward and put the heater on to its highest setting. As soon as the car became stifling, I turned it off and lowered my window all the way. It was crusted with ice and made a scraping noise as it went down.

It used to be a joke between us, that in everything I swing between extremes and he lives his entire life on the middle setting. Before I got out, I said, "That orange light is still on." Patrick told me he was planning to get oil the next day, turned off the car, and went into the house without waiting for me.

*

We took the house on a temporary lease, in case things didn't work out and I wanted to go back to London. Patrick had suggested Oxford because it is where he went to university and he thought that, compared to other places, commuter towns in the home counties, I might find it easier to make friends. We extended the lease by six months, fourteen times, as though things could not work out at any moment.

The letting agent told us it was an Executive Home, in an Executive Development, and therefore perfect for us—even though neither of us are executives. One of us is a specialist in intensive care. One of us writes a funny food column for Waitrose magazine and has googled "Kate Moss rehab which one?" while her husband is at work.

In physical terms, the Executive nature of it manifested as expanses of taupe carpet and a multitude of non-standard sockets and, to me, as a permanent sense of unease whenever I was there alone. A box room on the top floor was the only room that did not make me feel like there was someone behind me because it was small and there was a plane tree out the window. In summer it obscured the view of identical Executive Homes on the other side of the cul-de-sac. In autumn, dead leaves blew inside and mitigated the carpet. The box room was where I worked even though, as I was often reminded by strangers in social settings, writing is something I can do anywhere.

The editor of my funny food column would send me notes saying "not getting this ref" and "rephrase if poss." He used Track Changes. I pressed Accept, Accept, Accept. After he had taken out all the jokes, it was just a food column. According to LinkedIn, my editor was born in 1995.

*

The party we were coming home from was for my fortieth birthday. Patrick planned it because I had told him that I wasn't in the right place, re celebrating.

He said, "We have to attack the day."

"Do we."

We listened to a podcast on the train once, sharing the same headphones. Patrick had folded his sweater into a pillow so I could put my head on his shoulder. It was the Archbishop of Canterbury on Desert Island Discs. He told a story about losing his first child in a car crash a long time ago.

The presenter asked him how he coped with it now. He said that when it comes to the anniversary, Christmas, her birthday, he had learned that you have to attack the day, "so it doesn't attack you."

Patrick seized on the principle. He started saying it all the time. He said it while he was ironing his shirt before the party. I was on our bed watching Bake Off on my laptop, an old episode I had seen before. A contestant takes someone else's Baked Alaska out of the fridge and it melts in the tin. It made the front page of the papers: a saboteur in the Bake Off tent.

Ingrid texted me when it first aired. She said she would go to her grave knowing that Baked Alaska had been taken out on purpose. I said I was on the fence. She sent me all the cake emojis and the police car.

When he had finished ironing, Patrick came and sat seminext to me on the bed and watched me watching. "We have to—"

I hit the space bar. "Patrick, I don't really think we should co-opt Bishop Whoever in this case. It's only my birthday. Nobody has died."

"I was just trying to be positive."

"Okay." I hit the space bar again.

After a moment he told me it was nearly quarter to. "Should

you start getting ready? I'd like to be the first ones there. Martha?"

I closed the computer. "Can I wear what I'm wearing?" Leggings, a Fair Isle cardigan, I can't remember what underneath. I looked up and saw that I had hurt him. "I'm sorry, I'm sorry, I'm sorry. I'll get changed."

Patrick had hired the upstairs part of a bar we used to go to. I did not want to be the first ones there, unsure if I should sit or stand while I waited for people to arrive, wondering if anybody was going to, then feeling awkward on behalf of the person who had the misfortune of being first. I knew that my mother would not be there because I told Patrick not to invite her.

Forty-four people came in units of two. After the age of thirty, it is always even numbers. It was November and freezing. Everyone took a long time to give up their coats. They were mostly Patrick's friends. I had lost touch with my own, from school and university and all the jobs I have had since, one by one as they had children and I didn't and there was nothing left for us to talk about. On the way to the party, Patrick said if anyone did start telling me a story about their children, maybe I could try and look interested.

They stood around and drank Negronis—2017 was "the year of the Negroni"—and laughed very loudly and made impromptu speeches, one speaker stepping forward from each group like representatives of a team. I found an ambulant toilet and cried in it.

Ingrid told me fragapane phobia is the fear of birthdays. It was the fun fact from the peel-off strip from sanitary pads, which she says are her chief source of intellectual stimulation at this point, the only reading she gets time for. She said, in her speech, "We all know Martha is an amazing listener, especially if she's the one talking." Patrick had something written on index cards.

There wasn't a single moment when I became the wife I am, although if I had to choose one, my crossing the room and asking my husband not to read out whatever was on those cards would be a contender.

An observer to my marriage would think I have made no effort to be a good or better wife. Or, seeing me that night, that I must have set out to be this way and achieved it after years of concentrated effort. They could not tell that for most of my adult life and all of my marriage I have been trying to become the opposite of myself.

*

The next morning I told Patrick I was sorry for all of it. He had made coffee and carried it out to the living room but hadn't touched it when I came into the room. He was sitting at one end of the sofa. I sat down and folded my legs underneath me. Facing him, the posture felt beseeching and I put one foot back on the floor.

"I don't mean to be like this." I made myself put my hand on his. It was the first time I had touched him on purpose in five months. "Patrick, honestly, I can't help it."

"And yet somehow you manage to be so nice to your sister." He shook my hand off and said he was going out to buy a newspaper. He didn't come back for five hours.

I am still forty. It is the end of winter, 2018, no longer the year of the Negroni. Patrick left two days after the party.

My FATHER IS a poet called Fergus Russell. His first poem was published in The New Yorker when he was nineteen. It was about a bird, the dying variety. After it came out, someone called him a male Sylvia Plath. He got a notable advance on his first anthology. My mother, who was his girlfriend then, is purported to have said, "Do we need a male Sylvia Plath?" She denies it but it is in the family script. No one gets to revise it after it is written. It was also the last poem my father ever published. He says she hexed him. She denies that too. The anthology remains forthcoming. I don't know what happened to the money.

My mother is the sculptor Celia Barry. She makes birds, the menacing, oversized variety, out of repurposed materials. Rake heads, appliance motors, things from the house. Once, at one of her shows, Patrick said, "I honestly think your mother has never met extant physical matter she couldn't repurpose." He was not being unkind. Very little in my parents' home functions according to its original remit.

Growing up, whenever my sister and I overheard her say to someone "I am a sculptor," Ingrid would mouth the line from that Elton John song. I would start laughing and she would keep going with her eyes closed and her fists pressed against her chest until I had to leave the room. It has never stopped being funny.

According to The Times my mother is minorly important. Patrick and I were at the house helping my father rearrange his study the day the notice appeared. She read it aloud to the three of us, laughing unhappily at the minorly bit. Afterwards my father said he'd take any degree of importance at this stage. "And they've given you a definite article. The sculptor Celia Barry. Spare a thought for we the indefinites."

*

Sometimes Ingrid gets one of her children to ring and talk to me on the phone because, she says, she wants them to have a very close relationship with me, and also it gets them off her balls for literally five seconds. Once, her eldest son called and told me there was a fat lady at the post office and his favorite cheese is the one that comes in the bag and is sort of whitish. Ingrid texted me later and said, "He means cheddar."

I do not know when he will stop calling me Marfa. I hope never.

*

Our parents still live in the house we grew up in, on Goldhawk Road in Shepherd's Bush. They bought it the year I turned ten with a deposit lent to them by my mother's sister Winsome, who married money instead of a male Sylvia Plath. As children, they lived in a flat above a key-cutting shop in, my mother tells people, "a depressed seaside town, with a depressed seaside mother." Winsome is older by seven years. When their mother died suddenly of an indeterminate kind of cancer and their father lost interest in things, in particular them, Winsome withdrew from the Royal College of Music to come back and look after my mother, who was thirteen then. She has never had a career. My mother is minorly important.

*

It was Winsome who found the Goldhawk Road house and arranged for my parents to pay much less for it than it was worth, because it was a deceased estate and, my mother said, based on the whiff, the body was still somewhere under the carpet.

On the day we moved in, Winsome came over to help clean the kitchen. I went in to get something and saw my mother sitting at the table drinking a glass of wine and my aunt, in a tabard and rubber gloves, standing on the top rung of a stepladder wiping out the cupboards.

They stopped talking, then started again when I left the room. I stood outside the door and heard Winsome telling my mother that perhaps she ought to try and muster up a suggestion of gratitude since home ownership was generally beyond the reach of a sculptor and a poet who doesn't produce any poetry. My mother did not speak to her for eight months.

Then, and now, she hates the house because it is narrow and dark; because the only bathroom opens off the kitchen via a slatted door, which requires Radio Four to be on at high volume whenever anyone is in there. She hates it because there is only one room on each floor and the staircase is very steep. She says she spends her life on those stairs and that one day she'll die on them.

She hates it because Winsome lives in a townhouse in Belgravia. Enormous, on a Georgian square and, my aunt tells people, the better side of it because it keeps the light into the afternoon and has a nicer aspect onto the private garden. The house was a wedding present from my uncle Rowland's parents, renovated for a year prior to their moving in and regularly ever since, at a cost my mother claims to find immoral.

Although Rowland is intensely frugal, it is only as a hobbyist—he has never needed to work—and only in the minutiae. He bonds the remaining sliver of soap to the new bar but Winsome is allowed to spend a quarter of a million pounds on Carrara marble in a single renovation and buy pieces of furniture that are described, in auction catalogues, as "significant."

*

In choosing a house for us solely on the basis of its bones—my mother said, not the ones we were guaranteed to find if we lifted the carpet—Winsome's expectation was that we would improve it over time. But my mother's interest in interiors never extended beyond complaining about them as they were. We had come from a rented flat in a suburb much farther out and did not have enough furniture for rooms above the first floor. She made no effort to acquire any and they remained empty for a long time until my father borrowed a van and returned with flat-pack bookshelves, a small sofa with brown corduroy covers, and a birch table that he knew my mother would not like but, he said, they were only a stopgap until he got the anthology out and the royalties started crashing in. Most of it is still in the house, including the table, which she calls our only genuine antique. It has been moved from room to room, serving various functions, and is presently my father's desk. "But no doubt," my mother says, "when I'm on my deathbed, I'll open my eyes for the last time and realize it is my deathbed."

Afterwards my father set out to paint the downstairs, at Winsome's encouragement, in a shade of terra-cotta called Umbrian Sunrise. Because he did not discriminate with his brush between wall, skirting board, window frame, light switch, power outlet, door, hinge, or handle, progress was initially swift. But my mother was beginning to describe herself as a conscientious objector where domestic matters were concerned. Eventually the work of cleaning and cooking and washing became solely his and he never finished. Even now, the hallway at Goldhawk Road is a tunnel of terra-cotta to midway. The kitchen is terra-cotta on three sides. Parts of the living room are terra-cotta to waist height.

Ingrid cared about the state of things more than I did when we were young. But neither of us cared much that things that broke were never repaired, that the towels were always damp and rarely changed, that every night my father cooked chops on a sheet of tin foil laid over the piece from the night before, so that the bottom of the oven gradually became a mille-feuille of fat and foil. If she ever cooked, my mother made exotic things without recipes, tagines and ratatouilles distinguishable from each other only by the shape of the pepper pieces, which floated in liquid tasting so bitterly of tomato that in order to swallow a mouthful I had to close my eyes and rub my feet together under the table.

*

Patrick and I were a part of each other's childhoods; there was no need for us, newly coupled, to share the particulars of our early lives. It became an ongoing competition instead. Whose was worse?

I told him, once, that I was always the last one picked up from birthday parties. So late, the mother would say, I wonder if I should give your parents a ring. Replacing the receiver after a period of minutes, she would tell me not to worry, we could try again later. I became part of the tidying up, then the family supper, leftover cake. It was, I told Patrick, excruciating. At my own parties, my mother drank.

He stretched, pretending to limber up. "Every single birthday party I had between the ages of seven and eighteen was at school. Thrown by Master. The cake came from the drama department prop cupboard. It was plaster of Paris." He said, good game though.

*

Mostly, Ingrid rings me when she is driving somewhere with the children because, she says, she can only talk properly when everyone is restrained and, in a perfect world, asleep; the car is basically a giant pram at this point. A while ago, she called to tell me she had just met a woman at the park who said she and her husband had separated and now had half-half custody of their children. The handover took place on Sunday mornings, the woman told her, so they both had one weekend day each on their own. She had started going to the cinema by herself on Saturday nights and had recently discovered that her ex-husband goes by himself on Sunday nights. Often it turns out they have chosen to see the same film. Ingrid said the last time it was X-Men: First Class. "Martha, literally have you ever heard anything more depressing? It's like, just go the fuck together. You will both be dead soon."

Throughout childhood our parents would separate on a roughly biannual basis. It was always anticipated by a shift in atmosphere that would occur usually overnight and even if Ingrid and I never knew why it had happened, we knew instinctively that it was not wise to speak above a whisper or ask for anything or tread on the floorboards that made a noise, until our father had put his clothes and typewriter into a laundry basket and moved into the Hotel Olympia, a bed and breakfast at the end of our road.

My mother would start spending all day and all night in her repurposing shed at the end of the garden, while Ingrid and I stayed in the house by ourselves. The first night, Ingrid would drag her bedding into my room and we would lie listening to the sound of metal tools being dropped on the concrete floor and the whining, discordant folk music our mother worked to, carrying in through our open window.

During the day she would sleep on the brown sofa that Ingrid and I had been asked to carry out for that purpose. And despite a permanent sign on the door that said "GIRLS: before knocking, ask self—is something on fire?," before school I would go in and collect dirty plates and mugs and, more and more, empty bottles so that Ingrid wouldn't see them. For a long time, I thought it was because I was so quiet that my mother did not wake up.

I do not remember if we were scared, if we thought this time it was real, our father was not coming back, and we would naturally acquire phrases like "my mum's boyfriend" and "I left it at my dad's," using them as easily as classmates who claimed to love having two Christmases. Neither of us confessed to being worried. We just waited. As we got older, we began to refer to them as The Leavings.

Eventually our mother would send one of us down to the hotel to get him because, she said, this whole thing was bloody ridiculous even though, invariably, it would have been her idea. Once my father got back, she would kiss him up against the sink, my sister and I watching, mortified, as her hand found its way up the back of his shirt. Afterwards it wouldn't be referred to except jokingly. And then there would be a party.

*

All of Patrick's sweaters have holes in the elbows, even ones that aren't very old. One side of his collar is always inside the neck, the other side over it and, despite constant retucking, an edge of shirt always finds its way out at the back. Three days after he has a haircut, he needs a haircut. He has the most beautiful hands I have ever seen.

*

Apart from her recurrent throwing-out of our father, parties were our mother's chief contribution to our domestic life, the thing that made us so willing to forgive her inadequacies compared to what we knew of other people's mothers. They overflowed the house, bled from Friday nights into Sunday mornings, and were populated by what our mother described as West London's artistic elite, though the only credential for getting in seemed to be a vague association with the arts, a tolerance for marijuana smoke, and/or possession of a musical instrument.

Even when it was winter, with all the windows open, the house would be hot and heaving and full of sweet smoke. Ingrid and I were not excluded or made to go to bed. All night, we made our way in and out of rooms, pushing through throngs of people— men who wore tall boots or boiler suits and women's jewelry, and women who wore petticoats as dresses over dirty jeans, Doc Marten boots. We were not trying to get anywhere, only as close to them as possible.

If they told us to come over and talk to them, we tried to sparkle in conversation. Some treated us like adults, others laughed at us when we were not meaning to be funny. When they needed an ashtray, another drink, when they wanted to know where the pans were because they had decided to fry eggs at three a.m., Ingrid and I fought each other for the job.

Eventually my sister and I would fall asleep, never in our beds but always together, and wake up to the mess and the murals spontaneously painted on bits of wall that had not been Umbrian Sunrised. The last one ever conceived is still there, on a wall in the bathroom, faded but not enough so that you can avoid studying the foreshortened left arm of the central nude from the shower. When we first saw it, Ingrid and I feared it was our mother, painted from life.

Our mother who, on those nights, drank wine out of the bottle, plucked cigarettes from people's mouths, blew smoke at the ceiling, laughed with her head tipped back, and danced by herself. Her hair was still long then, still a natural color, and she was not fat yet. She wore slips and scraggy fox furs, black stockings, no shoes. There was, briefly, a silk turban.

Generally speaking, my father would be in the corner of the room talking to one person; occasionally, holding a glass of something and reciting The Rime of the Ancient Mariner in regional accents to a small but appreciative crowd. Either way, he would give up and join my mother as soon as she started dancing because she kept calling him until he did.

He would try to follow her lead and catch her when she had spun herself beyond standing up. And he was so much taller than her—that is what I remember, he looked so tall.

I had no way to describe the way my mother looked, how she seemed to me then, except to wonder if she was famous. Everyone drew back to watch her dance, despite the fact that it was only spinning, wrapping her arms around her own body, or waving them above her head like she was trying to imitate the movement of seaweed.

Worn out, she would sag into my father's arms but seeing us at the edge of the circle, say, "Girls! Girls, come here!" excited again. Ingrid and I would refuse but only once because when we were dancing with them, we felt adored by our tall father and funny, falling-over mother and adored, as the four of us, by the people who were watching, even if we didn't know who they were.

Looking back, it is unlikely our mother knew them either—the object of her parties seemed to be filling the house with extraordinary strangers and being extraordinary in front of them, and not a person who used to live above a key-cutter. It was not enough to be extraordinary to the three of us.

*

For a while, when I lived in Oxford, my mother sent me short emails with nothing in the subject. The last one said, "I am being sniffed by the Tate lot." Ever since I left home, my father has posted me photocopies of things written by other people. Open and pressed down on the glass, the pages of the book look like gray butterfly wings, and the fat, dark shadow in the center like its body. I have kept them all.

The last one he sent was something by Ralph Ellison. With a colored pencil, he had highlighted a line that said, "The end is in the beginning and lies far ahead." Next to it, his tiny handwriting in the margin: "Perhaps there is something in that for you, Martha." Patrick had just left. I wrote across the top of the page, "The end is now and I can't remember the beginning, that is the whole point" and posted it back.

It came back days later. His only addition, "Might you try?"

I WAS SIXTEEN the year I met Patrick. 1977 + 16 = 1993. It was Christmas Day. He was standing in the black and white checkered foyer of my uncle and aunt's house with Oliver, their middle child, wearing full school uniform and holding a duffel bag. I had just had a shower and was coming down to help set the table before we left for church.

My family never spent Christmas anywhere other than Belgravia. Winsome required us to stay the night on Christmas Eve because she said it made things more festive. And, she didn't say, it meant there would be no issues with lateness on the day—the four of us arriving at eleven-thirty for breakfast that was scheduled for eight a.m. BST, my mother would say, Belgravia Standard Time.

Ingrid and I slept on the floor in my cousin Jessamine's room. She was Winsome's late-in-life baby, five years younger than Oliver, who used to call her The Accident when adults weren't around and The WS, Wonderful Surprise, when they were, until he grew up enough to realize he was also a surprise—his older brother Nicholas is adopted.

He is the same age as me and was called something else when they got him. His origins were never discussed, beyond being referred to as his origins. But I have heard my uncle say, in his son's earshot, that when it comes to adopting babies in Britain, you can have any color you like as long as it's brown. I have heard Nicholas say, to his father's face, "If only you and Mum had ground away at it a bit longer you'd just have your two white ones." He was already going off the rails by Patrick's first year with us and has never got back on them.

Oliver and Patrick were both thirteen, at boarding school together in Scotland. Patrick had been there since he was seven. Oliver, who had been there a term, was meant to arrive on Christmas Eve but had missed his flight and been put on an overnight train. Rowland went to Paddington to pick him up in the black Daimler that my mother called the Twatmobile and came back with both of them.

As I was coming down the stairs, I saw my uncle, still in his coat, telling his son off for bringing a friend to bloody Christmas without bloody asking. I stopped halfway down and watched. Patrick was holding the hem of his sweater, rolling and unrolling it while Rowland was talking.

Oliver said, "I told you already. His dad forgot to book his ticket home. What was I meant to do, leave him at school with Master?"

Rowland said something sharp under his breath, then turned to Patrick. "What I want to know is what kind of father forgets to book his own son a flight home at Christmas. To bloody Singapore."

Oliver said bloody Hong Kong.

Rowland ignored him. "What about your mother?"

"He doesn't have one." Oliver looked at Patrick who kept going on his sweater, unable to say anything.

Slowly, Rowland unwound his scarf and once he'd hung it up, told Oliver that his mother was in the kitchen. "I suggest you go and make yourself useful. And"—turning to Patrick—"you, what did you say your name was?"

He said, "Patrick Friel, sir" in a way that made it sound like a question.

"Well you, Patrick Friel sir, can skip the waterworks since you are here now. And put your bloody bag down." He told Patrick he could call him and Oliver's mother Mr. and Mrs. Gilhawley, then stalked off.

I started walking down the stairs again. They both looked up at me at the same time. Oliver said, "That's my cousin Martha blah blah," grabbed Patrick's sleeve and pulled him towards the staircase that went down to the kitchen.

*

Months earlier, Margaret Thatcher had moved into a townhouse on the other side of the square. Winsome worked it naturally and unnaturally into every conversation and on Christmas Day, it was mentioned twice at breakfast and again as we were getting ready to walk to the church at the top of the square, towards a corner that made it nearer my uncle and aunt's house than the prime minister's.

What people notice, then eventually stop noticing about my aunt, is that whenever she is addressing a topic of importance, she speaks with her chin lifted and her eyes closed. At her crux, they spring open and bulge enormously as if she has been shocked awake. Ending, she sucks air into flared nostrils and holds it for a period that becomes worrying, before slowly expelling it. In the instance of Margaret Thatcher, my aunt always opened her eyes at the point of saying our lady prime minister had chosen "the less good side." It infuriated my mother, who wondered aloud on the way to church why it might be that, instead of walking straight there, Winsome was leading us around three sides of the square.

*

Before lunch I got changed into a Mickey Mouse sweatshirt and black bicycle shorts and came into the dining room with bare feet—I remember because when we were finding our places Winsome told me that I had time to go upstairs and change back since Lycra clothing wasn't really de rigueur at the Christmas table and perhaps I'd like to pop shoes on while I was up there. My mother said, "Yes Martha, what if Mrs. Thatcher is trotting across from the less good side of the square as we speak? Then where will we be?" She took a glass of wine from Rowland.

Watching her empty it, he said, "By God, Celia, it's not bloody medicine. At least look like you're enjoying it."

She was enjoying it. Ingrid and I were not. At home, at parties, our mother's drinking had always been a source of amusement to us. It was becoming less so now that we were older, and she was older, and her drinking was no longer dependent on there being interesting people in the house or any people at all. And it had never been amusing at Belgravia, where my uncle and aunt drank in a way that did not produce a change in mood, and Ingrid and I learned that bottles could be recorked and put away and glasses left on the table unfinished. That day, which ended with Winsome on her hands and knees on the floor next to our mother's chair, dabbing wine out of the carpet, it embarrassed us. Our mother embarrassed us.

Once we were all seated and Winsome started the platters going, requisite left around the table, Rowland, at the adults' end, asked Patrick, at the children's end, if he was of ethnic extraction.

Oliver said, "Dad, you can't ask someone that."

Rowland said, "Evidently you can, since I just did," and looked pointedly back at Patrick who obediently replied, saying his father was born in America but he is actually Scottish, and his mother was—his voice wavered at that point—his mother was British Indian.

In that case, my uncle said, it was peculiar that Patrick spoke with a smarter accent than his own sons if neither of his parents were English. Nicholas said oh my God under his breath and was asked to leave the room but didn't. In his critical years, my mother told us once, both Winsome and Rowland lacked follow-through when it came to their eldest son, a position that surprised Ingrid and me because she did not discipline us at all.

With forced brightness, Winsome asked Patrick his parents' names. He said his father was called Christopher Friel and, almost inaudibly, that his mother's name was Nina. Rowland began peeling bits of skin off the slices of turkey my aunt had arranged on his plate, feeding them one by one to the whippet sitting at his feet, which he had acquired weeks earlier and named Wagner. Unfortunately, people only got the joke if he explained it, the German pronunciation vs. the spelling. Often he had to write it down and show them. Appearing at breakfast that morning, my mother said she would have preferred to listen to the entire Ring Cycle performed by an amateur violinist than the dog's whining all night in the crate.

To Rowland's next question of what his father did, Patrick said he worked for a European bank but he couldn't remember which one, sorry. My uncle took a large swallow of whatever was in his glass, then said, "Tell us then, what befell your mother?"

The platters had finished going around but nobody had started eating because of the conversation being had from opposite ends of the table. Working hard not to cry, Patrick explained that she had drowned in a hotel pool when he was seven. Rowland said bad luck and shook out his napkin, indicating that the interview was over. Immediately, Oliver and Nicholas picked up their cutlery and began eating like a starter's pistol had just gone off, with their heads bowed, left arm circled around their plate as if defending it from theft while they shoveled food in with the fork in their right hand. Patrick ate the same way.

He was sent to boarding school a week after his mother's funeral. That is what kind of father manages to forget to book his own son a flight home.

A few minutes later, during a lull in the adults' conversation, Patrick stopped shoveling, raised his head and said, "My mother was a doctor." No one had asked him, then or earlier. He said it as if he'd forgotten, and just remembered.

I think, to prevent Rowland from reopening the topic or selecting a worse one, my father began to explain the Theseus Paradox to the whole table. It was, he said, a first-century philosophical conundrum: if a wooden ship has every single plank replaced during the voyage across the ocean, is it technically the same vessel when it gets to the other side? Or put another way, he went on, because none of us understood what he was talking about, "Is Rowland's current bar of soap the same one he purchased in 1980, or a different one entirely?"

At the end of lunch, Winsome invited us all to transition to the formal living room for "a little bit of opening." And, for Ingrid and me, a little bit of finding out that the money we lived on did not come from our parents.

Both of us, then, were at a school that was private and selective and single sex. I got a scholarship because, an older girl told me on my first day, I came number two in the exam and the number one girl had died in the holidays.

The uniform list was five pages long and double-sided. My mother read it out at the table, laughing in a way that made me nervous. "Winter socks, crested. Summer socks, crested. Sports socks, crested. Bathing suit, crested. Swim cap, crested. Sanitary towels, crested." She tossed it on the sideboard and said, "Martha, don't look like that, I'm joking. I'm sure you can use non-regulation pads."

Because she did not get a scholarship, our parents enrolled Ingrid at the high school near our house that was free and co-ed and offered female students two kinds of uniform, she told people, the normal one and the maternity one. But at the last minute our parents changed their minds and sent her to mine. My mother said she had sold a piece. Ingrid and I made a cake.

In the car, on our way to Belgravia that Christmas Eve, we had asked our mother why she didn't like Winsome, because she had spent the previous few hours refusing to get ready, issuing her annual threat of not coming whenever my father tried to chivy her along, only agreeing once there had been sufficient begging. She told us it was because Winsome was controlling and obsessed with appearances and, sister or not, she could not relate to someone whose twin passions were renovation and large group catering.

Even so, my mother always gave her extravagant presents— to everyone, but especially Winsome who would open hers just enough to see what was in it, then try to re-stick the tape, saying it was too much. Always, my mother would get up and leave the room aggrieved, and Ingrid would say something funny to make everything fine but instead, that year, she stayed where she was, threw up her hands and said, "Why, Winsome? Why are you never, ever grateful for things I buy you?"

My aunt looked deeply embarrassed, her eyes darting all over the room for anywhere to look. Rowland, who had just given her, per tradition, a Marks & Spencers voucher in the amount of £20, said, "Because it's our bloody money, Celia."

Ingrid and I were sharing the same armchair and found each other's hands. Hers felt hot, gripping mine, as we watched our mother struggle to her feet, saying, "Oh well Rowland, win some, lose some, I suppose." She laughed at her own joke all the way to the door.

As old as we were, it had never occurred to us that a blocked poet and a sculptor who was yet to achieve minorly important status would not earn anything and our crested swimsuits were, like everything else, paid for by my uncle and aunt. Once our mother was out of the room, Ingrid said to Winsome, "What is it? I'll have it as long as it's not a sculpture" and everything was fine.

*

It was the rule at Belgravia that children opened presents in ascending age order. Jessamine first, Nicholas and I last. As Oliver's turn approached, Winsome disappeared briefly and came back again with a present that, unnoticed by everyone except me, she put under the tree. A moment later, she retrieved it and said, "One for you, Patrick." He looked stunned. It was some kind of cartoon collection. Ingrid whispered "disappointing" when she saw what it was but I did not think I had ever seen a boy smile as hard as Patrick did when he looked up from opening it to thank my aunt.

How there was a present with his name on it even though no one knew he was coming remained a mystery to him until years later; we were packing to move to Oxford. Patrick found the book on a shelf and asked me if I remembered it. He said, "It was one of the best presents I got as a kid. No idea how Winsome knew to get it for me."

"It was from her emergency gift cupboard, Patrick."

He looked vaguely deflated but said, "Still," and stood reading it until I took it out of his hands.

*

Patrick returned the following year, this time by arrangement with Winsome, because his father had just got remarried—to a Chinese-American litigator called Cynthia—and was on his honeymoon. I was seventeen. Patrick was fourteen. I said hello when he appeared in the kitchen with Oliver; he stood near the door, doing the same rolling thing with the hem of his sweater while my cousin looked for whatever he had come in to find.

At some point that day, we all went up to Jessamine's room and sat on the unmade airbeds, except Nicholas, who went over to the window and took a cigarette out of his pocket, a roll-your-own that was loose and coming undone. Jessamine, who was nine, flapped her hands and started crying while he attempted to light it.

Ingrid said, "No one thinks you're cool, Nicholas," and got Jessamine to come sit between us. "It looks like a tea bag wrapped in toilet paper."

I offered to go and find him some sticky tape, then asked Jessamine if she wanted to see a trick. She nodded and let Ingrid wipe her face with the sleeve of her sweater. I had braces then and with everybody watching, I started moving my tongue around inside my cheek. A second later, I made my mouth into an O and one of my rubber bands shot out. It landed on the back of Patrick's hand. He looked at it uncertainly for a moment, then carefully picked it off.

At home later, Ingrid came into my room so we could lay out all our presents on the floor to see who had got more and divide them into Like and Don't Like piles, although we were getting too old for it. She told me she saw Patrick put the rubber band in his pocket when he thought no one was looking. "Because he loves you."

I told her that was gross. "He's a child."

"The age gap won't matter by the time you get married."

I pretended to throw up.

Ingrid said, "Patrick loves Martha," and took Hot Tracks '93 off my Don't Like pile and put it on my CD player.

That was the last Christmas before a little bomb went off in my brain. The end, hidden in the beginning.

ON THE MORNING of my French A level I woke up with no feeling in my hands and arms. I was lying on my back and there were already tears leaking from the corners of my eyes, running down my temples into my hair. I got up and went to the bathroom, and saw in the mirror that I had a deep purple circle, like a bruise, around my mouth. I could not stop shaking.

In the exam, I couldn't read the paper and sat staring at the first page until it was over, writing nothing. As soon as I got home, I went upstairs and got into the space under my desk and sat still like a small animal that instinctively knows it's dying.

I stayed there for days, coming down for food and the bathroom, and eventually just the bathroom. I could not sleep at night or stay awake during the day. My skin crawled with things I couldn't see. I acquired a terror for noise. Ingrid was constantly coming in and begging me to stop being weird. I told her to please, please, go away. Then I would hear her calling out from the hallway, "Mum, Martha's under her desk again."

My mother was sympathetic to begin with, bringing me glasses of water, trying to coax me to come downstairs in various ways. Then it started to annoy her and when Ingrid called out after that she would say, "Martha will come out when she wants to." She no longer came into my room, except once with the vacuum cleaner. She pretended not to notice me, but made a point of vacuuming around my feet. That is the only memory I have that involves my mother and any form of cleaning.

*

The Goldhawk Road parties were suspended at my father's behest. He told my mother, just until I was on the up. She said, "Who needs fun, I suppose," and subsequently cut her hair very short, and started dying it shades that do not appear in nature.

Supposedly, it was the stress of my illness that caused her to get fat. Ingrid says that if that is true, it is also my fault that she began wearing sack dresses; waistless, muslin or linen, invariably purple, layered over one another, so that their uneven hems fell around her ankles like corners of a tablecloth. She has not deviated from the style since, except for acquiring an additional layer for each additional stone. Now that she is essentially spherical, the impression is of many blankets thrown haphazardly over a birdcage.

Before I got ill, my mother's nickname for me was Hum because as a child I used to sing, one meandering, tuneless, made-up song that I started as soon as I woke up and continued until someone asked me to stop. The memories I have of it are mostly from other people—that I once sang about my love of tinned peaches for all of a six-hour drive to Cornwall, that I could be so affected by a song about a dog without a mother or a lost pencil, I made myself cry, so hard on one occasion I threw up in the bath.

In the only memory that is mine, I am in the garden sitting

on the unmown grass outside my mother's shed, singing about the splinter in my foot and her voice comes from inside and she is singing, "Come in here, Hum, and I will get it out for you." She stopped calling me Hum when I got sick, and began calling me Our Resident Critic.

Ingrid says she had always had bitch-like tendencies but it was me who really brought them out.

*

Last year, I got glasses that I do not need because the optometrist fell off his rolling stool during the eye-test. He looked so mortified I started reading the letters wrongly on purpose. They are in the glove box, still in the bag.

*

From the beginning, my father stayed up with me in the night, sitting on the floor, leaning against my bed. He offered to read me poetry and if I did not want him to, he talked about unrelated things in a very quiet voice, not requiring a response. He was never in his pyjamas, I think, because if he didn't change out of his clothes, we could pretend it was still just the evening and we were doing a normal thing.

But I knew he was worried and because I was so ashamed of what I was doing and, after a month, I did not know how to stop doing it, I let him take me to a doctor. On the way there, I lay down on the back seat.

The doctor asked my father some questions while I sat in the chair next to him looking at the floor, eventually saying that based on the fatigue, the pallor, the low mood, it was so likely to be glandular fever there was no point in a blood test. Likewise, there was nothing he could give me for it but, he said, some girls liked the idea of taking something, in which case, an iron tablet. He clapped his thighs and got up. At the door, he tipped his head at me as he said, to my father, "Evidently someone has been kissing boys."

On the way home my father stopped and bought me an ice cream, which I tried to eat but couldn't so that he had to hold the melting cone out the window for the rest of the drive. At the front door, he paused and said, instead of going straight back to my room, I could always come and have a rest in his study. It is the first room off the street. He said, for a change of scene, the scene being the space underneath my desk although he did not say so. He told me he had things to do—there didn't have to be any talking. I said yes because I knew he wanted me to and because I had just walked the short distance from the car and needed to sit down before taking the stairs up to my room.

I waited in the doorway while he cleared books and piles of paper off the brown sofa that had migrated inside again and was pushed against the wall under the front windows. Things slipped out of his arms because he was trying to do it so quickly, as though I might change my mind and leave if he took too long. Until then, I always thought I wasn't meant to go in there, but waiting, I realized it was only because my mother said why would anyone want to if they didn't have to? Out of all the rooms in the house, it was the one she hated most because, she said, it had an aura of unproductiveness.

Once he was finished, I went in and lay down on my side with my head on the sofa's low armrest, facing his desk. My father went around to his chair and adjusted a sheet of paper already in the typewriter, then he rubbed his palms together. Previously, whenever I heard the sound of his typing from another part of the house or passed his closed door on my way out, I imagined him in torment because he always looked drained when he emerged to cook chops. But as soon as he started pecking the keys with his index fingers, my father's face took on an expression of private bliss. Within a minute, he seemed to have forgotten I was there. I lay and watched him—stopping at the end of the line to read over whatever it was he'd just written, mouthing it silently to himself, usually smiling. Then, smacking the lever with his left hand so the carriage flew back to the margin, more palm rubbing, another line. The keys of his typewriter did not make a sharp crack so much as a dull thud. I was not agitated by the noise, only calmed to the point of drowsiness by the repetition of his process, and his presence—the feeling of being in a room with someone who did want to be alive.

*

I began to spend every day in there. After a while, I stopped lying down on the sofa and would sit and look out at the street instead. One day I found a pen between the seat cushions, and when my father noticed me drawing indifferently on my arm he got up and came over with some paper and a Shorter Oxford Dictionary. Perching next to me for a second, he wrote the alphabet down the left margin and told me to write a story in one sentence, using each letter in order. He said the dictionary was just to press on and went back to his desk.

I wrote hundreds of them. They are still somewhere in a box but I only remember one from that time because when I had finished it my father said it would one day be recognized as the high point of the oeuvre.

After
Barbara's
Contentious
Divorce,
Everyone
Felt
Genuinely
Hurt,
Including
Justifiably
Kin
Left
Melancholically
Noting
Or
Perhaps
Questioning
Rumors
Suggesting
That,
Unannounced,
Vincent'd

Wed an
uXorious
Young
Zimbabwean.

Sometimes still, when I can't sleep, I make them up in my mind. K is the hardest.

*

A friend of Ingrid's, who came over once when I was there, told me that the Headspace app had changed her life. I wanted to ask what her life had been like before and what it was like now.

*

I felt alright in September. My father and I decided I should start university. But I was only alright when I was in that room, with him. From the beginning, I couldn't last through an entire lecture. I missed whole days and then whole weeks. I began going back under my desk when I was at home. Towards the end of the term the dean put me on academic probation. He gave me a pamphlet on stress management and told me that I would need to make a good show in my exams if I decided to come back in January. I should use the holidays to have a serious think. Seeing me out of his office he said, "There's one of you in every cohort," and wished me a Merry Christmas.

*

On the highest floor of the Goldhawk Road house there is an iron balcony that we did not go onto because it was rusted out and coming loose from the wall. One night, in the holidays, I went out and stood on the grill floor in bare feet, staring over the rail to the long black rectangle of garden four stories below.

Everything hurt. The soles of my feet, my chest, my heart, my lungs, my scalp, my knuckles, my cheekbones. It hurt to talk, to breathe, to cry, to eat, to read, to hear music, to be in a room with other people, and to be by myself. I stayed there for a long time, feeling the balcony move sometimes according to the wind.

Normal people say, I can't imagine feeling so bad I'd genuinely want to die. I do not try and explain that it isn't that you want to die. It is that you know you are not supposed to be alive, feeling a tiredness that powders your bones, a tiredness with so much fear. The unnatural fact of living is something you must eventually fix.

*

This is the worst thing Patrick has ever said to me: "Sometimes I wonder if you actually like being like this."

*

Here are the reasons I went back inside. Because I did not want people to think my father was not a good parent. I did not want Ingrid to fail her exams. I did not want my mother to one day make art out of it.

But Patrick is the only person who knows the main reason

because it is the worst thing I have ever thought. I went back inside because, even as I was then, I thought I was too clever and special, better than anyone who would do what I had come out to do, I was not the one in every cohort. I went back inside because I was too proud.

Once, in my funny food column, I said that Parma ham had become pedestrian. After the magazine came out, a reader emailed me to say I came across as unpleasantly superior and she for one would continue to enjoy Parma ham. I printed it out and showed Patrick. He stood reading it with his arm around my shoulder, then pulled me in and said, his face turned down to the top of my head, "I'm glad."

I said, "That she's not going to give up ham?"

"That you're unpleasantly superior." He meant, since it is why you are still alive.

Probably, it is not the worst thing I have ever thought. But is in the top one hundred.

*

This is the worst thing Ingrid has ever said to me: "You've basically turned into Mum."

*

A few months ago, Ingrid called and told me about a kind of fade cream she had started using to get rid of a brown spot that had appeared on her face. On the back of the tube it said that it was suitable for most problem areas.

I asked her if she thought it would work on my personality.

She said maybe. "But it's not going to make it go away completely."

*

After that night on the balcony, I asked my father if I could see a different doctor. I told him what had happened. He was in the kitchen eating a boiled egg and stood up so quickly that his chair tipped over backwards. I let him hug me for what felt like a long time. Then he told me to wait while he found the list of other doctors he'd written on a pad that was somewhere in his study.

The doctor we chose from the list, because she was the only woman, slid a laminated questionnaire out of a standing file and started reading from it with a red whiteboard marker in her hand. The card was vaguely pink, from the marking and erasing of other people's answers. "How often do you feel sad for no reason, Martha? Always, sometimes, seldom, never?" She said, "Right, always," then as I answered each question after that, "Okay, always again; always for that one too; let me guess, always?"

She said at the end, "Well there's no need to score it then is there, I think we can safely assume . . ." and wrote a prescription for an antidepressant that was, she told us, "specially formulated for teenagers" as if it was a kind of acne cream.

My father asked her to elaborate as to how exactly this one differed from one formulated for adults. The doctor rolled her office chair towards him with a series of seated steps and dropped her voice. "It has a lesser effect on the libido."

My father looked pained and said, "Ah."

Still to him, the doctor said, "And I assume she is sexually active."

I wanted to run out of the room when she went on to explain, as quietly, that while the aforementioned libido would not be affected, I needed to take greater than usual precautions re accidental pregnancy because the medication was not safe for a developing fetus. She wished to be absolutely explicit on that point.

My father nodded and the doctor said, "Excellent," then walked her chair towards me and started speaking at a louder than normal volume, to reinforce the pretense that I wouldn't have been able to hear their exchange. She told me I was going to have a headache for two weeks, and possibly a dry mouth, but in a few weeks I would feel like the old Martha again.

She handed the prescription to my father and as we got up she asked if we had done all our Christmas shopping. She hadn't even started hers. It seems to come around faster every year.

Driving home, my father inquired if I was just crying in the usual way or for a specific reason.

I said, "The word fetus."

"Should I ask," his knuckles were white, gripping the wheel, "if she was right in assuming you are, in fact—"

"I'm not."

Parking in front of the chemist, he told me I didn't have to get out because he would be a mere moment.

*

The capsules were light brown and dark brown and because they were low dose, it was necessary for me to take six a day but essential that I built up to that number slowly, over the course of a fortnight; the doctor had wished to be absolutely explicit on that point too. Nevertheless, I decided to just start there and went into the bathroom as soon as we got home. Ingrid was already in there plucking her eyebrows. She paused and watched me try to put six tablets in my mouth at once. When they all fell out again, she said, "Hey, it's your old pal Cookie Monster," and mimed shoving them back in, saying "Me Cookie" over and over.

They felt like plastic in my mouth and left behind the taste of shampoo. I spat into the sink and went to leave but Ingrid asked me to stay for a bit. We climbed into the empty bath and lay at opposite ends with our legs pressed along each other's sides. She talked about normal things and did impressions of our mother. I wished I could laugh because she looked so sad when I didn't. Eventually she got out because she needed to check her brow work in the mirror and said, "Oh my God, why didn't you stop me?"

Still, every time I have to swallow a tablet, I think Me Cookie.

*

Out of Ingrid's sons, the middle one is my favorite because he is shy and anxious and ever since he could walk, a constant holder-on to things—handfuls of her skirt, his older brother's leg, the edge of tables. I have seen him reach up and hook the tips of his fingers into Hamish's pocket while they are walking next to each other, taking two steps to every one of his father's.

Putting him to bed once, I asked him why he liked having

something in his hand. At the time he was holding the strip of flannel he slept with.

He said, "I don't like it."

I asked him why he did it then.

"So I don't sink." He looked at me nervously, as if I might laugh at him. "My mum wouldn't be able to find me."

I told him I knew what that felt like, not wanting to sink. He held up the piece of flannel and asked me if I needed it; he would give it to me.

"I know you would but it's okay. Thank you. It's your lovely thing."

With the flannel still in his hand, he reached up gently, tugged the end of my hair until my face was very close to his and whispered, "I actually have two the same." If I changed my mind, I could tell him. He rolled onto his side and went to sleep with the fingers of his other hand curled around my thumb.

I HAD A headache for two weeks, and possibly a dry mouth. I still had the headache on Christmas Eve and told my mother that I didn't feel well enough to stay the night at Belgravia and I did not want to go the next day either.

The four of us were in the kitchen. We were already late, which was why my father was spreading pages of The Times Literary Supplement on the floor so he could polish his shoes, not the ones he was going to wear—all of his shoes—and my mother had just decided to have a bath, which was loudly filling next door. She was wearing a worn silk kimono that kept undoing itself. Each time, Ingrid, who was standing at the table wrapping presents quickly and badly, stopped and put her hands over her eyes, silently screaming like she had just been blinded in a factory explosion. I wasn't doing anything except sitting on a stepladder in the corner watching them all.

My mother went into the bathroom and came back with a laundry basket. I watched as she began packing the presents into it and vaguely heard her say that if we only went to Belgravia when we felt like it, she would have been there a total of once. I was distracted by the laundry basket because it was the one my father used when he moved to the Hotel Olympia.

I glanced at him, wiping brown polish off a black shoe with a tea towel. He had been leaving the house so rarely it was strange to see him making any kind of preparation to go out. Even when my mother told him to, or Ingrid begged him to drive her somewhere, he wouldn't. His reasons for refusing—that he was expecting a call from an editor, that he'd forgotten where he'd put his license—my mother found so specious, it was obvious he was trying to get out of helping her with us.

She said Martha. I blinked back at her. "Did you hear what I said?"

"I can just stay home by myself."

"Oh we'd all love to stay home by ourselves." She said she'd been denied that pleasure for months, with the briefest look at my father, and I wondered how it hadn't occurred to me until just then that since the night on the balcony, he had been making sure I was never, ever alone.

He looked extremely tired. My mother uncorked a bottle of wine and took it into the bathroom with her, flipping on the radio as she passed it.

*

Hours later, we got into the car and drove to Belgravia, the laundry basket full of presents on Ingrid's lap and my head on her shoulder. Winsome was the only one who had waited up for us. She was too furious to acknowledge my mother and only managed a crisp nod to my father. She kissed me and Ingrid, then told me that she'd made up a little bed on the sofa in the snug, which was what my cousins were required to call the TV room on the basement level, near the kitchen. She said, "Your father rang up this morning and said you've been poorly and wouldn't want to bunk in with the others," and now she'd seen me, I did look quite drawn.

I didn't come out in the morning. Nobody tried to make me. Ingrid brought me breakfast even though she knew I wouldn't eat it. She said I had to drink the tea.

I had been awake for hours, not feeling the sense of dread that seemed to precede consciousness or the consuming sadness that had accompanied it for so many months. In the dark, lying still, waiting for it, I had wondered if it was waking up in a different room.

After Ingrid went out I sat up and listened to the sound of voices from the kitchen and radio carols and my cousins thundering up the stairs and back down, Rowland's vibrato whistling as he passed the door and instead of terror, I felt reassured by the noise, even the sharp, isolated sounds of doors being closed too hard overhead and Wagner's demented barking. I wondered if I was better. I drank the tea.

Towards nine, the noise concentrated itself in the foyer, the shouting peaked and then the house fell into almost perfect silence. The only other person who hadn't gone to church, I knew when I heard the radio switch over from carols to a man's voice doing some sort of dramatic reading, was my father.

*

Jessamine knocked on the door soon after I heard them all come back. She was ten and dressed like one of the Queen's grandchildren. She was supposed to tell me lunch was ready and also supposed to tell me I didn't have to come and have any.

"Or"—she itched her tights—"if you want to eat in here, you are allowed and someone can bring it."

I said I didn't want anything. She went cross-eyed to indicate that I was insane and went out, leaving the door open.

I got up to close it. Patrick was hovering just outside. He was a foot taller than he had been the year before and said hello in a voice so unlike the one I was expecting, I laughed.

Embarrassed, he lowered his eyes. I was wearing the tracksuit bottoms and sweatshirt I had arrived in but I had taken my bra off and felt suddenly aware of it. I crossed my arms over my chest and asked him what he was doing. He said, fiddling with one cuff and then the other, that he was meant to be calling his father and Rowland had told him to use the phone in the snug but then Jessamine had just told him I was already in here.

"I can go out."

Patrick said it was fine, he could just go and find another one, then looked quickly in either direction as though checking for the sudden appearance of my uncle. I took a half-step to the side and he rushed in.

For a minute or two, he spoke to his father, in monosyllables. I waited outside the door until I heard him say goodbye. He was standing next to the phone table, staring blankly at a painting above it of a lion attacking a horse. A moment passed before he noticed me, apologizing for taking so long when he did. I thought he would leave then but he just stood there while I walked back to the sofa and sat down on the covers, crossed-legged, hugging a cushion in front of my chest and silently wishing for him to go so I could lie down again. Patrick stayed where he was. Because I could not think of another question I said, "How is school?"

"Good." He turned around, paused, then said, "Sorry you're sick."

I shrugged and pulled a thread out of the cushion seam. Although it was his third year with us, I could not remember talking to Patrick individually about something other than what time it was or where to put the plates he had brought down to the kitchen. But after another moment of him not leaving, I said, "You must miss your dad."

He smiled and nodded in a way that made it clear he didn't.

"Do you miss your mum?" As soon as I said it, his face changed, not towards an emotion I could name, more the absence of any. He moved over to the window, stood with his back turned and his hands by his sides, not speaking for such a long time that when he eventually said yeah it felt like it wasn't in reference to anything. His shoulders rose and fell with a heavy breath and I felt guilty that I had never considered how lonely he must be as the only unrelated person in the house, that having Christmas with someone else's family every year was less likely his preference than a source of shame.

I shifted a bit and said, "What was she like?"

He stayed at the window. "She was really nice."

"Do you remember specific things about her? If you were seven."

"Not really."

I pulled another thread out of the cushion. "That's sad."

Patrick finally turned around and said, quietly, that the only thing he did remember, which wasn't from a photo, was one time in the kitchen of the house they lived in before she died, he asked for an apple and as she was handing it to him she said do you need me to start it for you?

"I don't know why."

"How old were you?"

"Five or something."

I said, "You probably didn't have front teeth."

There isn't a name for the emotion that registered on his face then. It was all of them. Patrick left after that.

*

There was a café, a minute or two from the Executive Home, that I used to go to every morning. The barista was very young and looked like a non-specific famous person. One day I made a joke about it as he pressed the lid onto my coffee. He said something disappointingly flirtatious in response and by the end of the week I had entered into a mandatory banter relationship with him. It quickly became onerous and I started going to a café that was farther away, where the coffee was less good and where I did not have to talk.

*

Alone again, I got off the sofa and tried to find something to read. There was nothing except a Radio Times and a fully revised and updated edition of The Complete Whippet on the coffee table, and some sheet music on my aunt's writing desk.

I already knew that she had got into the Royal College of Music "at the tender age of sixteen" because, according to my mother, she would have whispered it over my crib. As such, it had never struck me as extraordinary. I had never thought about how she had managed it with a depressed seaside mother and a pointless father and no money. And, I realized, picking the music up and turning through the pages, astonished by the concentration of notes, that I had no memory of ever hearing her play. The grand piano in the formal living room I only thought of as something not to put drinks on.

While I was standing there, the door opened halfway and Winsome edged in with a tray. She was wearing an apron, wet with dishwater. I put the music down and apologized but as soon as she recognized what I had been holding, she looked delighted. I told her I had never seen such complicated music. She said it was just a bit of old Bach but seemed reluctant to turn the conversation to the topic of the tray and what was on it, only doing so once it became clear that I did not have anything else to say.

I went back to the sofa and sat down. It was, in her description, a little bit of leftovers, but once she had set the tray in my lap, I saw it was an entire Christmas lunch in miniature, arranged on an entrée plate, a linen napkin in a silver ring beside it, and a crystal glass of fizzy grape juice. My eyes filled with tears. Immediately, Winsome said I was under no obligation to eat it if I didn't feel like it. Since the summer, the sight of food had been unbearable to me but it was not why I could only stare at it. It was the care in my aunt's arrangement, the still-life beauty of it and, as I think about it now, the sense of safety that my brain construed from the child-sized portions.

My aunt said alright, well—perhaps she'd pop back later—and went to go.

As she got to the door, I heard myself say, "Stay."

Winsome wasn't my mother, but she was maternal—expressly not my mother—and I didn't want her to leave. She asked if there was something else I needed.

I said no, slowly, while trying to invent an alternative reason that would prevent her from going. "I was just wondering—before you came in, I was thinking about you getting into college. I was wondering who helped you."

She said, "No one helped me!" and charged softly back into the room after I picked up the tiny fork and speared a small potato and asked her how she did it in that case. Sitting in the space I tried to smooth out for her, Winsome began her story, undistracted by the fact that I was now eating the potato exactly the way her children weren't allowed to, off the end of the fork as if it was an ice cream.

She said she had taught herself to play on a piano in her school hall. Somebody had written the names of the notes in pencil on the keys and by the time she was twelve, she had finished all the grade books in the library and started sending away for sheet music. The Royal College of Music and its address on Prince Consort Road, London SW, was always printed on the back and she became, over time, desperate to see the place her music came from. At fifteen, she went to London on her own, intending only to stand in front of the building until her return train. But the sight of the students coming in and out, dressed in black, carrying instrument cases, made her jealous to the point of feeling sick and, somehow, she roused herself to go inside and ask the person on the front desk if anyone could apply. She was given a form, which she filled out at home that night, in pencil before pen and, two weeks later, she received an invitation to audition.

I interrupted and asked how she could prove what level she was, if she hadn't done any exams.

My aunt closed her eyes, lifted her chin, took a deep breath and said as her eyes sprung open, "I lied." Her exhale was glorious.

On the day, she played flawlessly. But afterwards the examiners asked her to produce her certificates and she confessed. "Anticipating arrest, but," Winsome said, "they gave me a place on the spot, as soon as they discovered I had never had a lesson." She brought her hands together and placed them one over the other in her lap.

I put my fork down. "If I came out, would you play something?"

She said she was far too rusty, but was instantly on her feet and whisking the tray off my lap.

I got up and asked her if she needed the music on the desk. My aunt laughed and ushered me out.

*

From where she told me to sit, I watched her open the lid of the piano, adjust the stool, then lift her hands, soft wrists rising before her fingers, and hover them there for some seconds before letting them fall onto the keys. From the first devastating bar of whatever it was she was playing, the others began drifting into the room one by one, even the boys, even my mother.

Nobody said anything. The music was extraordinary. The sensation was physical, like warm water being washed over a wound, agonizing and cleansing and curative. Ingrid came in and wedged herself into my chair, as Winsome was entering a section that got faster and faster until it no longer seemed like the music was being manufactured by her. My sister said holy shit. A series of violent chords followed by a sudden slowing down seemed to signal the end but instead of stopping, my aunt melted the final bars in to the beginning of O Holy Night.

My perception of Winsome belonged to my mother—I thought of her as old, punctilious, someone without an interior life or worthwhile passions. That was the first time I saw her for myself. Winsome was an adult, someone who took care, who loved order and beauty and labored to create it as a gift to other people. She lifted her eyes to the ceiling and smiled. She was still wearing her wet apron.

The first person to say anything aloud was Rowland, who had come in last and was standing in front of the fireplace with his elbow on the mantel like someone posing for a full-length portrait in oil. He called out for something a bit bloody cheerier and Winsome took a brisk turn into Joy to the World.

My mother stopped it by singing—a different song that my aunt could not follow her into because she was making it up. Her voice got higher and higher until Winsome improvised an ending and took her hands away from the piano, saying it was probably time for the Queen. But, according to my mother, we were all having fun. "And," she said, "I need to tell all of you, please, that when she was a teenager, my sister here was so convinced she was going to be famous, she used to practice with her head turned to the side—didn't you Winnie?—in preparation for when you'd have to play while gazing out at your vast audience." Winsome tried to laugh before Rowland said right, and ordered everyone born after the coronation to make themselves scarce, unnecessarily since Ingrid, my cousins, and Patrick had started evacuating during my mother's speech. I got up and walked to the door. I wanted to apologize to Winsome but as I passed her, I looked at the floor, and went back to the downstairs room. I didn't come out again until it was time to leave. In the back seat of the car, Ingrid told me she had unwrapped my presents for me. She said, "So much shit for the Don't Like pile."

I wasn't better. I had just been given some of Christmas Day off. The next time I went to Belgravia, the piano was closed and covered.

*

I went back to university in January and did my exams. Foundations of Philosophy 1 was a take-home. I did it on the floor in my father's study, pressing on the Shorter Oxford.

The paper came back with a comment at the bottom. "You write exquisitely and say very little." My father read the essay and said, "Yes. I think you chewed more than you bit off."

Here lies Martha Juliet Russell
25 November 1977—TBC
She chewed more than she bit off

*

The pills did not make me feel like the old Martha when they took effect a month after I started them. I was not depressed anymore. I was euphoric, all the time. Nothing scared me. Everything was funny. I started second semester and made friends, by force, with everyone in my classes. A girl said, "It's weird, you're so fun. We all thought you were a bitch." The boy with her said, "They thought that—we just thought you were cold." "The point is," the girl said, "you didn't speak to a single person for like, the whole start of the year." Ingrid said I was less weird when I was under my desk.

*

I lost my virginity to a doctoral student assigned when my probation was lifted, the dean said, "to find any gaps and fill them in." I left his flat as soon as it was over. It was the afternoon but still winter and already dark. On the street I only saw mothers with prams. It felt like a parade, converging from multiple directions. Passing under streetlights, their babies' faces looked pale and moonlike, tinged with orange. They cried and twisted uselessly against the straps that held them in. I went into a Boots and was told by the disapproving chemist that I needed a prescription for the morning-after pill, he couldn't just sell it to me like headache tablets. There was a clinic down the road that did walk-ins; if he was me, he'd go straight there.

I waited for hours to be seen and reassured by a doctor who did not seem much older than me that I was well within my window of opportunity—she said, "So to speak" and giggled.

That night, I did not take my medication. I did not take it the

next day or the next, until I was not taking it at all. The doctor
who had given it to me was non-specific about the harm it would
cause, she could not tell me how long it "lingered in the system."
But all I could think about was the way she had whispered the
word fetus.

And so, I did a pregnancy test, every day until I got my period, convinced despite the precautions I had taken during and
afterwards, despite the fact that every test was negative, that I
was carrying a writhing, moon-faced baby. The morning my period came, I sat on the edge of the bath and felt sick with relief.

Without my medication, I was not euphoric anymore. I was
not depressed, the old me or a new me. I just was.

*

I told Ingrid that I had slept with the student, none of what had
followed for me in case she laughed and told me I was paranoid.
She said wow. "Consider your gaps found and filled in." When
she asked me what it was like, the first time, I made it sound brilliant because she was actively looking, she said, to have her own
gaps filled in.

*

After I graduated, late, I got a job at Vogue because they were
starting a website and I said, in my application, that as well as
being a qualified philosopher, I was au fait with the internet. Ingrid said I got the job because I am tall.

The day before I started, I went to the Waterstones on Kensington High Street and found a book about HTML, which I stood reading in the aisle because the cover was such an aggressive shade of yellow, I couldn't bear the idea of owning it. It was so confusing, I got angry and left.

We—me and the one other girl who did the website—sat far away from the magazine people but unnaturally close to each other in a cubicle made out of shelving units. We were both, it transpired, anxious not to annoy the other, which was why I worked out how to eat an apple in absolute silence—by cutting it into sixteenths and holding each piece in my mouth until it dissolved like a wafer—and why, whenever her phone rang, she would lunge for the receiver, lift it an inch out of the cradle and put it straight back down to stop it ringing. The calls could not have been for us since no one knew we were there. We started calling it the veal crate.

In my first six months I lost twenty pounds. Ingrid said I looked amazing in a gross way and could I try and get her a job there too. It wasn't on purpose—I was told it happened to everyone as though subconsciously, we were all preparing ourselves for the day we'd come in and find that the doors had been modified in such a way that only girls with approved dimensions could pass through them, like the baggage-sizers at airports.

I loved it there. I stayed until they found out I was not au fait with the internet and arranged for me to move downstairs to World of Interiors where I wrote exquisitely about chairs and said very little. Ingrid says it's thanks to hard work and determination that I have been steadily descending the career ladder ever since.

After her A levels, Ingrid did the first year of a marketing degree at a regional university, which she said left her dumber than she was to start with, then moved back to London and became a model agent. She resigned as soon as she got pregnant and never returned because, she says, she has no interest in paying a nanny so she can spend nine hours a day looking at Eastern European sixteen-year-olds with negative BMIs.

*

On holiday one year, I read Money, thirty pages of it until I remembered that I do not understand Martin Amis. The main character in the book is a dedicated smoker. He says, "I started smoking another cigarette. Unless I specifically inform you otherwise, I am always smoking another cigarette."

Unless I inform you otherwise, at intervals throughout my twenties and most of my thirties, I was depressed, mildly, moderately, severely, for a week, two weeks, half a year, all of one.

I started a diary on my twenty-first birthday. I thought I was writing, generally, about my life. I still have it; it reads like the diary you are told to keep by your psychiatrist, to record when you are depressed or coming out of a depression or anticipating the onset of one. Which was always. It was the only thing I ever wrote about. But the intervals in between were long enough that I thought of each episode as discrete, with its own particular, circumstantial cause, even if most of the time I struggled to identify it.

Afterwards I did not think it would happen again. When it did, I went to a different doctor and collected diagnoses like I was trying for the whole set. Pills became pill combinations, devised by specialists. They talked about tweaking and adjusting dials; the phrase "trial and error" was very popular. Watching me dispense such a quantity of pills and capsules into a bowl once, Ingrid, who was with me in the kitchen, said, "That looks very filling," and asked me if I wanted milk on them.

The mixtures scared me. I hated the boxes in the bathroom cabinet and the bent, crushed packets and scraps of foil in the sink, the insoluble feeling of the capsules in my throat. But I took everything I was given. I stopped if they made me feel worse or because they had made me feel better. Mostly they made me feel the same.

That is why eventually I stopped taking anything and why I stopped seeing so many doctors, and then none for a long time, and why eventually everyone—my parents, Ingrid, and later Patrick—came to concur with my self-diagnosis of being difficult and too sensitive, why nobody thought to wonder if those episodes were separate beads on one long string.

THE FIRST TIME I got married was to a man called Jonathan Strong. He was an art broker with a focus on pastoral art and sourcing it for oligarchs. I was twenty-five and still Vogue weight when I met him, at a summer party put on by the publisher of World of Interiors, who was in his sixties, white-haired, and, in wardrobe terms, partial to velvet. His first name was Peregrine and, people in the office said, his surname had been set as a keyboard shortcut on all the computers at Tatler because it appeared so often in the social pages. As soon as he found out that my mother was the sculptor Celia Barry, he invited me to lunch because although, he said, he was unmoved by my mother's work, except on the occasions he was actively repelled by it, he cared for artists and art and beauty and madness and he assumed I would be interesting on all four subjects.

I expended what material I had before Peregrine had finished his oysters but he asked me to lunch again the following week, and every week from then on because he claimed to be captivated by my childhood, the stories I told about it—the parties, my father's artistic and domestic travail, the unfinished opus, the Umbrian Sunrise, and foil mille-feuille. Most of all, he was thrilled by my brushes with insanity. He said he did not trust anyone who hadn't had a nervous breakdown—at least one—and was sorry his own was thirty years ago and, unimaginatively, following a divorce.

I told him about my father's alphabet game. Peregrine wanted to try his hand at it straightaway. It became our habit after that to write them once he had ordered for us, on cards supplied from his breast pocket.

The day I produced—I do not remember all of it—one that began with A Bronze-Cast Degas Excites Feeling—Peregrine told me I'd come to feel like the daughter he had never had, even though he had two. But, as he went on to explain, instead of becoming artists as he'd hoped, at university they'd both come out accountants. He said "to the heartbreak of their father." Even now, years later, he found it difficult to accept their chosen lifestyles, which involved much dusting of semi-detached houses in unbeautiful parts of Surrey and buying things from supermarkets, having husbands, and so forth. Peregrine's lifestyle was sharing a Chelsea mews with an older gentleman called Jeremy who did all their shopping at Fortnums.

At the end of his talk, I asked Peregrine to read what he had written. He said, "Far from my best but as you wish. All Bernard Can Digest Easily, French Gammon. His Intestinal Juices—" and then he was cut off by the arrival of our oysters.

*

Ingrid's eldest son went through a period of writing pretend menus. She texted me pictures of them. On one he had written,

1. red Winh 20
2. wite winhs 20
3. mixcher of all the wihns, 10.

In the message, Ingrid said she had ordered a large number three, because it's basic home economics.

*

It was Peregrine who pointed Jonathan out at the summer party and, as he said a year later while begging my forgiveness for it, "unwittingly choreographed your devastating pas de deux."

Jonathan was standing in the middle of the room talking to three blonde women dressed in iterations of the same outfit. Peregrine said they were all in danger, at risk of being seduced or sold a horrible landscape, and apologized for having to leave me alone because he had to go and say hello to someone tedious.

I passed Jonathan on my way to the terrace and sensed him turn and watch me to the door. When I came back inside and returned to where I'd been standing with Peregrine, Jonathan stepped away from his group. I committed to hating him while he was cutting his swathe towards me because his hair looked wet even though it wasn't and, passing a waiter, he lifted two glasses of champagne off his tray without acknowledging him. He put one in my hand and, as he did so, the sleeve of his dinner jacket shifted to reveal a wristwatch the size of a wall clock.

Because he'd left a matter of inches between us, he clinked the rim of my glass by tilting his only a fraction and said, "I'm Jonathan Strong, but I'm much more interested in who you are."

I surrendered to him a minute later. He had an extravagant

energy that animated him and anesthetized whoever he was talking to and was in on the joke of how beautiful he was. When I told him he had the brilliant eyes of a Victorian child who would die the same night of scarlet fever, he laughed excessively.

His reciprocal comment was so banal—my dress, apparently, made me look like a 1930s movie star—I assumed he was joking. Jonathan was never joking, but I did not realize that for a long time.

I was taking something then that, in its reaction to alcohol, made me a cheap date and I was drunk before I had finished Jonathan's champagne. The distance between us had been diminishing all the time we had been talking, and once it became nothing, once he was whispering against my face, letting him kiss me felt like a continuation of our progress towards each other. Then, letting him take my phone number and the next day, agreeing to dinner.

He took me to a sushi restaurant in Chelsea that he was, for a brief time, one hundred percent in love with, before he decided that food going around and around on a little train was incredibly juvenile. I refreshed my commitment to hating him the moment we sat down and slept with him that night.

That was the root of the giant misunderstanding that was us getting married: the fact that he thought I was so uninhibited, fun, a skinny person interested in fashion, an attender of magazine parties, and I thought he had a sense of humor and didn't take immense amounts of cocaine.

*

Partway into the dinner, Jonathan delivered a disquisition on mental illness and the kind of people who choose to have it, that was unrelated to whatever we'd been talking about before.

Anyone who clamored to tell you they had some sort of psychological disorder was, in his experience, either boring and desperate to seem interesting, or unable to accept that they were fucked up in some ordinary way, probably by their own hand and not because of the childhood they were equally in a rush to tell you about.

I said nothing, distracted by the fact that while he was speaking, Jonathan lifted a dish of sashimi off the conveyer, removed the lid, ate half a slice off his chopsticks, grimaced and put the remainder back on the dish, replaced the lid and sent it on its way.

Jonathan went on, saying everyone was on meds of some kind now, but to what effect—the general populace seemed as miserable as ever.

I could not take my eyes off the dish as it continued around the circuit, passing in front of other diners. Remotely, I heard him say, "Perhaps instead of chomping on pharmaceuticals like bar nuts in the vague hope of getting better, people ought to think about toughening the fuck up."

I took a sip of the saké that I had declined and he'd poured anyway, and saw, over his shoulder, a man farther down the line take Jonathan's plate of leftovers off the belt and give it to his wife. She picked up her chopsticks and reached for the half-slice. I was spared the horror of watching her eat it by Jonathan saying my name and then, "I'm right, no?"

I laughed and said, "You're hilarious Jonathan." He grinned and refilled my saké glass. By the time he repeated his treatise on mental health a few weeks later, I was in love with him and still thought he was joking.

*

When I told Peregrine that I had started seeing Jonathan, he said he rather wished I'd let myself be talked into the awful painting instead of the sex.

INGRID MET HAMISH that same summer, on her way to a birth-day party Winsome was throwing for her at Belgravia. As soon as she fell over in front of his gate, Hamish abandoned his bins and ran out to see if she was alright. He helped her up and because my sister turned out to be bleeding from multiple sites, he offered to drive her to wherever she was going and said, according to Ingrid, "I am not a terrible murderer." She said if that meant he was a really good murderer, she would like a ride.

Arriving at the house, Hamish agreed to come inside for a drink because he had enjoyed being talked at by my sister, for most of the way, so much. I was already there and after Ingrid introduced us, Hamish asked me what I did. He said it must be exciting, working at a magazine, then told me he had a job in government that was too boring to go into. Ingrid said, just having heard it herself, she wouldn't contest him on that point. Before the end of the party, I knew she was going to marry him because although he was beside her all night, he did not challenge her on a single point of any anecdote while she was telling it, even though my sister's anecdotes are always a three-way combination of hyperbole, lies, and factual inaccuracy.

They had been together for three years by the time he pro-posed, on a beach in Dorset that was deserted because it was January and, as she described it later, the wind was so ferocious, sand cut at them sideways and Hamish did the whole thing with his eyes shut.

*

Jonathan proposed when we had been together a matter of weeks, at a dinner he put on for that purpose. Except for a stepsister, he was estranged from his own family but he invited mine: my parents and Ingrid, who brought Hamish, Rowland, Winsome, Oliver, Jessamine, and Patrick, who came in place of Nicholas— away, I was told, at a special farm in America.

He hadn't met them before that night or known me long enough to know that I would feel the same about such an intimate thing occurring in public as I had felt at fourteen when I got my first period at an ice rink. I wanted it, but not in those circumstances. Later, I understood it was because Jonathan needed an audience.

His apartment was on a high floor of an aggressively conceptual glass tower in Southwark that had been the subject of vigorous community opposition in the planning stages. Every feature of its interior was concealed, recessed, disguised, or cleverly obscured by something put there on purpose to draw the eye towards something else. Before I learned where everything was, I slid back a lot of panels and found something I wasn't looking for, something I wasn't supposed to see or nothing at all.

I was living at home when I met Jonathan, because the salary of a chair describer was in the lowest possible five figures and still was at the time of the dinner, because although he had asked me to move in with him almost immediately, being so high up, in an apartment banked on all sides by vast, hermetic windows, made me feel like there wasn't any air. I could not last for more than a few hours inside without having to take the silently plummeting elevator to the ground floor and stand outside for some time, breathing in and out in a way that was too fast to qualify as mindful. And so, I arrived that night with my parents and introduced them to Jonathan in the apartment's low-lit vestibule. He was wearing a navy suit with an open shirt and looked like a luxury estate agent, compared to my father who was wearing brown trousers and a brown cardigan and looked, conversely, like he drove a mobile library.

They were equally aware of the contrast but Jonathan stepped forward, grasped my father's hand and said, "The poet!" in a way that was rescuing for both of them and desperately enamoring for me. Next he turned to my mother, swept her over and said, "Darling, what have you come as?" She had come as a sculptor. Jonathan said he needed a moment so he could deconstruct her outfit, and although he was mocking her, my mother let herself be twirled.

The others arrived while we were still there and Jonathan repeated their names after me as though he was learning key words of a foreign language, while shaking their hands for what seemed like a second too long.

I introduced Patrick last and Jonathan said, "Right, right, the school friend," then went off to shepherd everyone into the apartment's vast entertaining area, leaving us by ourselves.

He looked well—I looked well. We had not established a topic beyond that before Jonathan jogged back in and said, "You two, Patrick, come, come."

*

I did not know that Jonathan was going to ask me to marry him at the dinner or that his doing so would come as the crescendo to a slideshow of photos charting our relationship to that point. By and large, they were individual shots, mine of him, his of me, taken with his amazing camera.

It was shown on a screen that descended from an invisible recess in the ceiling, and as it silently ascended again, Jonathan beckoned for me to come and stand next to him.

In the slowed-down moment of getting up, I looked at my weakly smiling father, whose desire to help me had always exceeded his ability, at Ingrid who was still in the stage of sitting on Hamish's lap, presently with her arms draped around his neck. I looked at my uncle and aunt and cousins in intimate conversation at the other end of the table, past Patrick who was only a place along but seemed on his own, to my mother who was splashing champagne into and nearly into her glass with her eyes fixed too adoringly on Jonathan who was, by then, standing with his arms out like he was about to take possession of a large object. I wanted to become someone else. I wanted to belong to anyone else. I wanted everything to be different. Before he actually asked me and so he wouldn't get down on one knee in front of my family, I said yes.

There was a second of intense quiet before my father started to applaud like a recent convert to classical music who is not sure if you are meant to between movements. The others began to join in except Ingrid, who just glared back and forth between me and Jonathan until my mother—beside her—shouted, "Whoop de doo, Martha's pregnant" over the gathering applause. Ingrid turned to her sharply and said, "What? No she isn't," and then to me, "You're not, are you?"

I said no and Ingrid reached for the neck of the fresh bottle my mother was trying to open and wrested it from her. She made Hamish take it as she got off his lap, coming up to where Jonathan and I were standing and somehow compelling him to move so she could hug me without also acknowledging him.

Seeing us like that, everyone seated would have assumed it to be a congratulatory embrace between two sisters. Not the effort of one to comfort the other, speaking quietly into her ear, saying, "Don't worry, she's drunk, she's an idiot," the effort of the other to stay where she was and not run out of the room because her humiliation was so profound. But the source of it was not my mother. There was no way to tell Ingrid just then that it was Jonathan who had responded to my mother's pronouncement with mock horror then turned to my father and said, "She better not be!" through gritted teeth. When my father didn't laugh, Jonathan repeated himself to Rowland who did, and from there it spread along the table.

It was only a half moment, but I did not know where to look as the laughter rose so I kept looking at Jonathan, who was also laughing, although real sweat had formed on his brow.

He did not want children. He told me at the sushi restaurant. I told him I didn't either and he picked up his glass and said, "Wow, the perfect woman." It felt decided from the beginning, there had been no need to revisit it. And I was glad, but not happy. The idea of being pregnant was not funny but people were laughing. I did not want to be a mother but the thought that I might, or the image of me becoming one shortly, they appeared to find hilarious.

Except for Patrick, solemn in his place. While the laughter went on, I had met his eye and he smiled, sympathetically—for which bit, I didn't know—but my mortification was complete. The school friend felt sorry for me.

Before Ingrid and I separated, I said thank you, "I love you," and lifted my face, a brilliant smile already on it for anyone who might be looking at me.

They were all up from the table. Jonathan and I were brought back together, enveloped in their congratulations. He said, "Thanks, guys. Full disclosure, I don't think I've been happier in my life. Look at her for God's sake." He picked up my hand and kissed it.

I went into Jonathan's en suite as soon as I could and was shocked by the unfamiliar version of myself in the mirror. Huge-eyed, with a smile on my face that looked like it had been there when I died and had been hardened by rigor mortis. I put my hands on my cheeks and opened and closed my mouth until it went away. By the time I went back out, Ingrid had gone home.

*

Late that night I took a taxi back to Goldhawk Road. Jonathan apologized for having to go to bed instead of helping me clean up. He hadn't expected a grand romantic gesture to be so knackering.

As I was being driven over Vauxhall Bridge, Ingrid called and told me to please listen to the reasons she didn't think I should marry him. "This isn't even all of them, but he never says yes. Always a hundred percent. Listed among his chief likes, coffee and music. Always says full disclosure before revealing information about himself—usually boring, e.g. I love coffee. Most shots in that slideshow were just of him. Asked you—you of all people—to marry him, in public."

I said that was enough.

"He does not know you."

I asked her to please stop.

"You do not love him—deep down. You are just a bit lost."

I said, "Ingrid, shut up. I know what I'm doing and anyway, Oliver beat you to it. I don't need your reasons as well."

"But the baby thing, him saying ha ha ha, she better not be."

I said he was being funny. "That's just what he is like. He is incredibly loving underneath."

"Really?"

"Yes. He is."

Ingrid said she would just have to take my word for it until he started to be incredibly loving on the surface, and hung up.

*

If my daughter thinks he's good enough, then so do I, was all my father said when I asked him if he liked Jonathan, the morning after the dinner. My mother said he absolutely wasn't the kind of man she had imagined I'd choose and consequently, she adored him. I told her I couldn't tell, especially not from the way she had flung her arms around Jonathan's neck and tried to initiate some sort of dance in the foyer as we were all standing around saying goodbye, or the fact that she'd laughed so hysterically when he'd leaned in to kiss her cheek and by some wrong angling of their heads, they had caught the corner of each other's mouths.

I moved in with him the following weekend.

*

Because Ingrid's children look like her, they look like me. People in the street—older ladies who stop me and say you have got your hands full or, alternatively, he is too big for a pram—do not believe me when I say I am not their mother, so I keep walking and let them think that I am.

*

There were two en suites attached to Jonathan's bedroom and he came into mine on Sunday morning as I was pressing a pill out of the sheet into my hand, saying he was bored and had started missing me the second I got up.

Before, we'd been lying in bed; Jonathan drinking a tiny espresso produced by the expensive coffee machine he'd bought himself as an engagement present the previous day, while I studied the ring he'd chosen on the way home and just given me, sliding it onto my finger with ease because it was too big.

Now, in the bathroom, he picked something of mine off the sink, then seeing the pill in my hand, asked me what it was. I said birth control and told him to please go out. Jonathan pretended to look wounded but left. I swallowed the pill and put the packet back in my makeup bag, a hidden pocket.

I came out and saw him back in bed, propped up against his European pillows, apparently in the throes of an epiphany. He patted the space beside him. Before I was all the way there, he grabbed my hand and pulled me onto the bed.

"Do you know what, Martha? Fuck the birth control. Let's have a baby."

I said, "I don't want a baby."

"Not a baby—our baby. Can you imagine? My looks, your brains. How can you wait?"

"I'm not waiting. I never want one. Neither do you."

"And yet, I just suggested it."

"You told me," I said his name because he wasn't listening, "you told me the second time we met that you didn't want children."

He laughed. "It was a precaution, Martha, in case you turned out to be one of those women who is desperate for—" Jonathan interrupted himself. "Imagine a girl. Me with a daughter, a tribe of them actually. It would be phenomenal."

Already and from then on, Jonathan was consumed by the idea, in the same way he would be if one of his university friends called to say they should go skiing in Japan ASAP or buy shares in a boat. He kicked the covers back and sprang off the bed, saying he was so convinced he could change my mind, he might as well put one in me now before he had to leave for the gym so that it was already underway by the time I did.

I laughed. He told me he was deadly serious, and went over to his wardrobes that looked like a stretch of mirrored wall.

My suitcases were in his way, open and empty but surrounded

by the clothes that I had taken out the day I arrived and was still in the process of putting away. He asked me to take care of it while he was out because the whole area was starting to look like the square footage beneath a TK Maxx sale rail.

"Have you ever seen inside a TK Maxx, Jonathan?"

"I've heard tell."

He opened the wardrobe doors and, as he was dressing, said, "Apart from the risk of you teaching my daughter to be slovenly, you'd be a ravishing mother, fucking ravishing."

Once he was gone, I went back into the en suite and started running the bath.

THE NIGHT I got engaged to Jonathan was also the night I found out, beside a row of commercial rubbish bins, that Patrick had been in love with me since 1994.

I had come down, hoping Ingrid might still be on the street. There was no one. I crossed over and stood under an awning, unready to go back upstairs. It was raining and water was sheeting off the sides and thundering onto the pavement. I had been there for a few minutes when Oliver and Patrick appeared out of the lobby. Seeing me, they bolted across and pressed in on either side. Oliver reached into his jacket pocket, took out a cigarette, lit it behind his hand, and asked me what I was doing.

I said mindless breathing. He said "in that case" and put the cigarette to my mouth. I inhaled and held in the smoke for as long as I could. Above the volume of the rain, Patrick said congratulations.

Oliver looked sideways at me. "Yes, bloody hell, that was quick work."

I let go of the smoke and said yes, well. A taxi came around the corner and drove towards us, spraying water from puddles. Patrick said he'd actually come down to leave and might make a break for it. He turned his collar up and ran out.

Oliver took the cigarette back and I put my head on his shoulder, exhausted by the prospect of having to go back inside and talk to people.

He let me stand like that, then a moment later said, "So you're sure about the getting married to Jonathan thing. He doesn't seem especially—"

I lifted my head and frowned up at him. "Especially what?"

"Especially your type."

I said since he had known Jonathan for two and a half hours I wasn't massively interested in his take on things. He offered the cigarette back and I accepted it, irritated by what he'd said, more at how sullen I'd sounded in reply.

Patrick had not stopped the taxi and was waiting for another one, unsheltered on the other side of the street. I smoked and stared ahead, aware that Oliver was observing me. After a minute he said, "So you're clearly not with child then. Seriously, what's the rush?"

I began to say that I didn't have any conflicting plans but stopped because acid was starting to come up my throat and then I was coughing.

After a series of painful swallows I said, "He loves me."

Oliver took back the last inch of cigarette and with it in the corner of his mouth said, "Not the biggest newsflash though, is it? It's been what, ten years?"

I asked him what he was talking about. "I'm talking about Jonathan."

He said, "Shit, sorry. I thought you meant Patrick. I assumed you knew. Sensing now, you didn't."

I turned and looked at him properly. "Patrick does not love me, Oliver, that's ridiculous."

He replied in the slow, over-articulated tone of someone trying to explain an obvious fact to a child. "Ah, yes he does. Martha."

"How do you know?"

"How do you not know? Everyone else does."

I asked him who everyone was in this instance.

"All of us. Your family. My family. It's Russell-Gilhawley lore."

"When did he tell you though?"

"He didn't need to."

I said oh right. "So he's never said so. You're just guessing."

He said no. "But it's—"

"Oliver, he's basically my cousin. And I'm twenty-five. Patrick's whatever, nineteen."

"Twenty-two. And he's not, by any definition, your cousin."

I looked out at the street again. Patrick had given up and was
walking away from us with his head bowed into the rain.

I had never consciously considered any mannerism or physical
aspect of his, but everything about him—the width of his shoulders, the shape of his back, the way he walked with his hands
pressed so deep into his pockets that his arms were straight and
the insides of his elbows faced forwards—were as familiar to me
in that moment as any known fact or person in my life.

At the end of the street, Patrick glanced over his shoulder and
briefly waved. It was too dark by then to see his face properly, but
for the split second before he went on, turning the corner and
disappearing, it felt as if he was looking only at me. And I realized then that it was true—Patrick loved me—and, in the next
instant, that I had known it for a long time. It wasn't sympathy I
had seen on his face, earlier, at the table, and that was why it was

unbearable: someone conveying love while everyone else laughed at me.

Oliver said nothing, only lifted one eyebrow when I told him it didn't matter either way since I was in love with Jonathan, then I ran through the rain and back upstairs.

My wedding to Jonathan cost £70,000. He paid for all of it. I let it be organized by his stepsister, who described herself as in events and shared his gift for creating unstoppable momentum. In emails that did not contain any capitals, she told me that she had about a million strings she could pull at soho house, or any hotel in w1, meaning she could get us a date in a month. She said she knew the gatekeeper at mcqueen and had gone to school with most of the girls at chloé so, whichever I preferred, and she didn't have to make an appointment with any of the florists on the list (attached below) like a pleb, she could one hundred percent just walk in and get everything sorted in half an hour, even if i was thinking out of season.

I said she could choose. At Soho House, wearing Chloé, holding lily of the valley flown in from somewhere, I told Jonathan I was so happy I felt like I was on drugs. He told me he was positively ecstatic, and actually was on drugs.

*

Patrick accepted the invitation to my wedding. Peregrine, walking the Camino de Santiago with Jeremy, sent his deepest regrets and an antique oyster knife.

*

We had a honeymoon in Ibiza, which was short but, in dog years, proportionate to our marriage. Jonathan said it was a crime he hadn't already taken me to his favorite place in the world, which was, he promised, nothing like its reputation. I said I would go as long as we stayed somewhere that was far away from everything.

In the members' lounge, waiting for our flight, I told Jonathan I had changed my mind. He was sitting in a deep armchair reading the Weekend FT with his feet up on the low table in front of him.

"Scratch too late, I'd say, darling. We're boarding in twenty."

I said no. "About having a baby."

His campaign had been relentless over the six weeks since he first suggested it, and he seemed unsurprised to have broken me so quickly; he said in that case, I could look forward to being thoroughly knocked up by the time we got back to London, unaware that the effort he had invested in changing my mind had been wasted. I had flushed the pills that I told him were birth control, and the pills that really were, down the toilet, while he was on his way to the gym.

It was not my intention, but as the bath was running I looked in the mirror and remembered how I had appeared in it on the night of Jonathan's dinner, the rictus expression on my face. I remembered the minutes after he proposed, standing in front of my family while they laughed and laughed at the idea of me being a mother. Jonathan did not think it was hilarious anymore. He thought I would be a fucking ravishing mother. Standing over the toilet I pressed the pills out of the foil one by one. They were already dissolving in the water before I pushed its hidden flush.

Once Jonathan had gone back to his newspaper I looked around the airport lounge for a moment, then got up to get a drink. A woman in the next circle of chairs was so enormously pregnant she had balanced a small plate of sandwiches on the top of her stomach. As I passed her, I tucked my hair behind my ears, both sides at once to hide my face because I was smiling in a way that would make me seem mad.

Jonathan and I flew business class. We drank champagne from miniature beakers. I found out that my new husband owned an eye mask that he had bought in a shop, not retained from a previous flight. All the way there, I thought about my baby.

*

We got to the villa in the early afternoon. While I was unpacking, Jonathan suggested a swim followed by some pre-prandial fornicating. I told him I felt tired, that I would sleep while he swam and join him for the sex part. He had already changed into his floral trunks and did his famous impression of a sulking child on his way to the door—the bottom lip, the crossed arms, the stomping. I had a shower and got into bed.

The housekeeper woke me up, apologizing that she needed to come in and close the shutters to keep the mosquitos out now that the sun was setting. She said the husband would be unhappy to come back and find she had let the beautiful wife get eaten to the death on the honeymoon. I asked if she knew where the husband was. He had gone in the taxi to the town and even though, she said, the husband had told her he would be back at eight, it was nearly nine and she did not know what to do with the dinner that had been ready for a long time.

I ate on the terrace, at a table that had been carefully set for two and was hastily reset for one while I stood waiting. Excessive sad-eyed smiling, and fussing with napkins and glasses, constant coming in and out to check if the lady likes what she is eating and if she would like more candle for the mosquito and compliments on her youth are the international signs for your marriage is bad.

Afterwards I lay on a lounger beside the pool with a towel around my shoulders, looking at the sea, which rose and fell on the other side of the low stone wall, black and straggled with bits of goldish moonlight. I stayed there until midnight. Jonathan came back early the next morning, his septum crusted with what could have been the fine white sand Ibiza's beaches are famous for.

*

While Jonathan had conceded to stay somewhere that was far away from anything, he couldn't bear days of it being just the two of us. I could not bear nights of it being just the five hundred of us at clubs he said he had been to once or twice, and where he would invariably turn out to be well known. He promised I would have fun if I let myself and although I stayed for as long as I could each time, when I became panicked by the music that sounded like the soundtrack to a session of electric shock therapy, we'd agree that there was probably no point. I took long taxi rides back to the villa by myself and went to bed.

The amount of sex he'd told me we'd be having—a medically inadvisable amount—was not had. Jonathan was too dazed when he came back in the morning, too haggard in the afternoons, too agitated as it got towards his standard departure time. The only time he attempted it, returning to the villa after a twenty-six hour absence once and finding me still awake, I pushed him off me and told him my period had started. He got up and struggled back into his jeans, saying too loudly that if girls got their periods at thirteen or something, surely by twenty-five I should know how to game the system. I said, "It's not the fucking stock market, Jonathan." He didn't respond, except to say to himself as he kicked his shirt up off the floor, that with any luck the taxi that had just dropped him off might still be outside.

A moment later I heard tires on the gravel, and then I was alone again.

*

Although he accepted the invitation, Patrick did not come to my wedding. He called my mother in the morning and said he had fallen off his bike.

*

In the short time we'd known each other, Jonathan had never been exposed to the one of me who can cry for days and days, without being able to say why, or when I am going to stop. It began on our early flight back to London. I took the window seat and, after watching the island recede beneath us and the view become sea, I put a pillow against the cabin wall and rested my head against it. When I closed my eyes, tears started to slip down my face. Jonathan was choosing a movie and didn't notice.

I went to bed as soon as we got back to the apartment. Jonathan said he was going to sleep in another room, since I was obviously coming down with some hideous flu thing—why else the trembling and looking like death on legs and the weird breathing—and he had no interest whatsoever in catching it.

He went back to work in the morning. I didn't get up then, or the next day. I stopped leaving the apartment. In the daytime, I could not make the rooms dark enough. Light sliced through the curtains, found cracks under the pillows and T-shirts I put over my head and hurt my eyes even when, trying to sleep, I covered them with my hands.

In ascending order, Jonathan said when he came home in the evenings and found me still there:

Are you sick?
Should I be calling someone?
Genuinely, Martha, you're giving me the creeps.
Ah, what the fuck?
It looks like you've had another productive day, darling.
Do you think we could find it in ourselves to return
our sister's calls so our husband isn't assaulted by her
messages while he is at work?
I might as well go out then. No, truly, don't get up.

God, you're like some kind of black hole sucking in all my
energy—a force field of misery that just drains me.
Feel free to avail yourself of another bedroom if this is
going to be you, in perpetuity.

Weeks passed that way. Letters came from my work, which I did
not open. Then Jonathan booked a buying trip and said he would
be gone for ten days; in that time, I should, with all love and re-
spect, think about skedaddling. But, he said, hand on the door
frame, he had googled it and I would be pleased to know that my
chastity had spared us the faff of an actual divorce. A download-
able PDF, £550, and six to eight months of twiddling our thumbs
and it would be, at least in the eyes of the law, as though the
whole thing had never happened.

As soon as Jonathan left the apartment, I turned my phone on
and texted Ingrid. She arrived with Hamish half an hour later
and helped me get up. While she worked my arms into my coat,
Hamish filled my suitcases with whatever he thought might be
mine.

*

The elevator dropped us to the ground floor and as the lobby
doors slid open, air hit my face, hot and cold and human-
smelling, exhaust and asphalt. I dragged it into my lungs like I
had been too long under water, and for the first time in weeks I
felt like I wasn't about to die.

My father was double-parked on the other side of the street.
Behind the car was the row of commercial rubbish bins, next to

an awning. I was too worn out by pain to think, anymore, about what would have happened if instead of running back inside, I had run in the other direction, the way Patrick had gone.

With her arm through mine, Ingrid led me to the car and helped me into the front. My father leaned over to do up my seatbelt and at every set of traffic lights on the journey home, he reached across the divide and squeezed my hand, saying my lovely girl, my lovely girl, until the lights changed and he had to drive on.

As he parked in front of the house, I saw my mother standing in the front window. I knew everything she was going to say, if not the order in which she would say it on this—my latest—occasion. I was not sick, I was highly strung. I could not self-regulate. And if I had a depressive bent, I also had an unbelievable knack for timing my dark periods with, for example, other people's career-making exhibitions. I thrived on negative attention and if I had to break something or scream or, she would say in this case, leave a marriage to get it, I would. But, like a toddler flailing on the floor of a shop, the best thing was to ignore me. And once I had calmed down, I could be invited to consider how my behavior affected other people, setting back their careers, costing them a son-in-law they'd come to adore even more intensely since they first discovered him to be their fellow in the art world, a recipro-cal flirt, someone who always supported the finishing of a bottle and the opening of another one.

I did not want to get out of the car.

Hamish and my father went in with the bags. Ingrid waited until I said okay, and walked me inside. By then, my mother was elsewhere. Ingrid took me up to my room. The bed had been made up and next to it, on a chair that had always been my bed-side table, there was a ceramic jar full of ivy branches, cut from a vine that grew up the side of my mother's shed. I thanked Ingrid for putting it there. She said, "I didn't. Here—" she pulled the covers back.

For a while she lay next to me and stroked the inside of my arm, talking to me about Hamish's annoying sister and the te-nets of the South Beach Diet. Eventually she said she was going to go so I could sleep. She put her feet on the floor but remained on the edge of the bed. "Martha, it's going to be okay. You'll get over it much faster than you think, I promise."

I sat up and leaned against the wall, arms around my legs. "We were going to have a baby."

Ingrid's face fell. She reached for my foot and held it. "Martha." Her voice was so quiet. "You said—"

"It was Jonathan's idea."

"So you didn't really want one. He talked you into it."

"I let him."

She frowned, I first thought at me, but it was disdain for Jona-than. "He is such a fucking car salesman." She squeezed my foot and said she was so sorry. But then, "Thank goodness it didn't happen. Can you imagine, having Jonathan Fucking Annoying Face for a father."

Ingrid let go of my foot and said she'd come back later; that it was still going to be okay.

My mother entered as she was going out, stopped a short way in and looked at the ivy for a moment. "I can't remember if I put water in that or not." Then she turned to leave again but paused at the door and said, "Martha. Jonathan is a shit."

*

In the morning, I started putting away the clothes Hamish had packed then stopped, realizing I did not want any of them. Things I had acquired while Jonathan and I were together, things that I had owned before, now poisoned by some association with him. The drawer I had opened wouldn't close again. Behind it, I found a half-used box of pills from a previous era, a brand I didn't recognize, prescribed by a doctor whose name meant nothing, for whichever pathology he/she thought I had. I took some and hoped they would make me feel better even though they were so far past their use-by date.

*

It was a sort of muscle memory that compelled me out of my room and down flights of stairs to the kitchen when the phone started ringing. Answering it had been added to the list of duties my mother conscientiously objected to a long time ago, an interruption to her repurposing like cleaning and cooking and raising daughters. Often her shrieking somebody bloody answer that would see my father and Ingrid and me congregated in the same room, a minute later, as if we had been mustered by a fire alarm. I had forgotten about it, and although I resented it at the time, the same feeling of slipping in socks off the front of each carpeted stair made me feel nostalgic for the four of us at home. But only by the definition Peregrine taught me once, later—"the original Greek, Martha."

It was Winsome, ringing to talk to my mother about plans for

Christmas, which, she pointed out, was nearly upon us, with it being suddenly September. She did talk about Christmas—to me, because my mother did not respond to my calling out—rapidly and with an edge of hysteria in her voice for a number of minutes after I answered her question as to why I was there.

She was flirting with the idea of a buffet, Jessamine was bringing a boyfriend, something was being painted, something may or may not be finished in time—I was looking out the window at a blackbird pushing its beak into the same bit of grass over and over again. "And Patrick won't be with us." He was overseas—Winsome could hardly imagine the day without him but, she said, in compensation we would be seeing much more of him afterwards, now that he was near finishing at Oxford and coming up and down to organize a job, staying with Oliver who had just bought in Bethnal Green—why there, she did not know.

She went on to list the deficiencies of the flat itself, but I could not move past the image of Patrick in the street outside Jonathan's apartment, the sense of him looking only at me before he turned the corner. Then, I believed what Oliver said. I didn't anymore. In the short course of my marriage the idea had come to feel absurd. Winsome concluded her list but said, "At least it isn't in one of those awful glass towers that are all surfaces and sharp corners." Her first and final word on Jonathan.

*

The lady behind the counter at the Hospice Shop would not accept my wedding dress. Piece by piece, she was emptying my clothes out of the plastic bags I had carried in. I was wearing the only outfit I would own once I left—jeans and a Primark sweatshirt that Ingrid bought two of because they were £9 and had the word University printed on the front, which, she said, made it clear to people that we'd been educated at tertiary level but weren't so desperate for approval we needed them to know where.

My wedding dress was underneath other things and when she tugged it out by its sleeve, the lady gave a little gasp. Aside from the fact something as lovely as that should be in tissue paper and a proper box, she was sure I would regret parting with it. Her eyes darted to my left hand. I was still wearing my wedding rings and, assured by their presence that she had not said something unfortunate, the lady smiled and said, "You might have a daughter to give it to one day." She was going to pop out to the back and see if she had something better for me to take it home in.

Once she was through the curtain, I left without my dress and started walking home. It had begun to rain and water was sluicing across the pavement and spilling into the gutters. At the first corner, a storm drain had flooded, forcing pedestrians to cross one at a time. In the queue, I twisted off my rings, meaning to drop them into the drain when my turn came. But waiting, I realized it was the kind of gesture that would have made Jonathan roar with laughter, and I zipped them into the coin bit of my wallet before moving ahead.

Hamish put them on eBay. With the money, I bought my father a computer and gave the rest to a community organization that opposes the development of apartment buildings like Jonathan's.

THE JOB I never went back to after my honeymoon was my job at World of Interiors. A final letter, readdressed by Jonathan, arrived at Goldhawk Road. Due to my delinquency, I had been formally released from employment.

Sitting on my bed, I wrote to Peregrine. I wanted to apologize for disappearing instead of resigning properly, and not being brave enough to tell him why I couldn't come back. I tried but could not, after many drafts, make the real reason sound amusing. In the letter I sent in the end, I told him that I had run out of descriptors that could be applied to chairs. I said I had nothing left except "nice" and "brown" and I was so grateful and sorry and I hoped we could stay in touch.

His reply came back on a monogrammed card the same week. It said, "Better for a writer to run than give in to the siren call of thesaurus.com. Lunch soon/always."

*

According to my father I needed to recuperate emotionally before I even thought about trying to find another job. I was in his study looking at a recruitment website and had selected Greater London, then found myself at a loss.

Because recuperating emotionally was impossible in my room, the soundtrack of my mother's repurposing coming constantly through the window, he invited me to spend time in his study like I was seventeen—he didn't say that part, but we were both aware of it. For a few days I did, but the work of writing poetry had become visibly less enjoyable since then. Now, it involved more getting up and chair scraping, walking around the room and sighing and reading the poetry of other writers aloud, which he said helped him get in the zone, although obviously not enough.

I moved downstairs to the kitchen and started writing a novel. The sound of his labor was audible from above. I began going to the library. I liked it there but the novel kept steering itself towards autobiography and I couldn't steer it back. I imagined myself speaking at a writers' festival and being asked by someone in the audience how much of the book was based on my own life. I would have to say all of it! There's not a single shred of invention in its four hundred pages! Except the section where the husband—who is blond in real life and unmurdered—decides to relocate his expensive coffee machine to another part of the kitchen and when he picks it up, brown water from the collection tray cascades down the front of his white jeans.

That scene and every other seemed to vibrate with brilliance and humor as I typed them. The next day they read like the work of a fifteen-year-old with encouraging parents. Altogether, I could see how much it lurched in style towards whatever I was reading at the time. A confusing mix of Joan Didion, dystopic fiction, and an Independent columnist who was serializing her divorce.

I gave up and started reading large-print romance until I realized I had made friends with the elderly contingent who also spent their days in the silent area because, by the time they invited me to lunch at The Crepe Factory, it did not seem remarkable that I said yes.

*

Nicholas moved into Goldhawk Road a month after I did, making the house feel, to my mother, like a temple of unemployment. He arrived from residential rehab unannounced and told us he would be back to self-medicating in twenty-four hours if he had to go back to Belgravia.

Because he had always been unpredictable in ways that reminded me of my mother, and periodically depressed in ways that reminded me of me, I had always liked Nicholas the least out of my cousins. But his being there meant Oliver began coming over at night to watch television with him, or sit while he step-nined his former friends by phone.

Oliver brought his laundry, and he brought Patrick whenever he was in London because although the flat in Bethnal Green was conveniently situated, he told me, between a takeaway that specialized in all world cuisines and Yesmina Fancy USA, purveyor of human and artificial hair extensions, it did not have a washing machine, hot water after five p.m., or what the estate agent said he was legally allowed to advertise as a bathroom.

Patrick and I met in the kitchen, the first time he came to the house. I was emptying the dishwasher and a wet bowl slipped out of my hand when he came in.

He looked the same. I had moved in and out of an apartment, been married, abroad, ill and thrown out, and Patrick was wearing the shirt he'd had on at Jonathan's dinner, the last time I had seen him. I could not make sense of it, that I was entirely changed and he wasn't changed at all. I got down and started cleaning up, remembering it had only been three months.

He came over to help me and there with him, kneeling opposite, not saying anything except to tell me that some of the smaller bits were really sharp, Patrick's sameness seemed to collapse time, until none had passed, nothing had happened and it was just the two of us, picking up bits of bowl.

I did not expect him to say, all of a sudden, "I'm sorry about Jonathan."

I said yes, right and got up quickly to go and get a broom because I did not want to cry in front of him. He wasn't in the kitchen when I came back with it, and there weren't any broken pieces left on the floor for me to sweep up.

Oliver and I hadn't revisited the topic of our conversation under the awning or acknowledged the conversation itself since we had it. I did not know if he had told Patrick, whose level of discomfort in the kitchen wasn't obviously higher than it always was whenever he was around me. I did not know if Patrick had detected mine. Because of it, I didn't join them in the living room that night, or any night afterwards. Still, when they were there and I could hear the television, the sound of their voices, the thump of the dryer in the under-stairs cupboard, food being delivered, I felt less on my own.

*

Early in the morning, Nicholas went on walks and filled the rest of his day by going to meetings and journaling and talking to his sponsor on the phone. Having deduced, in a short time, that I had even less to do than he did, he asked me if I wanted to go with him.

That day, we made our way from Shepherd's Bush to the river, along it as far as Battersea; the next, all the way to Westminster. From then on, we took circuitous routes to the city, followed canals, went up into Clerkenwell and Islington, inventing ways home that took us through Regent's Park, eventually walking for so many hours a day that we started buying energy bars and Lucozade. By the time we had worked through every flavor varietal, I loved Nicholas. He felt like my brother, and never asked why I was twenty-six and jobless and living with my parents and why I only owned one outfit. When I volunteered it, he said, "I wish marrying a total fuckwit was the worst life-choice I'd ever made."

But, he told me, "Everything is redeemable, Martha. Even decisions that end up with you unconscious and bleeding in a pedestrian underpass, like me. Although ideally, you want to figure out the reason why you keep burning your own house down." We were somewhere in Bloomsbury, sitting on the edge of a fountain in a gated garden. I asked him why he kept burning his house down, then said he didn't need to talk about it if he didn't want to.

He did. He said no one ever talking about anything when he was growing up was the reason.

I told him Ingrid and I were always desperate to ask about his origins.

Nicholas said, "God, my origins."

I'd pronounced it the way Rowland did. I thought he would find it funny but it was clear he didn't.

I apologized. "It must have been horrible, having something about you that was unspeakable."

Nicholas sniffed. "Being something unspeakable, you mean. If you were so desperate to ask questions, why didn't you? Did your parents tell you not to or something?"

I said no. "We just assumed we weren't allowed. I don't know why. Probably because we never heard anyone in your family mention it and," I considered it, "I think, for me, it was like I didn't want to be the one to break the bad news."

"It's not like I didn't know I was adopted though, is it?"

"No. The bad news you weren't white."

He said what? so loudly that people turned around, then grabbed me by my shoulders. "Why am I only hearing this now, Martha?"

"I'm so sorry, Nicholas, I thought you knew."

He released me with a little backwards push and said he needed to keep walking, to process. Maybe, he said, on a level he'd suspected but still, it's a massive shock, hearing someone say it. I told him I understood it would be a huge blow.

Out of the gate Nicholas put his arm around me and said, "Martha, you are a fool." We walked like that for a while, back through Fitzrovia. Later, we turned up towards Notting Hill. I asked him if he thought we should be eating more carbohydrates. He said, Martha, we should be getting jobs.

*

There was a sign in the window of a small organic supermarket we passed on Westbourne Grove advertising casual vacancies in all departments. Even though we lacked essential retail experience, we were both hired, I think, because as a recovering addict and spurned wife who walked for miles every day, we both had the requisite pallor and wasted bodies of health shop employees.

Nicholas was put on the night shift, stocking shelves. The manager asked me if I would prefer register or café. I told her that, as an insomniac, I was also interested in evening work. She glanced at my biceps, said, "Register," and sent me home with a sample of herbal sleep tonic that tasted like supermarket salad leaves that had decomposed in the bag.

We didn't go on walks anymore. On breaks, I ate ham sandwiches from Pret and drank the ultimately best flavor of Lucozade, hiding in the stockroom because meat is murder and, I overheard the manager telling a customer, sugar is microbial genocide. Even though Nicholas stayed on at Goldhawk Road, I missed him.

THE LAST TIME I saw Jonathan was at his office. I went there to sign our finalized annulment papers. It had been six months by then since I had skedaddled. I stood in front of his desk waiting as Jonathan checked every page with uncharacteristic diligence then pushed them towards me, smirking. "All I can say is thank God you didn't manage to get pregnant. Someone with your tendencies."

I snatched up the papers and reminded him that it had been his idea. "But yes, thank God you didn't manage to get me pregnant, Jonathan. A baby I didn't want in the first place turning out to have a genetic predilection for cocaine and white jeans." I left before he could say anything else.

*

Outside, on my way to the bus, I walked past a rubbish bin and tossed the papers in without stopping, unable to imagine a situation that would require me to present a hard copy record of my abortive marriage or where I would keep them in my bedroom at Goldhawk Road unless I dragged one of my father's filing cabinets upstairs and put them under A for Agonizing Fuck Ups '03–'04.

At a set of lights, I got off the bus and walked half a mile back to the rubbish bin. The papers were still there, under a McDonald's cup that had been tossed in full. Without them I had no proof that I wasn't married to a man who, Ingrid told me while evacuating me from his apartment, scored nine out of ten on an online questionnaire she had done on his behalf called Are You a Sociopath? I lifted them out, the pages now a single clod, and carried them by one corner to find another bus, dripping Fanta down the side of my leg.

For half an hour, the bus crawled along Shepherd's Bush Road. Traffic lights changed, and changed again, without admitting any cars to intersections already jammed. There was no one else on the upper deck and I sat with my forehead against the glass, looking down at the street and then, as it came into view, through the wide front window of a café where a woman was breastfeeding a baby and reading. To turn the page, she had to put the book on the table and keep it open with the heel of her hand while swiping her fingers right to left. Before she began reading again, she would drop her face enough to kiss the baby's hand that had got a tiny grip on the edge of her shirt. After a few minutes, I saw a pregnant woman get up from another table and go over. They started talking to each other, the one touching her stomach and laughing, the other patting her baby's back. I could not tell if they were friends, or like-strangers compelled to acknowledge their shared fecundity. I did not want to be either of them.

I told Ingrid that I had let Jonathan change my mind. As she understood it, it was a brief reversal of a life-choice.

I had never been able to tell her about my terror of pregnancy at the time I acquired it or as I got older and, instead of diminishing, my teenage fear intensified until I was a woman not just afraid of being pregnant, a damaged fetus, a damaged baby, but of babies in general, mothers and the concept of motherhood itself—one person charged with creating and keeping safe an entire human being. Ingrid would declare my fear irrational, illegitimate as the basis of an adult decision. And now, I did not want her to know that, so afraid, I'd still let Jonathan's assured way of being and his propulsive energy overwhelm me and make me think I wasn't scared at all. So quickly and so easily, I'd let him convince me I was someone else or that I could be simply by choosing and that I wanted a baby.

But I couldn't compel myself into becoming someone without tendencies. Circumstances had no bearing, time wasn't progressing me towards any other way of being. I was already at my final state. I was childless. I didn't want children. I said, "So that's good" aloud, to no one. The women in the café were still talking when the traffic suddenly dissipated and the bus drove on.

*

At home, Oliver and Patrick were in the living room with Nicholas, watching television. Although it had been their practice for months and I'd had enough incidental conversations with Patrick to no longer feel awkward, I still didn't join them and hadn't meant to then. But as I passed the open door on my way to the stairs and saw them, shoulder to shoulder on the too-small sofa, loneliness collected me with such force I felt like I had been winded. I just stood there with my bag on my shoulder and my papers still in my hand, feeling the fast up and down of my chest, the in and out of my ribcage, until Oliver noticed me and said that, as I could see, they were watching competition darts and since it was the penultimate round, I needed to come in and sit down properly or continue on my way.

I saw myself, in a minute, sitting on my bed scrolling through listings for share houses in suburbs of London I only recognized as terminating destinations of various Tube lines, pretending I was still on the cusp of moving out.

I let my bag slide off my shoulder and went in. Patrick acknowledged me with a silent wave and Nicholas with the observation that I looked like shit. He asked me where I had been.

"Town."

"Doing what?"

"Divorcing."

He said, "Shame" and turned back to watch a man with a stomach that hung over his trousers aiming a dart at a red circle and punching the air when it struck the center. After that, Nicholas got up, stretched, and told me I could have his spot because he just remembered a girl he needed to make amends with because his final act before rehab was putting a nine iron through her windscreen after taking more than his recommended daily intake of methamphetamine. "Which I've discovered is none. Back shortly."

Patrick made a gesture of moving over to make more room, although there was none. Sitting between Patrick and Oliver, my arms pressed against theirs, all I wanted to do was stay there and watch competition darts while my cold empty body absorbed their warmth. The only thing Patrick said, turning his head but avoiding my eye, was, "I hope you're okay."

I pretended not to hear him because there was no way to bear the kindness of it, and instead asked Oliver why the men needed to wear moisture-wicking polos and sporty trousers to play a game that fat men play in pubs. He said, "It's a sport, not a game," and we were all silent until its protracted finish and the presentation of a trophy that was so modest, I had to look away when the winner lifted it above his head with both hands as if its weight demanded it.

Oliver said, "Right, let's see what else your parents' terrestrial channels have to offer us, Martha." I knew he wouldn't leave until Nicholas came back and I hoped that it would be a long time before he did. I did not want to be alone. Partway into the movie that Oliver chose for its promise of coarse language and sexual references, I felt myself falling asleep and just before I did, someone shifting so that my heavy head could rest against their shoulder.

⁕

The television was off and the windows black when I woke up. Only Patrick was still in the room. I was lying on my side, curled around a cushion. My head was in his lap. As soon I moved, he shot up and went over to the bookcases on the other side of the room, as though he'd been waiting for an opportunity to retrieve the Encyclopedia of Middle English from my father's shelves, which he opened to a random page and stood reading. I asked him what time it was and where my cousins were. It was midnight, Nicholas had gone to bed and, he said, Oliver left a while ago.

"Why didn't you go with him?"

Patrick hesitated. "I didn't want to wake you up."

"It would have been fine."

"Right, obviously. I just thought—no, don't worry." He put the book under his arm and began patting his pockets. "Sorry, I should have—"

"You've missed the last Tube. How are you going to get home?"

"I'm going to walk."

"From Shepherd's Bush to Bethnal Green."

He said it wouldn't take that long and he really felt like it—he'd been planning to walk. I glanced at his feet, sockless in canvas tennis shoes that were, for some reason, missing their laces.

"Is this the first time you've ever lied, Patrick? You're not very good at it. Seriously, why didn't you go with Oliver?"

Patrick cleared his throat. "I just thought it probably hasn't been the best day and maybe you'd want company when you woke up. But you're absolutely fine, so that's great. I'll get going."

I asked if he was planning to borrow the book that was still under his arm.

He produced a laugh and said he'd forgotten it was there, extracting it and momentarily pretending to read the back. "I might leave it. I might put it back." I said I would get the door for him because only lifetime inhabitants of Goldhawk Road know the exact sequence of locks required to open it, and left him to reshelve the book.

The bulb in the hall light had been blown for some time. Trying to get around my father's bicycle propped against the wall, my hip caught the handlebar and I unbalanced it. I stepped back to let it fall over. I didn't know Patrick was already behind me, and I stumbled against him. He put his hands on my waist and because he did not take them away, even after I had righted myself, I said, "Do you love me, Patrick?" Instantly he let go and stepped back. In the dark, I couldn't see his face.

He said no. "Or do you mean as a friend?"

I moved and switched on the outside light. It shone dimly through the glass above the door. I said, not as a friend.

"Then no. I don't." He said not like that and edged past me, then picked his way over the bike and began working the locks in any combination.

"Oliver told me that you have been in love with me since we were teenagers."

With his back to me, Patrick said, "Did he?"

"On the night Jonathan proposed."

"Right, well I don't know why he did that."

I reached past him for a high bolt he hadn't seen, skimming his arm. Patrick pressed himself against the wall and went out as soon as I had opened the door wide enough for him to get through it.

"Patrick."

He was taking the steps two at a time and didn't turn around until he had reached the bottom. I followed, then stopped halfway.

"Is it true?"

He said no, definitely not. "I really don't know what Oliver was thinking." He said, "Sorry, I need to get going," already walking away.

*

The bell rang while I was still in the hallway, righting my father's bicycle.

"Hi."

"Hi."

"Sorry—"

"What for?"

On the top step, hands in his pockets, Patrick said, "I just felt like I should say, I wasn't a hundred percent honest with you just then."

I said okay.

He paused, evidently unsure if he was required to elaborate or if, having confessed, he could rightfully leave. A second later, pushing his hands deeper into his pockets, he said, "No, it's just at one stage . . ."

I scratched my arm, waiting. I thought I wanted to know, in the hallway I felt like I needed to know if Patrick loved me. I no longer did. I was embarrassed and wanted him to leave because I was convinced—irrationally but still convinced—it was obvious to him that the second his hands were on my waist and the half-second they'd remained there had been enough to make me believe that he did love me as Oliver said. And I had wanted him to say it because now, in Patrick's mind, I was in love with him.

"At one stage"—he shifted his weight—"I did think I was, you know."

"When?"

"One year, after I saw you at your aunt and uncle's, at Christmas." He said I probably didn't remember it. "We were teenagers. You were sick and I had to come in to—"

"You told me about your mother."

Patrick looked overly surprised, as though he did not think any conversation we'd ever had would be memorable to me.

"Why did that make you think you were in love with me?"

"I think, just because you asked me about her. No one else had or has really, if you don't count Rowland wanting to know how she died, the first time I came."

I shivered and folded my arms, although the air coming from outside wasn't cold. "We are awful, Patrick."

He said, "You weren't. You're not. Anyway the point is, I did think I was in love with you then and apparently told Oliver, which is a shame." Patrick scratched the back of his head very briskly. "But I obviously wasn't and figured it out eventually. So please don't worry, I have never loved you." He heard himself and said, "Sorry, that sounds—"

"It's fine." I told him I shouldn't have asked him in the first place. "You can go."

"Are you alright though?"

I said yes, sharply. "I'm fine, Patrick. It's just been a full day of men who loved me once then stopped or thought they were in love with me, then realized they were just hungry or something." I stepped back into the house, telling Patrick that I would see him later.

*

Instead of sleeping, I lay awake until morning, my mind shifting between the memory of Jonathan behind his desk, his smirk as he told me I shouldn't be a mother, and Patrick on the street outside my parents' house and returning to the door. Jonathan was savage but at least in breaking my heart he'd kept it quick and dirty. In explaining that he'd never loved me, Patrick had been so concerned not to hurt me, it was like having the adhesive bandage removed from a wound, peeled away from the corner too slowly, with such excessive care that before the wet flesh is halfway exposed you want to rip it off yourself.

It was during those hours, when I had thought about both of them, that Jonathan and Patrick became connected in my mind. And it was because they had both rejected me, on the same day, that afterwards, whenever I thought about Jonathan and my failed marriage, I thought about Patrick as well. That is what I decided in the following days and that is what I believed for a while.

NICHOLAS CAME INTO the kitchen the next morning while my father and I were sitting at the table reading newspapers. He wanted to know if there were any spare boxes in the house because he had decided to move in with Oliver. He wanted to be nearer the city. He wanted to try and get a proper job. He said his brother was coming to get him that afternoon.

My father got up and said he'd see what he could rustle up. Nicholas made toast and brought it over, sitting in an opposite chair. He began to talk about his plans. I brought my elbow onto the table and continued reading with my hand across my forehead, holding the weight of my head and shielding my face at the same time.

I did not respond to anything he said. I felt like a schoolgirl trying to hide the fact she is crying at her desk because the worksheet in front of her is too hard. I was trying not to cry because the prospect in front of me, of Nicholas leaving and it all of a sudden becoming just me and my parents in the house, was too hard. As he continued, I tried to concentrate solely on the fact that his going meant Patrick would stop coming over.

After a few minutes, he gave up and dragged my father's paper towards him, turning each page without pausing to read anything. I sat motionless in front of mine, reading everything on the spread open in front of me until there was nothing left except the Court Circular. The previous day Princess Anne had opened a customer service center at the Selby District Council and attended a reception afterwards. I felt sorry for her and worse for myself, especially once Nicholas stood up, put his plate in the sink, and said he should probably crack on.

Eventually I left the house and went for a walk. As I was trying to find my way out of Holland Park, my phone rang. It was Peregrine. My apology letter and his reply had been our only contact. I was not brave enough to initiate a lunch, in spite of my missing him, more than seemed reasonable.

Now, he said, he was in a car heading generally westward and wanted to know exactly where I was. He had just found out—he said never mind from whom—that my marriage had flopped and while he did not need to ask who was at fault, he felt desperate that I hadn't rung him up when it happened.

I told him I was in Holland Park, and Peregrine said how convenient. He would divert his driver. "You can scurry up and meet me at the Orangery in quarter of an hour."

I told him I was wearing jeans. He disapproved of denim in any incarnation, on any occasion, and I hoped the fact would get me out of going. I wanted to see him but not as I was.

I heard him give some instruction to his driver and then, coming back, Peregrine said he would overlook it since sartorial standards were always the first thing to go after heartbreak.

*

In lieu of hello, Peregrine said, "I have never understood why people think of champagne as celebratory rather than medicinal." A waitress was pouring it, clearly to his mind the wrong way and as she moved to fill the second glass, he thanked her and said that we could manage things from here. I sat down and he put a glass in my hand. "Surely the only time one needs one's blood effervesced is when life is utterly flat."

He watched as I sipped it, then said that although it pained him to say, I looked terminally ill. "Anyhow"—he leaned back and steepled his fingers—"what are we doing next? Do we have a plan?"

I began to tell him that I was living with my parents and working at an organic supermarket but he shook his head. "That's simply what you're doing. It isn't a plan and I would say you're very unlikely to strike upon one, languishing in darkest W8."

I touched the side of my glass. It sent a ribbon of condensation down the stem. I did not know what to say.

Peregrine put his palms on the table. He said Paris, Martha. "Please go to Paris."

"Why?"

"Because when suffering is unavoidable, the only thing one gets to choose is the backdrop. Crying one's eyes out beside the Seine is vastly better than crying one's eyes out while traipsing around Hammersmith."

I laughed and Peregrine looked unhappy. "I am not being whimsical, Martha. Short another, beauty is a reason to live."

I told him that it was a lovely idea but I didn't think I had the energy or money to go abroad.

He said first of all Paris is hardly abroad. "And secondly, I have a little pied-à-terre, purchased many years ago for the girls. I'd imagined them Zelda Fitzgeralding their way around Montparnasse or at the very least Jean Rhysing the time away in a darkened room, but the Beautiful and the Damned preferred the suburbs of Woking and so it sits, furnished and vacant."

He told me that while it wasn't in disrepair, the décor could only be described as character-building. "Still, it is yours, Martha. A home, for however long it is needed."

I said it was so kind of him and I would absolutely think about it.

"That is precisely what you shouldn't do." Peregrine looked at the time. "I must get back to the factory but I will have the key bicycled over this afternoon." It was, he said, decided. Separating at the corner of the park, Peregrine kissed me on both cheeks and said, "The Germans have a word for the sickness that attends heartbreak, Martha. Liebeskummer. Isn't it awful?"

*

At home, I googled my bank account and proceeded through the Forgot Password? process to see how much money I had accumulated since I came back to Goldhawk Road, all my assets held in wedding rings and a wardrobe I divested to the Hospice Shop. At the organic supermarket, I earned an hourly rate equivalent to a wheatgrass smoothie, small, with no additions. But I bought nothing—for months only ham sandwiches and sports drinks for my walks with Nicholas.

The key arrived midafternoon. The address was on a monogrammed card and written above it, "A Bride, Cruelly Dismissed, Experiences Felicity, Going Husbandless, In Jeans . . . etc. etc. and ring me up as soon as you arrive." I had enough money, so I went.

I LIVED IN Paris for four years and worked the whole time at an English language bookshop near the Notre Dame, selling Lonely Planets and paperback Hemingways to tourists who only wanted to take photographs of themselves inside the shop.

My boss was an American who lived in its converted attic. He was trying to be a playwright. On my first day he showed me where everything was, his tour culminating at the shelves nearest the door. He said, "And all the reputable authors are here." I asked him where the disreputable authors were and he clicked his tongue against the roof of his mouth and said, "We've got ourselves a live one" to a doleful Danish girl who was serving out her last day. I slept with him for three and a half years and never loved him.

Before he stuck up a sign banning le camera à l'intérieur, and subsequently le iPhone and encore plus, le bâton de selfie, I was captured in the background of a thousand photographs, sitting behind the counter reading new releases or looking at the slice of the river visible between buildings if the only new releases were crime or magical realism.

*

Peregrine was the first person who visited me in Paris and, apart from Ingrid, the person who visited me most, only ever for the day, arriving before noon and leaving late. We would meet at a restaurant, Peregrine preferring one that had just lost a Michelin star because he considered it an easy form of charity, and, he said, in Paris it was the only guarantee of attentive service. Whatever time of year it was, we walked to the Tuileries afterwards and from there along the river and up into the Marais, avoiding the Center Pompidou because the architecture depressed him, and on to the Picasso Museum, staying until Peregrine said it was time to find somewhere louche to drink Dubonnet before dinner.

I measured out my time in Paris by Peregrine's visits. I think he knew, because he would never leave without telling me when he planned to return. And he always came in September, on what he called the anniversary of my sacking—by Jonathan, not by the magazine.

I was happy whenever I was with him, even on those anniversaries, except for the year I was about to turn thirty. Entering the forecourt of the museum, Peregrine said that he had been finding my behavior all day somewhat challenging. Thus, instead of going inside, we were going to walk all the way back and he would describe his life at precisely my age; since I would find it a very grim picture, he said, I might stop feeling so despondent about mine and walking with dreadful rounded shoulders.

On the street again, Peregrine brushed his coatsleeves then said alright, well, and we started walking. "Let us think. My wife had just given me the boot, having found out that my tastes ran in a different direction and while Diana set about making sure I'd get none of our money or see the children again, I moved to

London, into the awfulest room in Soho, became partial to various substances and was, in consequence, given the heave-ho by my magazine at the time. I was out of money in a day and forced to return to my family seat in Gloucestershire, where I was very much unwelcome, both personally and as one of my kind, and there followed the nervous collapse. What do you think?"

I told him it was quite a grim picture and I was sorry that he had been through it, and sorry that I had never asked him about any life he'd lived before the present one.

He said yes. "However, the benefit of exile—one was forced to clean up one's act because Quaaludes simply could not be got in Tewkesbury in 1970."

I said, "Like pesto," and put my shoulders back. Peregrine took my arm and we kept going.

*

Usually we parted outside the Gare du Nord but I did not want him to leave, and asked if I could go inside with him and wait until his train. We stood at a café counter and I told him that, although I was ashamed about it, sometimes I missed Jonathan. I hadn't told anyone else.

He said there was no shame in it, none at all. "Even now I find myself recalling the years I was married to Diana with immense nostalgia." He sipped the coffee, set it down and said, "Per the original Greek definition of course, which is utterly unrelated to the way members of the public use it to describe how they feel recounting their school days." Peregrine looked at the clock and put money from his breast pocket on the counter. "Nostos,

Martha, returning home. Algos, pain. Nostalgia is the suffering caused by our unappeased yearning to return." Whether or not, he said, the home we long for ever existed. At the gate to his platform, Peregrine kissed me on both cheeks and said, "November," and I knew it would be my birthday.

*

In between: I loved Paris, the view out of the pied-à-terre window, of zinc roofs and terra-cotta chimneys and tangled power lines. I loved living alone after the months at Goldhawk Road. I spoke to my father on weekends and Ingrid every morning as I walked to a café on the corner to get breakfast. I started writing a different novel.

And I hated Paris, the pied-à-terre's red linoleum floor and the communal bathroom at the end of a dark passage. I was so lonely without my father, without Nicholas and Oliver and Patrick, the sound of their activity downstairs as I tried to sleep, without Ingrid. I hadn't been there very long when she called and told me that Patrick had started dating Jessamine, which she found hilarious and I didn't for reasons I couldn't explain. But afterwards the novel kept setting itself at Goldhawk Road and the protagonist, who I had made a man so it couldn't be me, kept becoming Patrick instead. And then there was a girl. Everything that happened to her happened unexpectedly, and no matter what I did, she never seemed to be anywhere except on the stairs.

When I told Peregrine I was writing a book that was constantly turning into a love story set in an ugly house, he said, "First novels are autobiography and wish fulfillment. Evidently, one's got to push all one's disappointments and unmet desires through the pipes before one can write anything useful."

I threw the pages out when I got home. But I tried in other ways, and kept trying per Peregrine's wish for his daughters to be Zelda Fitzgerald, all the time. I walked along the river and spent money, and went to markets and ate cheese out of the paper with my fingers while I wandered around. I painted the pied-à-terre's walls and covered its floors. I went to the cinema alone and bought dress rehearsal tickets for the ballet. I taught myself to smoke and like snails and went out with any man who asked me.

But I Wikipedia'd the other writer he had mentioned that day at the Orangery—I had not heard of her then—and I read her book, the one set in Paris. More often I was its main character, a woman who lies in a darkened studio thinking about her divorce for 192 pages. Wikipedia said "critics thought it well written, but ultimately too depressing."

And—and so—I learned medical French, by immersion. Je suis très misérable. Un antidépresseur s'il vous plaît. Ma prescription has run out et c'est le week-end. Le docteur: How often do you feel triste, sans a bonne raison? Toujours, parfois, rarement, jamais? Parfois, parfois. As time wore on, toujours.

*

I went home once, a month or so before I returned to London for good. It was January, wet and dark in Paris when I got back, the shop deserted like it always was between Christmas and Valentine's Day. The American had gone home for a holiday and I just sat catatonic behind the counter for hours and hours with a book open in my lap.

The American came back, unexpectedly betrothed to a man, and fired me because I could not pay for all the books I had made unsaleable by cracking their spines and wetting the pages. I did not want to be in Paris anymore. The reason I had gone to London was for Peregrine's funeral.

He had fallen down the central staircase at the Wallace Collection and died when he struck his head on a marble newel post at the bottom. One of his daughters gave the eulogy and looked earnest when she said it was exactly how he would have wanted to go. I wept, realizing how much I loved him, that he was my truest friend, and that his daughter was right. If it hadn't been him, Peregrine would have been acutely jealous of anyone who got to die dramatically, in public, surrounded by gilt furniture.

On my final day in Paris, I ate oysters at the out-of-favor restaurant he had taken me to on my thirtieth birthday. Walking afterwards from the Tuileries to the Picasso Museum, I thought about a time we had said goodbye at the Gare du Nord. It was evening, the sky was violet. Peregrine was wearing a long coat and a silk scarf and after the kiss on both cheeks, he dropped his hat on his head and turned towards the station. The impression of him, walking towards its blackened façade, the crowd of ordinary people parting in front of him, was so sublime I called out his name and he glanced back. Regretting it, even as I spoke, I said, "You are very beautiful." Peregrine touched the brim of his hat and the last thing he ever said to me was, "One does one's best."

At the museum, I sat for a long time in front of a painting that was his favorite because, he said, it wasn't typical and therefore the masses didn't understand it. Before I left, I wrote on the back of my ticket and when the guard was not looking, I slid it behind the painting. I hope it is still there. It said, "A Better Companion Didn't Exist For Girls, Heartbroken etc. etc."

The daughters sold the pied-à-terre.

INGRID MET ME at the airport, said "Bonjour Tristesse," and hugged me for a long time. "Oh my gosh, I've been sitting on that forever." She let me go. "Hamish is in the car." On the way home she told me now that they had picked a date, fucking finally, as her bridesmaid I had two months to put on preferably a stone, but even half a one would do. "You don't have to get me a gravy boat as well."

According to a subsequent visit to conceptioncalculator.com, Ingrid got pregnant for the first time between her April wedding and the cocktail reception that followed at Belgravia. Winsome had every bathroom in the house renovated immediately afterwards, despite only walking in on Ingrid and Hamish in one of them.

Before, in the moment of waiting to go into the church, my sister turned back to me and said, "I'm going to do Princess Diana walking."

"Really?"

"I've come this far, Martha."

*

Ingrid had told me he was coming and even though the entire congregation turned around as we entered and my sister and I walked up the aisle watched by two hundred people, even though I did not find him until the final feet of it, I was only conscious of myself in terms of Patrick; whether I was, just then, being looked at by him, if so how he perceived me. My bearing and my expression, the direction of my gaze—it was all for Patrick.

Because. Over time, I'd thought less and less about Jonathan, realizing after two years in Paris that I only thought about him when prompted by some external stimulus. And now, not even when a man in the street walked past me trailing Acqua di Parma.

But I did not think less about Patrick. I was right that it was in association with Jonathan to begin with and solely to replay, and compare and contrast, their separate methods of rejection. Then he dated Jessamine, and invaded my novel, and it wasn't only then anymore. Considered on its own, disconnected from Jonathan's, Patrick's crime no longer seemed like one and when I replayed it, I could see his goodness. And I was alone so much, there was comfort in remembering Patrick as good, in imagining his sameness, imagining he was with me as I walked along an unpopulated street or marked hours in an uncustomered shop.

He was standing in the middle of the family row, next to Jessamine, visible when a couple cleaved to talk to the people on either side of them. He was wearing a dark suit. That was the only thing that was identifiably different from the various pictures of Patrick I held in my mind, which featured him always in jeans and a shirt, ironed badly and partially untucked. His face was the same; his hair was still black and still needed cutting. He was in those ways unchanged. But he had a different air, discernible even at a distance.

As the first hymn began, he passed an order of service to Ol-

iver who was on the other side of Jessamine. The transaction required Patrick to reach behind her and retreating, he put his hand
on the small of her back. He said something, which she inclined
her head to hear and appeared to find very funny. Then with the
same hand he reached into his breast pocket and took out a pair
of glasses, opening them with some sort of unconscious flicking
action, before casually taking up his own order of service. Patrick did nothing casually. No practice of his ever seemed innate.
As I knew him, being physically proximate to a woman made
him so nervous he could appear unwell. As the hymn was finishing, I was dismissed from the altar, and required to walk past
him on the way to where I was meant to stand. He acknowledged
me, smiling and adjusting his cuff at the same time. I'm not sure
I smiled back or not as I continued to my place, trying to locate a
description for the way he looked, self-conscious when it came to
mind as though I'd spoken it aloud to the congregation. Patrick
looked intensely masculine.

And the way I felt, seeing him for the first time in four years,
was the way I felt every time I saw him in public all the years
we were together. If I arrived somewhere and saw him already
waiting for me, or walking in my direction, if he was talking to
someone on the other side of a room—it wasn't a thrill, a rush of
affection, or pleasure. Then, in the church, I didn't know what it
was and spent all of the service trying to diagnose it.

*

At the reception, Jessamine told me and Nicholas and Oliver a
story about the first time she went into town at night, as a teen-

ager. Winsome was supposed to pick her up at nine but she wasn't there. By nine-thirty all Jessamine's friends had gone home and she was alone in a crowd at Leicester Square, embarrassed, then angry, then afraid because the only reason Winsome would be late was if she was dead.

Oliver said, "Yeah, even then she would have made it."

Jessamine said exactly. "But then, at like ten, I saw her shoving through a group of drunk people, I honestly felt like I was going to vomit and cry, I was so relieved. It's like, one second you can be alone and terrified in a crowd of scary idiots and the next you know you're completely safe."

Oliver asked where their mother had been.

Jessamine said she didn't know. "That isn't the point of the story."

"What was the point? It was bloody long."

"Oliver, shut up. I don't know." She flicked her hair. "Just that feeling of like, thank God when you see that person. Martha, do you know what I'm talking about?"

I said yes. Thank God is how I felt when I saw Patrick that day. Not a thrill or affection or pleasure. Visceral relief.

*

Later, once Ingrid and Hamish had gone, the guests left, the staff quietly finished, Winsome and Rowland went to bed, and it was just my cousins, me, and Patrick, sitting in the garden, in the dark, at a table that hadn't been cleared of bottles and empty glasses. Apart from Patrick, we were all half-drunk, in wedding clothes and jackets found inside.

Lighting a cigarette, Oliver asked Patrick why in all the Christmases he came to when we were teenagers, he never drank the alcohol we stole from Rowland's liquor cabinet or climbed out onto the roof to try Nicholas's joints and why, when we were ordered out of the house during the Queen's Speech, he'd still walk all the way around the gardens while we just sat on a park bench for an hour before going home. Why he felt like he had to be such a good boy when we were a pack of shits.

Patrick said, "You weren't trying to be invited back."

Three of us at once said God, very quietly.

*

Because it was early in the morning but still dark when I wanted to leave, Patrick said he would drive me home and for the minutes it took him to go back inside and get his coat, I was by myself in his car. If I could have called my sister just then, I would have asked if she wanted a rundown of its interior because she would have said yes and "I am dying" when I told her about Patrick's pocket tissues and pound coins in a little console tray, the roll of wine gums that he had opened without tearing the foil and closed carefully after eating one. "And," I would have said, "instead of the earth's layers of shit you would expect to find at your feet in the car of a twenty-seven-year-old single man, there is nothing down here except vacuum lines in the carpet."

I got out my phone and started a text, but didn't send it because she was somewhere with Hamish and I did not want her to know that I was sitting in a car at four o'clock in the morning, alone and tired, and trying to fend off my rising sadness at the thought that she had chosen Hamish over me, by going through Patrick's glove box.

He opened the door and got in while I was looking at his hospital ID. "Can I just say I had been awake for twenty-six hours when that was taken? That's why I look like that. Sorry I took so long."

The light came on when he started the car and Patrick glanced down for the gearstick. My gaze had followed his and in the second before it was dark again, I noticed his hand and his wrist, and the way the tendons moved as he tightened his grip, and as he let go and moved it to the wheel, the run of his forearm below his rolled-up shirtsleeve. When he became aware of it and went to say something, I reached forward and pushed all the buttons on the radio until a country song came on, fading towards its finish.

I said, "Oh my gosh, Patrick. What station is this?"

He said, looking straight ahead, "It's a CD," and tried to turn it off because I was laughing.

"No don't. Don't. It's amazing."

After it finished, I told him we were going to need to listen to it again because we had missed its emotional apogee. Patrick said fine and skipped back.

I loved it and did not let the fact that I had never heard it before stop me from singing. Patrick claimed not to be enjoying my extemporaneous lyrics but he kept laughing. It finished and I tried to play it again but could not find the button. I was surprised by Patrick reaching for my hand and transferring it back to my lap. I asked if I could have a wine gum, already picking up the packet and tearing it open, the sensation of contact still on my skin.

He did not want one and with my mouth full I said, "Are you exclusively into country, or do you like other kinds of music as well?"

"I don't like country. I just like that song."

"Why?"

He told me he appreciated the key change. Later I found out it was because, at an airport once when he was young, it started playing over the speakers and hearing it, his father said casually, "This was your mother's favorite song." Personally, he said he'd never understood how such an intelligent woman could bear its cloying sentimentality and over-egged melody. At some point, before it finished, it occurred to Patrick that he was listening to words his mother would have known by heart. He had already lost his memory of her voice but from then on, whenever he listened to the song, Patrick felt as though he could hear her. That is why he still played it whenever he was by himself in the car.

I was suddenly tired, and hungry, and asked Patrick to tell me about what he had been up to for the last four years and said I would be listening even though my eyes were going to be shut. He told me that he'd planned to do obstetrics but had changed to intensive care at the last minute, and was applying for an overseas placement, somewhere in Africa, because you got extra points or something.

Without opening my eyes I said, "Are you still with Jessamine?" knowing he wasn't. Ingrid had called to tell me they had broken up, weeks after she'd called to tell me they were together.

He said, "What? No. That was short-lived. And regrettable. Nothing to do with Jessamine. Just, we're quite different people."

"What happened?" I opened my eyes.

"It was when I started to think about the Africa thing and when I told her about it, she said that although she adored me, the whole Médecins Sans Frontières vibe didn't really work for her. She said I should be a dermatologist."

"A famous one?"

"Ideally. I believe she's only dated men in finance since then."

I said, "In three out of five cases they are called Rory."

"So you already knew we—"

"It was four years ago, Patrick, of course I did."

In a movie, if someone who is happy coughs, the next time you see them they will be dying of cancer.

In real life, if someone realizes when the car stops in front of her house that she is disinclined to get out and knows it isn't just the idea of going inside and passing her parents' closed door on the way to her room that is keeping her from undoing her seatbelt; if she knows it is because she does not want to say good-bye to the person who has driven her home and would rather sit and keep listening to him talk even though what he has been talking about is mostly quite boring, to do with his work; if it seems like he does not want her to get out either from the way he keeps looking down at her hand to see if she has moved it yet to the buckle, the next time you see them they will be walking to a terrible but open café that she points to at the end of the street and says, "We could have breakfast if you want." "Although," she adds "we will both come out smelling like fat" to make it easy for him to turn her down.

But he says, "That's okay. Good idea" and undoes his own seatbelt, trying to get out while it is still retracting because he wants to open her door and she does not understand what is happening, why he has suddenly appeared on her side of the car when the inside handle doesn't seem to be broken because no one has ever opened the door for her before, not even as a joke. He will say, once she is out of the car, "Do you want to get changed first," and she will look down at her uncle's dog-walking jacket over her silk bridesmaid's dress but say, "No, it's fine" because she does not want to leave him, standing here, on this part of the pavement. She worries that he would be gone when she gets back because this is where he said he didn't love her and never had and there is no chance he wasn't instantly aware of that too. And if he is made to stand there by himself for however long it takes her to get changed, he might decide it isn't what he wants to do—eat fried eggs with someone who would ask him a question like that. And if he waited for her, it would only be to say, "Do you know what, I'm pretty tired. I should let you go."

She doesn't want to be let go. People letting her go has become a theme. For once, she would like to be detained. That is why when they arrive at the café and he takes a long, long time over the menu, she isn't annoyed. Eventually it will annoy her so much that one day she will say, "For fuck's sake, he'll have the steak," and actually grab his menu from him and hand it to the waiter who will look embarrassed for both of them because he mentioned, as they were sitting down, that it was their wedding anniversary. But that is a long time away. Now she is happy at how long it takes him to decide, then happier when he says, "I think I will have the omelette," and the waitress who's been sniffing and shifting her weight from foot to foot says, "Just to let you know, the omelette takes fifteen minutes," and he will say, "Does it? Okay," and look back at the menu as though he should probably choose something else but she tells him she's not in a rush, to which he says, "Really, okay," and to the waitress, "I will have the omelette in that case." And although omelettes are disgusting, she orders the omelette too because otherwise her meal will arrive way before his and it will be awkward, as if it wasn't awkward enough, being by themselves for the first time, on opposite sides of a small table. That is why as soon as they sat down, she had said, "This feels like a date," and they had both laughed self-consciously and were glad that the waitress came over then and asked them if they wanted the table wiped.

*

I ate all of the toast and the edges of the omelette and drank too much coffee before Patrick said he probably did need to go. We walked back and reaching the house, he stopped and put his hands in his pockets, the way he had the last time.

"What?"

"No, it's just, you probably don't remember—"

"I do."

He said, ah. "Okay, well, I should have apologized."

I said it was my fault. "What were you supposed to say?"

"I don't know, but the way I said it. I upset you and I was sorry. I came back to tell you that, a few days later, but you were already in Paris. So, anyway, if it's not too late, I'm sorry I made you cry."

I said, "It wasn't you. I thought so, at the time, but it was just Jonathan, I was so humiliated and that's why I was so rude to you. So I'm sorry as well. And sorry if you smell like fat."

We both smelled our sleeves. Patrick said wow. "Anyway"—

he got out his keys—"you probably need to go to sleep." He unlocked the car and thanked me for the breakfast he had paid for. It was ten o'clock in the morning. I said, "Goodnight Patrick," and watched him get in and drive away, standing there by myself, in my bridesmaid's dress and my uncle's jacket.

PATRICK TEXTED ME. It was still the day after Ingrid's wedding, the afternoon.

"Do you like old movies?"

"No. Nobody does."

"Do you want to see one with me tonight?"

"Yes."

He said he would pick me up at 7:10ish. "Do you want to know which one?"

I said, "They are all the same one. I will come outside at 7:09ish."

There was a bar at the cinema. The film started but we never went in. At midnight, a man with a mop said, sorry guys.

*

I had just started a job at a small publishing house that specialized in war histories written by the man who owned it. He was old and did not believe in computers or women coming to work in trousers. There were four of us in the office, all women, similar in age and appearance. The only thing he required us to do was bring him a cup of tea at eleven-thirty and shut the door on the way out.

We took turns. Once, on mine, I asked him if I could show him my father's poems. I said he'd been called a male Sylvia Plath. The owner said, "That sounds painful" and "Please don't let it slam," gesturing towards the door.

Spring, then summer and we gave up the pretense of working and began spending our days on the roof, lying in the sun reading magazines with our skirts rolled to the tops of our thighs and eventually off altogether, as well as our tops. Patrick's hospital was visible from up there and the sound of ambulance sirens carried across the rooftops and the clump of green that was Russell Square.

That is where we saw each other, coincidentally the first time, both of us on our way to the Tube. Then by arrangement, sometimes, then every day. Before work, when the park was empty and the air was still cold, at lunchtime when it was hot and crowded and strewn with litter, after work, sitting on a bench until there was no daylight left and no more office workers cutting through the park on their way home and no more tourists standing in their way and it was just us again. Then at some point Patrick would say, "I should walk you to the Tube. It's late and presumably you've got to be in at the crack of nine-thirty."

Sometimes he was late and so sorry although I never minded waiting. Sometimes he was wearing his hospital outfit and his junior doctor sneakers, which I made fun of to cover how desperately endearing I found them, with their puffy soles and, I said, jazzy purple bits.

Once, a lunchtime, Patrick put his hand out to take the sandwich I had brought him and we both saw there was something that looked like blood on the inside of his forearm. He apolo-

gised and went to a drinking fountain to wash it off and apologized again as he sat down.

I said it must be strange to have a job where people around
you are dying. "Not of boredom, as in my case. What's the worst
thing about it? The children?"

He said, "The mothers."

I picked up my coffee, embarrassed just then by the intensity
of his job, against the stupidity of mine. I said, "Anyway, do you
want to know the worst things about my job?"

Patrick said he felt like he already knew them all. "Unless
there are some new ones from today."

"Ask me something else then."

He had been about to eat but put his sandwich back in the
box and the box down on the bench. "What was the worst thing
about Jonathan?"

I covered my mouth because I had just tipped coffee into it
and I was shocked, then laughing and unable swallow. Patrick
handed me a napkin and waited for me to answer.

I said the stupid things first: his wet-looking hair, the way he
dressed. That he never waited until I was out of the car before he
started walking away, that he wasn't sure what his cleaning lady's
name was even though she had worked for him for seven years. I
told him about the room in Jonathan's apartment that had nothing in it except a drum kit that faced a mirrored wall. And then I
took the lid off my cup and said, the worst thing is that I thought
he was funny because he made everything sound like a joke. "But
he meant everything he said, at the time. Then he would change
his mind and mean the opposite, as absolutely. He said I was

beautiful and clever, then insane and I believed all of it." I stared into my cup. I wished I had stopped at the mirrored wall.

Patrick rubbed underneath his chin. "Probably, the worst thing to me was the tan."

I laughed and looked at him smiling at me and then not as much when he said, "and being there when he proposed to you." A feeling, like fizzing, moved up the back of my neck. "Seeing you say yes and not being able to stop it." The fizzing spread out, across my shoulders, down my arms, upwards into my hair.

My phone rang. I had not managed to say anything. Patrick said don't worry and told me to answer it.

It was Ingrid. She said she was in a disabled loo in Starbucks, in Hammersmith, and she was pregnant. She had just done a test.

Because she was talking so loudly, Patrick heard and did a thumbs-up, then pointed to his watch and stood up, simulating walking back to work and texting me later. I mimed him taking our empty cups and sandwich packets with him but said good-bye out loud.

Ingrid asked me who I was talking to.

"Patrick."

"What? Why are you with Patrick?"

I said, "Something weird is happening. But, you're pregnant. I am so excited. Do you know who the father is?"

I let her talk about it for as long as I could, about the baby, morning sickness, names, then said, "I'm so sorry, I have to get back to the office. I've got so much work to invent."

Ingrid said okay. "Don't get stuck there. Burning the five p.m. candle on a Friday."

I was so happy for her and did not know how I was going to survive it.

*

I didn't want to see anyone the next day. I was supposed to go to a thing at the Tate with Patrick. He had already paid for the tickets. In the morning he texted me and I said I couldn't go and, because he said okay and didn't make me feel guilty, I texted back and said I actually could go.

It was an exhibition of works by a photographer who only seemed to photograph himself, in his own bathroom. Patrick became despondent as we entered the third room of it. We were both looking at a picture of the artist standing in his bath, wearing an undershirt and nothing else.

I said, "I don't know much about art but I know I would rather be at the gift shop."

Patrick said I'm really sorry. "Someone at work said it was amazing. I thought it sounded like your kind of thing."

I put my hand on his arm and kept it there. "Patrick, my only thing is sitting, drinking tea or something else and talking, or even better, not talking. That is the only thing I ever want to do."

He said good, okay, noted. "I think there is a café here. On the top floor."

*

In the elevator, he said, "You must be excited about Ingrid." I told him I was and felt glad that the doors were opening. We sat at a table by the window, sometimes looking at the river and sometimes at each other, and drank tea or something else, talking for a long time about other things than Ingrid being pregnant. Patrick, about being an only child and how much he used to envy Oliver for having a brother, then his memory of meeting me and Ingrid for the first time, how inscrutable our relationship had been to him, for years afterwards. He said, until then, he hadn't known it was possible for two separate people to be that connected. From looking alike and talking alike and, in his memory, never being apart, it felt like there was a sort of force field around us, impenetrable to other people. Weren't there matching sweatshirts at one point, with something weird written on the front?

I told him there was—I still had mine but now, "nivers" and a spray of sticky white bits was the only thing left across the chest. He said he remembered me wearing it every single time he ever came to Goldhawk Road in the months I lived there.

Ingrid and I were aware of the force field, I said, and it felt like it still existed sometimes but I knew it wouldn't be the same once she was a mother and I wasn't. "It's why I'm not overburdened with female friends, because they all have children now and—" I just said well and moved the sugar.

"But it will evolve, don't you think, once you do too."

"I don't want children." I was suddenly thinking about Jonathan, taking precautions, and I did not hear Patrick's reply at the time; only later that night, replaying the conversation while I lay awake. He hadn't asked why not. Only said, "That's interesting. I've always imagined myself having children. But I guess just in the way everyone does."

*

It had become Saturday night by the time we emerged from the gallery, and I wanted to go nowhere less than home. My parents had established some sort of salon and artists less important than my mother and writers more successful than my father would be packed into the living room, draining bottles of supermarket Prosecco and waiting for turns to talk about themselves. Because I couldn't say where I did want to go when Patrick asked me, we crossed over the river and started walking along the Embankment until it became so crowded we kept being forced apart by the shoals of people coming the other way.

I could see Patrick was annoyed by the over and over of it— having to separate, having to find each other again a second later. For me it was so many tiny bursts, a salvo, of the Thank God feeling, which was why I wanted to keep walking. Finally, as a couple unready to give up their dream of rollerblading hand in hand down the Thames came towards us, he took my hand and pulled me to one side. He said, "Martha, we need an objective. I am worried we're risking our lives only to end up at a Pizza Express that will make you sad if it's empty and anxious if it's full." I did not know how he knew that about me. "Can we go back to your house?" He clarified—he meant, could he come with me on the Tube to Goldhawk Road in a protective capacity and leave me at the front door.

I thought about it, then said, "Do you know what's funny? I've known you for however long, fifty years, and I've never been to your house."

When Patrick pulled me out of their way, it had been so that

my back was against the plinth of a statue and when the roller-
bladers turned around and came back, uncoupled and both out
of control, he was forced to step in so that we were face to face
and close enough that breathing out, our bodies were barely separate. I wondered if Patrick was aware of it too, at all or as power-
fully as I was, before he said, "This way, then," and led off in the
direction of his flat.

*

Patrick promised me it was usually much tidier than this as he
opened the door, then stood aside so I could go in first. It was on
the third floor of a Victorian mansion block in Clapham, on a
corner of the building so the living room overlooked a park from
tall, perpendicular windows. He bought it after he graduated and
lived there with a flatmate called Heather who was also a doctor.
A mug on the arm of the sofa seemed to represent the total mess
Patrick was talking about. Because it had lipstick on the rim, I
assumed Heather was the sloven.

She came home while he was making me a bacon sandwich,
wandered into the kitchen and went up behind him, picking a
burned bit out of the pan he was holding. She ate it like it was
a delicious little sweet, then wafted over to a cupboard and got
something out like she knew where everything was and had
agency in it being there in the first place. I felt like I had never
hated another woman so much.

Once we had eaten, I watched him do the dishes. Patrick dried
things. I told him if he just left them on the board, physics or
whatever would dry them so he didn't have to.

He said he wasn't sure it was physics. "I don't mind doing it. I have a bit of a completist mentality. I'll be finished in a minute. Do you know how to play backgammon?"

I said no and conceded to being taught. We went into the living room and while he was setting up the suitcase thing, Patrick said, "I meant to tell you, I'm going to Uganda."

I frowned and asked him why.

"For work, a placement. I told you I was applying. A while ago, I guess."

"I remember. I just didn't think that you would still—" I wasn't sure what I meant, then I was and couldn't say it.

"Still what?"

I meant, I didn't think you would still want to go because of me. I said, "I just didn't realize it was still happening, that's all."

Patrick asked me if I minded. He was joking but I felt exposed and said no. "Why would I mind? That would be weird." I picked up one of the pieces and turned it over. "When are you leaving?"

He said in three weeks. "The tenth. Back at Christmas. I think, the day before."

"That is five months."

Patrick said, "Five and a half" and finished setting up the board. I tried to focus on his explanation of the rules but I was preoccupied with the idea of him being away for so long and said, when he kept reminding me whose turn it was, "You just roll for me and I'll watch."

How long the man had been standing there I don't know but when I raised my head because I had heard somebody say, "Hello there," it sounded like it wasn't the first time he had said it. It was October and cold. I was at Hampstead Heath sitting in an area of tall dead grass between the gravel path and a narrow stream with my arms around my shins and my forehead on my knees. I had cried enough that the skin on my cheeks felt sore and tight like it had been soaped and over-scrubbed.

The man, in his oilskin jacket and tweed hat, was smiling cautiously. He had a dog on a leash, a large Labrador that was standing obediently beside him, beating its tail against his leg. I smiled back, involuntarily, like someone who has just been tapped on the shoulder at a party and is turning around in happy anticipation of seeing who it is and hearing whatever wonderful thing it is they've come over to say.

He said, "I couldn't help but notice you here." His tone was very fatherly. "I didn't want to invade your privacy but I said to myself, if she is still there on my way back—" he did a single nod to indicate that I was, indeed, still there and asked me if I was alright.

I was sorry and wanted to apologize for becoming a factor in his afternoon, for complicating his walk and demanding to be thought about. The dog put its nose down and sniffed towards me, as near as it could get on the leash. I reached out and the man gave out more so it could put its nose in my hand. He said, "Ah there, she likes you. She's rather old and doesn't like many people."

I squinted up at him. I wanted to tell him that my mother had just died to justify why I had been crying so hard in public. But it would be beyond this nice man's solving. I went to say that I had dropped my phone in the stream but I did not want him to think I was stupid or offer to retrieve it.

I said, "I'm lonely." It was the truth. Followed by some lies, told to absolve him of concern. "I'm just lonely today. Not in general. Generally I'm completely fine."

"Well, they say London is a city of eight million lonely people, don't they?" The man gently tugged the dog back to his side. "But this too shall pass. They also say that."

He nodded goodbye and moved off along the path.

*

As a child, watching the news or listening to it on the radio with my father I thought, when they said "the body was discovered by a man walking his dog," that it was always the same man. I still imagine him, putting his walking shoes on at the door, finding the leash, the familiar dread as he clips it onto the dog's collar, but still setting out, regardless, in the hope that, today, there won't be a body. But twenty minutes later, God, there it is.

*

I stayed sitting by the stream after he walked on, but kept my head up so as not to attract any more concerned persons. I wasn't alright. I hadn't been from the time Patrick went away. Sitting there, I thought about other times that I had felt like this—the months I was with Jonathan, on and off in Paris, the past few weeks—the lowest points of my adult life were related by the factor of his absence. It was so clear. And there had been that day in the summer—I stood up and brushed the back of my jeans. That is when I began to think of Patrick as the cure. By the end of our marriage, I saw him as the cause.

I WENT TO the airport to meet Patrick, early in the morning, the day before Christmas. We hugged each other like two people who had no practical experience of embracing, had only taught themselves the theory from a poorly worded manual.

He did not smell amazing. He had a very saddening beard. But, I said, aside from that I was so happy to see him. I did not say, beyond description, beyond what I had imagined.

Patrick said you too. And my name. "You too Martha."

In front of the ticket machine, he asked if I wanted to come home with him. It felt like a stone dropping—the disappointment—when he said "not in that sense obviously" and laughed. I told him I did, not in that sense either.

The flat was quiet, with the air of a long absence, and neat although Heather was supposedly still in residence. Patrick opened windows and asked me what I wanted to do. I said let's shave that beard off and I sat on the closed lid of the toilet while he did it, in humorous increments—Charles Darwin to suspected attacker via Mr. Bennet, BBC adaptation.

I went out afterwards so he could have a shower and sat in the living room, reading a book I found under his coffee table, trying not to think about the sound of running water and the steam and soap smell that was either carrying from the bathroom or being produced by my imagination. I wondered what he was doing. I wondered what he was doing, too exactly, and left the house to buy breakfast and food for his fridge, staying out until I was sure he would have finished.

We talked until it was too late for me to go home; Patrick gave me his bed and slept on the sofa.

*

In the morning, we walked all the way to Belgravia, along Battersea Park, over Chelsea Bridge. Winsome opened the door and looked surprised to see us together but suppressed her desire to remark on it while we took off our coats, by remarking on my hair instead.

Before lunch I went into the dining room and found her rearranging the place cards because, she said, having now seen Ingrid, she thought it would be better to have her on the end, to make it easier for her to get in and out. My sister was thirty-six weeks pregnant by then and had put on a significant amount of Toblerone weight.

Now, Winsome went on, she was wondering if Ingrid might also be more comfortable on a sturdier alternative to the formal dining chairs which, she pointed out, had such silly thin legs.

Perhaps I could suggest it to her. My aunt said, "She wouldn't be offended, would she?" and touched her pearls.

Ingrid was offended and refused to take the sturdier alternative, despite the additional inducement of a cushion. Once we were sitting down, she told us she was going to try and force out her mucus plug in the hope of ruining the upholstered seat of the thin-legged one she had made Hamish give up. He was next to Patrick, and glanced at him for reassurance after suggesting to my sister that perhaps all the pretend bearing-down wasn't the best idea, as funny as we were obviously all finding it.

She started laughing. "A woman can't dislodge her mucus plug by pretending to."

He looked back to Patrick and asked if that was true.

Ingrid said, "He's been a doctor for ten minutes, Hamish. I doubt he knows. No offense, Patrick."

"He's nearly a senior registrar, darling."

"Okay well I don't know the difference but fine, I will leave my mucus plug in situ."

Jessamine, next to her, said, "I am so excited for when we all stop saying mucus plug," and got up.

A moment later, Rowland appeared and took her seat. He had just acquired a sibling pair of whippets to replace Wagner, lately deceased, and he was hoping Patrick could advise him on their problem of nervous urination, he said, "In your capacity as a medic." Ingrid said he's actually a registrar and got up, announcing to the table that she was going upstairs to lie down because she felt sick. I went with her and stayed until she was asleep. By the time I came down, everyone had left on the walk. I was sitting at Winsome's piano, trying to play something, when she texted me. "Fck pls come up here and ring Hamish."

I found her in Jessamine's bathroom, kneeling in front of the sink and pulling down on the edge like she was trying to rip it out of the wall. The floor around her was wet and she was crying. She saw me and said, "Please don't be angry. I was joking. I was joking."

I went over and knelt beside her. She let go of the basin and lay on her side, curled up with her head in my lap. I rang Hamish. He said okay, okay, okay, okay, okay until I told him I had to go. A contraction was coming. My sister's body went rigid, like she was being electrocuted. With her jaw clenched she said, "Martha, make it stop. I'm not ready. The baby will be too small." As soon as the contraction had passed, she asked me to go please google how to keep a baby in. "Its birthday is going to be fucked, Martha." Laughing, or crying, she said, "Please. It's going to get a combined present."

There was nothing on Wikipedia. I asked her if she wanted me to distract her by reading aloud from the Daily Mail celebrity sidebar. She batted the phone out of my hand and told me to die in a hole, then screamed at me to get it again because another one was coming and I was supposed to be timing them or something.

For however long, we stayed like that. I told her it was going to be completely fine, desperate for it to be true, desperate that nothing happen to my sister and her baby. The contractions got closer, then joined together until Ingrid was racked by sobs and saying she was going to die. Hamish walked in as she was getting onto her hands and knees, screaming that something was coming out of her.

It had not occurred to me that Patrick would be with him, but he entered first. I moved out of his way and went and stood by Hamish who had stopped just inside the door because, as soon as she saw him, Ingrid said she didn't want him there anymore.

Patrick told her he needed to check what was happening. Ingrid said, "Fuck off, Patrick. Sorry, I am not having a family friend look between my legs."

Probably, Hamish said, she did need to let someone have a

quick squiz, particularly as he'd just realized he hadn't thought to ring an ambulance.

Patrick had, but told my sister then that if she could feel something, it wasn't going to arrive in time.

"She can do it then," Ingrid said. "Martha can. You can just tell her what to do."

I looked at him hoping he would shake his head because I was desperate not to have to assess a cervix but his expression was so commanding, I found myself already moving towards him.

Patrick told Hamish to go and get some scissors, reassuring my sister that it wasn't, as she instantly thought, so he could do a floor Caesarean with no fucking anesthetic.

Something was definitely coming out of her. I started to describe what it looked like until she told me, between breaths, that Patrick didn't need me to paint a fucking word picture and ordered me to move.

It was the last thing Ingrid said before she pushed up off her hands and released a long animal groan. Hamish was back to see her deliver an impossibly small, angry baby into her own hands. He went pale and listed towards the wall, not immediately responding to Patrick's request for the scissors he was holding. He apologized, saying they were the only ones he could find. "Winsome's sewing room."

Ingrid, slumped, holding her baby, said, "Oh my God, no Hamish. They're pinking shears. Patrick?"

He said they would be fine.

She looked at me, pleadingly. I told her they would give a lovely effect and went to turn away, overwhelmed by the quantity of blood on the floor but then Patrick reached out, and took the baby, cut the cord, and returned it to my sister's arms in a series of movements so swift and silent, it seemed like a routine they had been practicing. I was so transfixed, it was only the echo of Patrick's voice in my head, asking me to go and find more towels, that prompted me to go out and get as many as I could find.

Ingrid tried to wrap the baby up in one of them and started crying. She said to Patrick, "Do you think I'm hurting him? He's too small, he shouldn't be here yet." She said, "I'm so sorry, I'm so sorry," looking from him to me then Hamish, as if she'd sinned against each of us individually. I felt tears in my eyes when she looked down and apologized to the baby.

Patrick said, "Ingrid, he was going to come anyway. It was nothing you did."

She nodded but wouldn't look at him.

Patrick said, "Ingrid?"

"Yes." She raised her head.

"Do you believe me?"

"Yes."

"Good." Patrick took the rest of the towels I was holding and put them around her shoulders and over her legs. My sister—I had never loved her more intensely than I did then—wiped one of her cheeks dry and tried to smile and said, "Martha, I hope these are Winsome's good towels." She was still crying, but in a different way then, as though everything was suddenly alright.

*

Patrick and I stayed with her while Hamish went to meet the ambulance. I said no but she made me hold the baby and I let myself be obliterated by the intensity of my love for this almost weightless thing. In front of Patrick, she said, "Are you sure you don't want one?"

"I want this one. But you got him so I will have to go without."

Patrick said, "He's lovely, Ingrid," looking at the baby in my arms.

*

Hamish came back accompanied by a man and a woman in dark green uniforms jointly carrying a stretcher. He described the situation downstairs now that everyone had returned from the walk as controlled mayhem but nothing compared to the state of up here which, he said, really struck you afresh once you'd had a minute away from it.

He came over, and gently touched his son's forehead, then said to Ingrid already on the stretcher, "I expect we ought to call him Patrick."

Ingrid turned her head on the pillow and looked at Patrick, who was moving a towel back and forth with his foot, smearing blood more widely across the tiles. Then, to Hamish, she said she would have, if she was more of a fan of Patrick as a name, but unfortunately she wasn't. The ambulance people started wheeling her towards the door. As she passed him, Ingrid reached out and got Patrick's forearm. For a second she just held it, as if searching for words, then said, "You are doing an amazing job of the floor."

*

He and I were alone then. I sat on the side of the bath and told him to give up—it still looked like there had been a murder and Winsome was probably going to have the tiles ripped up anyway.

Patrick came and sat down. I asked him if he'd been terrified, delivering a baby in circumstances like that.

He said it wasn't the circumstances. "It was just because, I've seen a lot of births, obviously, but never," he said, you know, "done one."

While we were talking, Winsome tapped the open door and, putting her head in, said it looked like the battlefield of a particularly bloody civil war. She told us there was a change of clothes waiting for each of us in different bathrooms, "and towels etcetera" then said she needed to go and get rubber gloves and, with a sad look at the floor, "something to put those in," the towels that had so recently been her best.

*

I spent a long time in the shower and a long time changing into the clothes I found folded on a bathroom chair and a long time texting Ingrid, expecting no reply, before I finally went downstairs. Everyone was in the kitchen. The controlled mayhem Hamish had described was now absolute. My father and Rowland were having a conversation from opposite sides of the room, the subject of which I couldn't grasp. It was clear that my father was upset and my uncle was irritated. The dogs were yelping and running in circles around Rowland's ankles. Winsome was washing pots and Jessamine was putting plates into the dishwasher without being especially close to it, forcing them both to raise their voices further over the irregular clatter of china against china. My mother was sitting on a chair, straddling it like Liza Minnelli, and doing some sort of performance, regardless of the fact that no one except me was looking at her.

Patrick wasn't there. I went up to Winsome, who told me I looked very fresh, and asked if she knew where he was. She said he had left; whither, she could not say.

I went in a taxi to his flat, not knowing if he would be there and not knowing what I would say if he was, but he was the only person I wanted to be with.

I ARRIVED, IN Winsome's clothes. Patrick opened the door, still dressed as Rowland. He asked me if I wanted a cup of tea. I said yes and while we were waiting for the water to boil, I told him that I loved him. Patrick turned around and leaned against the counter, folded his arms loosely and asked me to marry him.

I said no. "I don't mean it like that. I'm saying it because I don't think we should spend as much time together as we were before you went away. I felt like your girlfriend and it's not fair for me to be with you all of the time, because even if I was your girlfriend, it couldn't go anywhere. Even though I do"—I picked the edge of the table—"want to be with you, all the time."

Patrick remained exactly as he was. "I want you to be with me all the time."

The way he said it made me feel like my body was suddenly full of warm water.

In which case, he went on, "It seems quite straightforward."

"It isn't though because I'm saying, I can't marry you."

He asked me why not. He did not seem perturbed, reaching around and tucking in the back of his shirt.

"Because you want children and I don't."

"How do you know I want children? We've never talked about it."

"You told me at the Tate that you always imagined yourself having children."

"That isn't the same thing as actively wanting them."

"I just saw you deliver a baby, Patrick. It is obvious. You do, and I would be Sophie's Choicing you because you can either marry me or be a father with someone else." I went on, so he would not say the thing I had been told so often by people who knew me and people who didn't. "I won't change my mind. I promise, I'm not going to and I don't want to be the reason you don't get to be a father."

Patrick said, "Interesting, okay" and went back to making the tea. He brought mine over and put it in front of me. He had taken the bag out because he knew with it in, I would feel like I was trying to drink out of the Ganges without getting any semi-submerged litter in my mouth.

I thanked him and he went back to where he was before. Leaning against the counter again, the folded arms. "The thing is, I will never change my mind about you." He said, he hadn't read Sophie's Choice but nevertheless, he understood the reference. "And this isn't an impossible decision, Martha. This is no decision. Whether or not I want children, I want you more."

I just said, "Okay, well" and touched the rim of my mug. It was strange, to be wanted so much. I said well again. "There's also the issue of my predisposition."

"What predisposition?"

"Towards insanity."

He said, "Martha" and for the first time sounded unhappy. I glanced up. "You're not insane."

"Not presently. But you have seen me like that."

That day in summer: he came to pick me up from Goldhawk Road at lunchtime. I was still in bed because my dreams had been grotesque and they had lingered like a physical presence in the room after I woke up, making me too afraid to move. I knew it was the beginning of something.

Patrick had knocked and asked if he could come in. I was crying and couldn't get the air to say anything.

He came over and felt my forehead, then said he was going to go and get me a glass of water. When he came back, he asked me if I wanted to watch a movie and—I remember—if I was okay with him sitting on the bed next to me, he said "with my legs up, I mean." I moved over a little bit and while he was choosing something on my laptop, he said, "Sorry you're not feeling great." I had known Patrick for so long. Most of the time—still sometimes then—my ordinary presence made him nervous. This way, he was so calm.

He stayed with me all day, and that night he slept on the floor. In the morning I felt normal. It was already over. We went to a pool. Patrick swam laps and I watched, holding a book, feeling mesmerised by the continuous movement of his arms, the way he turned his head, his endless progress through the water. Afterwards he drove me home and I apologized for being weird. He said, "Everyone has bad days."

I do not know if it was on purpose that he repeated it then, in the kitchen, everyone has bad days. "And I'd be fine with it, if you actually were. Insanity," he said, "is not a deal-breaker. If it's you."

I looked down and picked the edge of the table again. "Can I please have a biscuit?"

He said, "Yes, in a second. Could you look up, Martha?" I did.

We had the same conversation again. I told him we shouldn't see each other and he asked me to marry him. That time, with his hands in his pockets, the same as always and I started laughing because it was just him. It was just Patrick.

I said, "If you are serious, why aren't you kneeling down?"

"Because you would hate it."

I would hate it.

"Fine."

"Fine what?"

"Fine I will marry you."

Patrick said, "Right, okay," surprised and not immediately coming over. I had to get up before he moved and then, standing in front of me, he asked how I felt about—he said "you know" and meant, being kissed.

I said incredibly uncomfortable.

"Good. So do I. Let's just ah—"

"Get it over with." I kissed him. It was peculiar and extraordinary and of some duration.

Separating, Patrick said, "I was going to say, shake hands."

It is hard to look into someone's eyes. Even when you love them, it is difficult to sustain it, for the sense of being seen through. In some way, found out. But, for as long as the kiss had lasted, I didn't feel guilty for being so happy, when I had just taken something away from Patrick so that I could have what I wanted.

He asked me if I still wanted a biscuit. I said no.

"Come with me then. I have something for you." He said he had been waiting to give it to me for a long time and now that I had made him the happiest man alive by saying fine, he was going to go and get it.

I let him lead me by the hand into his bedroom. I knew it would be his mother's wedding ring. I stood and waited while he looked for it in his drawer with a gathering sense of not wanting it.

He said, "It might not be in very good condition. I haven't got it out for ages. It might not even fit." I was holding my hands together and wasted the final seconds of being able to tell him to please keep it—something so precious, which had belonged to a woman he loved who we could only assume would have hated me—by silently rubbing the back of my left hand as though the ring was already on it and I could somehow rub it off.

He found the box and took the band out. He held it out, between two fingers. It was amazing. Patrick said, "As it turns out, Martha, despite what I may have said at different times, I have been in love with you for fifteen years. Since the moment you spat this onto my arm." It was the rubber band from my braces.

He took my hand and tried to slide, and ultimately, stretched it over my finger. I looked at my hand and told him I would wear it forever, although it was already cutting off the blood supply. He kissed me again. Then, I said, "So just to confirm. When I asked you, that time, if you were in love with me—"

"Utterly," he said. "I loved you utterly."

*

I told Patrick I couldn't sleep with him that night because Heather was shortly due home, and I needed her to not be in the next room. He said he didn't want to anyway because he was saving himself for the right person and offered to take me back to Goldhawk Road.

In the car, doing up his seatbelt, Patrick said, "It is going to be rubbish the first time. You know that, don't you?"

"I do."

"Because I've had a decade or so to overthink it."

I told him I hated that term, because people were constantly accusing me of it. "I think they are underthinking everything. But I don't say so because it would be rude."

Patrick said yes, okay. "That's the most important thing to establish in this conversation, not how to negotiate our sex life" and started the car.

*

One day, years later, my mother would tell me that no marriage makes sense to the outside world because, she would say, a marriage is its own world. And I would dismiss her because by then ours had come to its end. But that was what it felt like, for the minute before we said goodbye outside my parents' house, Patrick's arms around me and my face turned into his neck. I hadn't said I loved him, properly in the way he just had, but it is what I meant when I said, "Thank you, Patrick," and went inside.

We went to the hospital the next day to see Ingrid. My parents, and Winsome and Rowland, were already there with Hamish, crowded into a room that was small and overly supplied with chairs.

As we were getting ready to go, Patrick said, "Just quickly, everyone, I asked Martha to marry me last night and she said fine."

Ingrid said oh my gosh, finally. "It's been a real will they, will they situation." My father did a triumphant movement with both fists, like someone who has just discovered they're the winner of something, then tried to make his way over to us, pushing through the surfeit of chairs. "I'm parked in—Rowland, move, I need to shake my son-in-law's hand." Patrick went over instead and I was, for a second, by myself.

Ingrid said, "Hamish, hug Martha. I can't get up." While I was being hugged stiffly by my sister's husband, I heard my mother say, "I thought they were engaged already. Why did I think that?"

Hamish released me and my father said, "It doesn't matter. They are now. What do you think, Winsome?"

My aunt said it was lovely because it made everything so tidy. And we were welcome, she said, to have it at Belgravia, should we so wish. Rowland, beside her, said, "I hope you've got £50,000 on hand, do you, Patrick? Bloody expensive business, weddings."

When my father finally reached me, he pulled me into a crushing hug and kept me there until Ingrid said, "Can you all leave now please?" and Hamish showed us out.

*

Patrick and I went back to his flat. There was a note on the table from Heather, reminding him that she had gone away and wouldn't be back until the weekend. I read it over his shoulder. He said, "I promise I didn't arrange that. Do you need a cup of tea first or anything?"

I said we should have it afterwards, as a reward, and pulled my T-shirt off.

*

Patrick wondered if it was the worst sex that had been had by two people in the UK since records began. For the few minutes it lasted, he had the set expression of someone trying to endure a minor medical procedure without anaesthetic. I could not stop making small talk. We had got out of bed straightaway and dressed with our backs to each other.

In the kitchen, drinking tea, I told Patrick that it was like a terrible party.

He asked me if I meant highly anticipated but then disappointing.

I said no. "Because only one person came."

The second time, we agreed, was motive to continue.

The third time, it felt like we had been melted down and made into another thing. We lay for so long afterwards, facing each other in the dark, not talking, our breath in the same pattern, our stomachs touching. We went to sleep that way and woke up that way. It was the happiest I have ever felt.

*

In the morning, after he gets out of the shower, Patrick puts his watch on first. He dries himself in the bathroom and leaves the towel behind. It is more efficient, he says, not having to make a return trip just to hang it up. I was still in his bed, the first time he performed the routine in front of me, coming into the room, wandering from his drawers to his wardrobe. Naked except for the watch. I observed him for as long as I could before he noticed and asked me what was funny.

I said, "Do you have the time, Patrick?"

He said, I do actually, and went back to his drawers.

Men describe themselves as real leg men. A tits man. With Patrick, I found out I am a real shoulders man. I love a good set of delts.

The fourth time, the fifth time . . .

*

Ingrid wanted to know what it had been like, sleeping with Patrick. We were walking to a park close to her house. It was intensely cold but she had not been out of the house since she was discharged from the hospital and had begun to feel delirious. She was pushing the pram. I was carrying a heavy seat cushion from her sofa because she needed to feed the baby and the only way it didn't hurt was with the cushion—only this cushion—underneath him. We found somewhere to sit down and while she was getting ready she said, "Just tell me one thing about it. Please."

I refused, then relented because she kept asking. "I didn't know it could be like that." I said I hadn't known that was what it was for. "How you were meant to feel afterwards. That the afterwards is why sex exists."

She said, that's nice. "But I meant an actual detail."

On the way back to the house Ingrid said, "Do you know what annoys me so much? If I got hit by a car while we're crossing and died, in the newspaper it would say a mother of a something-day-old baby was killed at a notorious intersection. Why can't it say a human who incidentally has a baby was killed at a notorious intersection?"

"It makes it sadder," I said. "If it's a mother."

"It can't be sadder," Ingrid said. "I'm dead. That is the saddest it can be. But apparently I just exist in terms of my relationship to other people now and Hamish still gets to be a person. Thanks. Amazing."

I helped her get the pram inside, reestablished the sofa, and went to make her tea. The baby was feeding again when I came back from the kitchen. She kissed his head and looked up. I saw her hesitate before she said, "I think you and Patrick should have babies. I'm sorry. I know you're anti-motherhood but I do. He isn't Jonathan. Don't you think, with him—"

"Ingrid."

"I'm just saying. He would be such a good—"

"Ingrid."

"And you could do it. I promise. It's not even that hard. I mean look at me." She directed my attention to her unclean clothes, her swollen chest, damp spots on the cushions and looked about to laugh, then like she was going to cry, then merely exhausted.

I asked her what she wanted for her birthday.

Ingrid said, "When is it?"

I told her it was tomorrow.

"In that case, a bag of salty licorice. The kind from Ikea."

The baby squirmed and pulled off. Ingrid let out a little cry and covered her breast. I helped her turn the cushion around and once he was on again, I asked if I could get her a kind of licorice that didn't require a journey to Croydon. She did cry then, telling me through tears that if I understood what it was like, being woken up fifty times a night and having to feed a baby every two hours when it takes an hour and fifty-nine minutes and feels like being stabbed in the nipple with four hundred knives, then I would be like, do you know what? I think I will just get my sister the licorice she specifically likes.

I drove directly from her house to Croydon and left on her step the next day £95 worth of salty licorice in the blue bag and a card. It said "Happy birthday to the world's best mother, daughter, wife of a mid-ranking civil servant, neighbor, shop customer, employee, council-tax payer, crosser of roads, recent NHS admission, her sister's entire universe."

Days later, Ingrid texted me to say that after the third packet, she'd really gone off it. Then she sent a photo of her hand, holding a Starbucks cup. Instead of asking her name, the person who took her order had just written LADY WITH PRAM.

WE GOT MARRIED in March. The first thing the minister said when I got to the altar and stopped next to Patrick was, "If anyone needs the toilets, they are through the vestry and to the right." He made the gesture of a cabin steward pointing out the exit on one side. Patrick tilted his head towards me and whispered, "I think I'll try and hang on."

The second thing the minister said was, "I believe this day has been rather a long time coming."

*

I wore a dress with sleeves and a high neck. It was made of lace and looked vintage and came from Topshop. Ingrid helped me get ready and said I looked like Miss Havisham, pre her big day turning to absolute shit. She gave me a card that said "Patrick Loves Martha." It was attached to the present, Hot Tracks '93.

*

When my cousins were teenagers, Winsome could correct their posture at the table by silently getting their attention and, once they were looking at her, reaching up her arm and taking hold of an imaginary string attached to the crown of her head. Then as they watched, she would tug it upwards, lengthening her neck and drawing her shoulders down at the same time in a way they could not help imitating. If they were sitting slack-mouthed, Winsome would touch the underside of her chin with the back of her hand, and if they were not smiling while they were being spoken to, she would smile at them in the hard, artificial manner of a school choir mistress reminding her performers that this is their happy number.

At the reception, my mother stood up in the middle of my father's speech and said, "Fergie, I will take it from here." She was holding an overfilled brandy balloon and every time she lifted it to toast one of her own remarks, the contents spilled over the rim. When, at one point, she raised her arm so she could lick brandy off the inside of her wrist, I looked away and saw Winsome, beside her, flashing her eyes at me. As I watched, my aunt's hand went to her crown, then she pinched the invisible string and I felt myself rise, in unison, as she pulled it upwards. She was smiling at me but not as the choir mistress, as my aunt telling me that we were going to be brave.

But in a second, my mother started saying something about sex; instantly Winsome brought her hand down and knocked over her own glass. Wine flooded across the table and began running off the front onto the carpet. Leaping up she said, "Celia, napkin" over and over until my mother was forced to stop talking. By the time Winsome finished her show of cleaning up, my mother had lost her train of thought.

*

Jessamine was the only other person who drank too much at the reception. As Patrick and I were leaving, she wrapped her arms around my neck and kissed me and whispered, loudly into my ear, that she loved me so much and she was so, so glad I was marrying Patrick. Probably—no, definitely—she was still in love with him but it was fine because I might get tired of being with someone so boring and good and hot and then she could have him back. She kissed me again, then apologized because she had to quickly go and be sick in the loo. Patrick believed that it happened but not that it was true; Ingrid believed both.

*

His father did not come to our wedding because he was in the process of divorcing Cynthia. I told Patrick we should go to Hong Kong and stay with him. He said, "We really shouldn't." I didn't meet Christopher Friel until much later when he had a coronary incident and Patrick finally agreed to go. I did not like him after the first five to ten minutes in his company. Patrick had been charitable in every story he'd ever told about him.

Nothing in Christopher's apartment testified to the existence of a son. I asked if he had anything of Patrick's from childhood that I could look at but he said he'd got rid of it all years ago. He sounded proud. But, as we were packing to leave, he brought out a small collection of letters Patrick had written to his mother while she was overseas for a number of weeks. They'd somehow survived the cull, Christopher said, and offered them to me, in their Ziploc bag.

I read them during the flight home. The cabin light was low

and Patrick was sleeping with his arms folded and his shoulders drawn up. He was six when he wrote them. He had signed all of them "Lost of love, Paddy." I touched his wrist. He stirred but didn't wake up. I wanted to say, if you ever write me a letter, please sign it that way. Lost of love, Paddy.

*

He chose St. Petersburg for our honeymoon, and the hotel because although I had said I could do it, I fell at the first hurdle, which was the travelers' photos on TripAdvisor: an infinity of towel swans and seafood platters and unacceptable stray hairs.

On the plane, he asked me if I was going to change my name. He had just finished a crossword in the in-flight magazine that a previous passenger had already started.

I said I wasn't.

"Because of the patriarchy?"

"Because of the paperwork."

A steward came past with a cart. Patrick asked for a napkin and told me he was going to write a list of pros and cons about name changing. Ten minutes later he read it to me. There were no cons on it. I told him I could think of some and took the pen out of his hand. He said I should press my button and ask for a packet of napkins since I was a pro at thinking up cons.

*

We lost each other in the Hermitage on our first morning. I went to the café and ordered jasmine tea and waited for him to find me. Before it arrived, I heard his voice on the loudspeaker. "Mrs. Martha Friel, née Russell. Your husband would like you to come to the main lobby."

Next to the desk, a stand of brochures, doing something with his collar—thank God.

*

On the Nevsky Prospekt, Patrick bought me a figurine of a horse from a teenage girl who was selling them. She had a baby with her. Waiting as he chose, I felt like I couldn't breathe for the sorrow of its smiling at me, and the way it grabbed its little feet at the same time, happy even though its life was sitting for hours a day in a metal pram with dirty white wheels while its mother sold horses.

Patrick paid £50 for the worst one, not the 50p she asked for it, pretending he didn't realize his mistake. As we walked away, Patrick handed me the horse and asked me what I was going to call it. I said Trotsky and burst into tears. Afterwards I apologized for not being fun. Patrick said he would have been worried if I was fun in this scenario.

*

That night it was snowing too hard to go out. We ate in the hotel restaurant. Instead of going in by the lobby, Patrick led me out onto the street. The air was so cold, it made me cover my eyes. He took my elbow and we ran along the short stretch of pavement to an external entrance. Back inside, Patrick said, "Totally independent restaurant." I could not remember if or when I had told him that my reaction to hotel restaurants ranges between ennui and despair.

I finished reading my menu and told Patrick, who was on the second page of his, that I would be taking his name after all.

He looked up. "Why?"

"Because," I said, thanks to my mother obviously, "I am expert in all forms of passive aggression and I can't let such an emotionally manipulative public announcement go unrewarded."

He leaned across the table and kissed me, even though I had just put a piece of bread in my mouth. He said I'm so glad Martha. "I had to give the man a hundred dollars to let me use the microphone. I mean, American dollars."

I swallowed. "You're probably going to Siberian prison."

He said absolutely worth it and went back to his menu.

Out loud, because I had nothing else to do, I analyzed the particular pathos of hotel restaurants. I said maybe it was the lighting, or the fact they were always carpeted, the higher than usual concentration of people eating alone, maybe it was just the concept of an omelette station that made me question the meaning of everything.

Patrick waited for me to finish, then asked me if I'd ever had borscht.

I said, "I love you so much," then a maître d' came over with two green glass bottles and said, "Water with gas or no gas?"

*

At Heathrow, waiting for our bags, Patrick said, "Remember that wedding we had?" I had just asked him how he was planning to get back to his flat. He had his arm around me and kissed the side of my head. I said, "Sorry. I'm so tired." It had been so much effort, telling myself and making myself believe that coming back from a honeymoon is when marriages start, not when they end.

I did not know how to be a wife. I was so scared. Patrick looked so happy.

IN THE TAXI and again as I followed him up the stairs, Patrick told me I could do whatever I wanted to the flat to make it feel like mine. It was a Friday. On Saturday he went to work and I took everything out of the kitchen cupboards and put it all back in, one cupboard over, so that if Heather visited, she would not know where anything was. I couldn't think of anything else.

I had decided to be neat and I was for a number of days. But Patrick preferred the flat the way it was now, he said, with clothes on the floor, magazines and hair elastics and an astonishing number of glasses, and everything so generally accessible because cupboards and drawers were never, ever shut. The way he laughed as he spoke did not make me feel guilty, and he made no effort to move anything. Maybe that was why his flat felt like my home so quickly.

The only things he asked if I could do, a few weeks later, was not to leave medication lying around—he said, "It's just my training"—and try to use the spreadsheet he had made me for financial record-keeping, instead of my method, which was stuffing receipts into a ragged envelope, then losing it.

He opened it on his computer to teach me how it worked. I told him that seeing numbers in such concentration caused an invisible membrane to come down from underneath my eyelids, blinding me until the numbers went away. There were many categories. One of them was called Martha's Unexpecteds. I said I had not expected him to be so Stasi-like in his financial oversight. He said he didn't realize anyone would suggest a Word document and the calculator on their phone as an alternative to an actual spreadsheet. I told him I would try and use it, but it would be in a spirit of self-denial. Patrick said later, it was genuinely incredible how many Unexpecteds one person could attract.

*

In bed, on the nights he wasn't working, Patrick would do a difficult Sudoku from a book of only difficult Sudokus and I would ask him when he was going to turn the light off. I told him that was when I felt the most married.

Once he had finished, he would put the Sudoku book away and read articles from medical journals. If I lay with my back to him, Patrick would absentmindedly begin pressing his thumb into places that hurt at the base of my spine. He bought massage oil from somewhere and when he found out that things with fake perfume in them make me feel like I am being slowly asphyxiated he bought coconut oil, a kind from the supermarket that came in a jar and had a high smoke point which, the label said, made it suitable for all kinds of frying. Even when he put the journal away, he kept rubbing my back. Sometimes for the whole of Newsnight, sometimes after he would turn off the light. That was when I felt the most loved.

One night, I rolled over in the dark and asked if he had any feeling left in his thumb. I said, "How can you do that for so long?"

He said, "I'm hoping it turns sexual."

I told him that was a shame. "I'm hoping it turns into me being asleep." I heard the lid come off the jar.

Patrick said, "May the best man win."

Our sheets smelled like a Bounty Bar.

*

Then Patrick moved to a different hospital on the other side of London. It felt like he was never home. I was still working at the publishing house. Although spring, it was cold and constantly gray and when no part of the working day could be spent on the roof with the only other girl who was left at the company besides me, it was impossible to sustain activity beyond lunchtime. The editor started telling us to go home if we had nothing to do because he couldn't bear our salad lunches and the sound of ladies' voices, talking and talking. I felt like I was always at home. I would invite Ingrid to come over or would ask if I could go there. She always said yes but if the baby had not slept, or was sleeping or nearly asleep, she would text and cancel at the last minute. Or I would go, and she would have to feed him in the other room because he was distractible, or she would complain or talk endlessly about the women in her baby group and I would go home, feeling guilty that from the moment I had arrived I had been trying to think how to leave.

In bed, on those nights when Patrick was at work and I had

seen no one all day, I missed him so much it made me angry. I stayed up late reading Lee Child novels I bought on his Kindle and composing arguments to have with him when he got back. I told him I did not feel married. I told him I didn't feel loved, in which case, what was the point.

That was also when I started throwing things. The first time, a fork at Patrick because he walked away from me when I was upset. About something so small—as he was getting ready for work, he mentioned that he had got two more Amazon receipts that day and because I had previously told him I was going to read all of James Joyce including the shit ones by the end of summer, he was starting to worry that the Jack Reacher thing was a cry for help.

I remember him stopping when the fork hit the back of his leg and rang onto the floor, looking back and laughing, out of shock. I laughed too so then it was a joke. My funny impression of a wife going insane from loneliness. He said ha, okay. "It seems like I should go then." And I threw something at the door as he shut it behind him and no one laughed.

The next day, Patrick did his impression of a husband who hadn't had things thrown at him the night before. I kept waiting for him to mention it. He didn't. At dinner I said, "Are we going to talk about the fork?" And he said, "Don't worry, you weren't feeling great." I said fine, if you don't want to. I sounded angry but I was grateful that he hadn't made me apologize or explain why I had reacted that way to a joke, because I didn't know. I said, "I'm sorry anyway" and told him I wouldn't do it again, "obviously."

But I kept throwing things, in moments of rage that were unpredictable and incommensurate with whatever had happened.

Except once—a hairdryer, hard enough that it left a bruise where it hit him, because I had complained about being lonely and he said, laughing, that I should have a baby for something to do.

As soon as I had done it, I would go out of the room, leaving the pieces of whatever I had broken on the floor. They would have been swept up and disposed of, always, by the time I came back.

As a teenager, whenever she was getting ready to go out, Ingrid would have a tantrum about what to wear, becoming so hysterical so quickly, she seemed like a different person. She pulled outfits out of her wardrobe, tried them on, wrenched them off, sobbed, swore, screamed that she was fat, told my parents she hated them and wanted them to die, tipped her drawers out until everything she owned was on the floor. Then she would find something and instantly she would be fine.

As an adult, she told me that it felt so real in the moment, but afterwards she couldn't believe she'd got so upset and thought she would never do it again. She never apologized afterwards and my parents did not make her. But, she said, "it didn't matter, she knew they were still thinking about it" and her shame was so intense it made her angry at us. "Instead of like, hating myself."

Throwing something at your husband is the same. I was so ashamed afterwards, it made me angrier at Patrick than I had already become for his never being around.

*

When you are a woman over thirty, with a husband but without children, married couples at parties are curious to know why. They agree with each other that having children is the best thing they have ever done. According to the husband, you should just get on with it; the wife says you don't want to leave it too late. Privately, they are wondering if there is something medically wrong with you. They wish they could ask directly. Perhaps, if they can outlast your silence, you will offer it up of your own accord. But the wife can't resist—she has to tell you about a friend of hers who was told the same thing but as soon as she gave up hope . . . the husband says bingo.

In the beginning, I told strangers I couldn't have children because I thought it would stop them from continuing beyond their initial inquiry. It is better to say you don't want them. Then they know straightaway that there is something wrong with you, just not in a medical sense. So the husband can say, oh well, good for you, focusing on your career, even if, to that point, there had been so little evidence of a career being focused on. The wife doesn't say anything, she is already looking around.

*

By summer I had read four and a half pages of Ulysses and all of Lee Child. Patrick took me out to dinner to celebrate. I told him the shit James Joyces turned out to be all of them. During dessert, he gave me a library card. He said it was a present to go with the £144 worth of Jack Reachers he had already given me.

I got out one book. An Ian McEwan that I thought was a novel and put it in a drawer when I realized it was short stories. I called Ingrid and told her I had accidentally invested in two characters who would be dead in sixteen pages. She said seriously. "Who has the time?"

ALTHOUGH FROM THE age of sixteen, she smoked every day in high school at the bottom of the playing fields, and was regularly caught, Ingrid graduated without any detentions on her record. It was so easy for her to talk her way out of them. Although from age seventeen to that summer, I was regularly ill, I had never been admitted to the hospital. It was so easy for me to talk my way out of it.

It was August, nearly September. Patrick went to Hong Kong for his father's third wedding, to the twenty-four-year-old daughter of one of his colleagues. For weeks the headlines had been about the weather, about London putting Greece in the shade and giving the Costa del Sol a run for its money. I didn't go with him because I had started to feel unwell. Two days after he left, I woke up and everything was black.

I tried to go back to sleep, hot and tangled and sick with guilt that I wasn't getting up and going to work. A dog was barking from the flat below, and somewhere outside road workers were breaking up the street. I listened to the relentless jangle and bleat of the pneumatic drill. It wouldn't stop it wouldn't stop it wouldn't stop.

As the noise got louder and louder, it felt—it always felt—like pressure building in my skull, like air is being pumped and pumped and pumped in until it's hard like a tire, but still more air pushes in and in and it begins to hurt so much, knife hot and migrainous, that you cry and imagine a fissure in the hard bone becoming a crack and the air finally rushing out and then relief from the pain. You are terrified. You are going to vomit. Your lungs are closing. The room is moving. Something bad is about to happen. It's already in the room. It is making your back cold. You wait and wait and wait and then it doesn't happen. The thing has left the room and it has left you behind. It isn't going to end. There isn't day and night. There isn't time. Only pain, and the pressure and the terror that is like a twisted cord running down the center of your body.

Late, in the afternoon, I got up and went to the kitchen. I tried to eat but couldn't. Water made me feel nauseous. My hips ached from lying on my side in a ball. Patrick called and I cried on the phone and said sorry, sorry, sorry. He said he would change his flight. He said, "Can you try and go out? Go to the Ladies' Pond. Take a taxi the whole way." He said, "Martha, I love you so much." I hung up, promising to call Ingrid, but was too ashamed once he had gone, imagining her arriving and finding me this way.

From above, I watched myself get up and move slowly around the flat like I was so old, a woman at the end of her life. I dragged on my swimsuit, put clothes over it, put toothpaste in my mouth, left the flat. The effort of pushing open the building's heavy outer door took my breath away.

There was too much noise, heat, too many people coming towards me and buses thundering past me so near the curb, I went home again. Patrick called, I cried on the phone. He said his plane was leaving in an hour, he would be back so soon.

I asked him to stay on the phone and talk to me and I could just listen. I told him I was very scared.

"Of what?"

"Me."

He said, "You won't do anything, will you?" He wanted me to promise. I said I couldn't. He said in that case, Martha, please go to the hospital straightaway.

I knew that I wouldn't. But as it got dark again, I began to feel scared of the flat, its ringing silence, the dead air. Patrick was out of reach on the plane by then. I crawled on my hands and knees to the door and waited outside for a taxi with my back pressed against a brick wall. My brain laughed at me, look at how stupid you are, crawling across the floor, look at you being scared to go outside.

*

The doctor in emergency said, "Why have you brought yourself here today?" He didn't sit down.

My hair was in my eyes and sticking to my wet face and the stream running from my nose but I didn't have the energy to lift my arm and push it away. I told him it was because I was so tired. He said I needed to speak up, and asked if I was having thoughts about hurting myself. I said no, I said I just wanted to not exist anymore and asked if there was something he could give me that would make me go away, but in a way that wouldn't hurt anyone or make a mess. Then I stopped talking because he said I seemed more intelligent than that, sounding frustrated.

Although I didn't look up from the spot of floor I had been

staring at since I was put into the room, I sensed him looking at my notes, then heard the door open, suck across the linoleum and click shut. He was gone for so long that I began to believe the hospital had closed and I was alone, locked in. I scratched my wrists and stared at the floor. He came back, it felt like hours later. Patrick was with him. I didn't know how he knew where I was, and I was filled with shame because he had to come home for me, his miserable wife slumped in a plastic hospital chair, too stupid even to raise her head.

They talked about me between themselves. I heard the doctor say, "Listen, I can find her a bed but it would be an NHS facility and," more quietly, "you'll know that public psych wards are not nice places." I didn't interrupt. "In my opinion, she's better off going home." He said, "I can give her something that will calm her down and we can touch base in the morning."

Patrick crouched beside my chair, holding the armrest, and moved my hair. He asked me if I felt like I should go in, just for a bit. He said it was up to me. I said no thank you. I had always been too afraid to be among those people in case they didn't think it was weird I was there. In case the doctors wouldn't let me go. I wanted Patrick to grab me by the wrists and drag me there so that I did not have to decide. I wanted him not to believe me when I said it was fine.

"Are you sure?"

I said yes, and pushed my hair off my face properly as I stood up. I said he didn't have to worry, I just needed some sleep.

The doctor said, "There we go, she's already perking up."

Patrick drove us back without speaking. His expression was blank. At home, he could not get his key in the lock and, just once, he kicked the base of the door. It was the most violent thing I have ever seen him do.

In the bathroom I swallowed all of what the doctor had given me without reading the dose, took off my clothes and the swimsuit, which had left red lines all over my body, and slept for twenty-three hours. In brief moments of consciousness, I would open my eyes and see Patrick sitting in a chair in the corner of our room. I saw that he had put a plate of toast on the bedside table. Later, that he'd taken it away again. I said sorry, but I'm not sure it was ever out loud.

He was in the living room when I finally woke up and went out to find him. It was dark outside. He said, "I was going to get pizza."

"Okay."

I sat down on the sofa. Patrick moved his arm so that I could be against his side, facing into him, with my knees up so that I was a ball. I never wanted to be anywhere except for there. Patrick, working around me, called the delivery place.

I ate. It made me feel better. We watched a movie. I told him I was sorry for what had happened. He said it was fine . . . everyone has etc.

*

I met Ingrid for lunch in Primrose Hill. It was the first time she had left the baby, even though he was eight months old. I asked her if she missed him. She said she felt like she had just got out of high security prison.

We had manicures, went to a film and talked through it until a man in the next row asked us to please put a sock in it. We walked to the Heath, looked at the Ladies' Pond, swam in our knickers. We laughed our heads off.

As we walked back through the park, a teenage boy approached us and said, "Are you the sisters from that band?" Ingrid said we were. He said, "Go on then, sing us something." She told him we were on vocal rest.

I felt intensely good. I didn't tell Ingrid that a week ago, the same day, I was in the hospital because I had forgotten.

Patrick never mentioned it again but a short time later he said maybe we should leave London, in case London was the problem. At the beginning of winter, tenants took over our flat and we moved to the Executive Home.

As we were driving out of London, Patrick asked me if I would consider making friends in Oxford. Even if I didn't want to and I was only doing it for him, he didn't mind. He just didn't want me to start hating it too soon. He said, at least until we've unloaded the car.

I was in the passenger seat looking for pictures of Drunk Kate Moss on my phone to send to Ingrid because at the time we were communicating primarily by that means. She was four weeks pregnant, not intentionally, and she said seeing pap shots of Kate Moss falling out of Annabel's with her eyes a bit shut was the only way she was getting through the day.

I told Patrick I would, although I didn't know how.

"Maybe, not a book club obviously but like a book club." He said, "You don't have to get a job straightaway either if—"

I said there weren't any jobs anyway, I had already looked.

"Well in that case, it makes sense to focus on the friends thing. And maybe you could think about doing something else work-wise, if you wanted to. Or, I don't know, do a master's."

"In what?"

"In something."

I screen-shotted a picture of Kate Moss in a fur coat ashing a cigarette into a hotel topiary, and said, "I'm thinking about re-training as a prostitute."

In the middle of overtaking a van, Patrick shot me a look. "Okay. First, I don't think you're supposed to use that term any-more. Second, you know this house is in a cul-de-sac. There won't be the foot traffic."

I went back to my phone.

Nearing Oxford he asked me if I wanted to drive past the al-lotment garden he had put his name down for. I said that un-fortunately I didn't since it was winter and presumably it was a square of black mud at the present time. He told me to wait—by summer we would be entirely self-sufficient, in the area of let-tuce.

That night we slept on our mattress in the living room sur-rounded by boxes, which I had opened one by one and become overwhelmed by when none of them were all just towels. The heating was too high and I lay awake thinking through the cata-logue of terrible things I have done and said, and the much worse things I have thought.

I woke Patrick up and gave him one or two examples. That I sometimes wished my parents had never met each other. That I wished Ingrid didn't get pregnant so easily and that everyone we knew had less money. He listened without opening his eyes, then said, "Martha, you can't honestly think you're the only one who thinks things like that. Everyone has terrible thoughts."

"You don't."

"Yes I do."

He rolled away from me, and started to fall asleep again. I got up and turned the ceiling light on. Back beside him I said,

"Tell me the worst thing you've ever thought. I bet it's not even remotely shocking."

Patrick moved onto his back and bent his arm over his eyes. "Fine. At work a while ago they brought in a man who was in his nineties. He was brain dead from a stroke and when his family got there I explained that there was no chance he was going to recover and that it was a question of how long they wanted to keep him on the ventilator. His wife and son said, essentially, to go ahead but his daughter refused and said they should wait in case of a miracle. She was incredibly upset but it was midnight, and I'd been there since five o'clock in the morning and all I could think was hurry up and sign the jolly thing so I can go home."

"Gosh. That is quite bad."

He said, "I know."

"Did you actually say the jolly thing to their faces?"

He said okay shut up, and felt on the floor for his phone. He started streaming Radio Four. It was the Shipping Forecast. "You will be asleep by the time he gets to the Scilly Isles, I promise. Please can you turn off the light."

I did, and lay looking at the unfamiliar ceiling, listening to the man say, Fisher, Dogger, Cromaty. Fine, becoming poor.

He said, Fair Isle, Faeoro, the Hebrides. Cyclonic, becoming rough or very rough. Occasionally good.

I turned my pillow over and asked Patrick if he thought the forecast for the Hebrides was really a metaphor for my interior state but he was already asleep. I closed my eyes and listened until God Save the Queen and the end of transmission.

The next morning, in the kitchen while he looked for the kettle, I said, "What did you do about the man in the end?"

"I stayed for another six hours until the daughter changed her mind, then I managed his death. Martha, why did you label every single box Miscellaneous?"

*

There was a gate at the bottom of the Executive Development that gave access to the canal and the muddy towpath on the other side. We walked along it in the afternoon. On the other side of the canal, Port Meadow was a flat, silver expanse stretching towards a low black line of trees and behind them the outline of spires. Horses were grazing half-hidden in the mist. I did not know who they belonged to.

At its end, the towpath joined a street into town and we kept going. Patrick showed some sort of card to the man inside the gatehouse of Magdalen College and took me in. He promised me close-up deer but they were standing together, in a distant corner of the park, and the only thing roaming freely on the grass were young, vital people, students who called out to each other, broke into little sprints for no reason, existed as though nothing bad had ever or would ever happen to them.

*

I found a book club and went to it. It was at someone's house. The women all had doctorates and did not know what to say when I told them I didn't, as if I had just confessed to having no living relatives or an illness with a residual stigma.

I found a different book club, in a library. The women there all had doctorates, too. I said mine was on the Lancashire Cotton Panic of 1861 because I had listened to an episode of In Our Time about it while I walked there. A woman I talked to afterwards said she would love to hear more about my area of research next week, but I had already told her all the things I could remember. I left knowing I could not go back because I would have to listen to the episode again, and one of the three male experts on the panel had been a compulsive throat clearer, and kept interrupting its sole female.

*

Sometimes, during the day, I sat in the front window of the Executive Home and stared at the facing Executive Home, trying to imagine myself inside it, living a mirror image version of my exact life.

The actual woman who lived there at the time had boy-girl twins and a husband who was, according to the magnetic signs that he pressed onto his car doors in the morning and peeled off at night, The Chiropractor Who Comes To You.

One day she knocked on the door and apologized for not coming over sooner. We were wearing the same top and when she noticed and laughed, I saw she had adult braces. While she was talking, I imagined what it would be like to be her friend. If we would visit each other without texting, if we would drink wine in each other's kitchens or outside in our gardens, if I would tell her about my life and she would be forthcoming about a childhood in which braces were not possible.

She said she hadn't noticed any children and asked what I did. I told her I was a writer. She said she actually had a blog, and blushed telling me the name of it. It was mostly funny observations about life, and recipes, and she said I obviously didn't need to read it.

The main thing: what did I think of the house? I said oh my gosh, like we were friends who have been talking for an hour and have finally got to the good part. "I feel like I've been in a dissociative fugue since we drove in the gates." I told her I had only lived in London and Paris and wasn't sure I'd known places like this really existed. "Are we supposed to believe we're in Regency Bath, despite the satellite dishes?" I was talking too fast by then because Patrick was the only person I had spoken to for a period of days but I thought I was being interesting and funny from the way she was smiling and furiously nodding. "I've come home about ten times and not been able to get the door open and then I realize I'm standing in front of the wrong house." I made a joke about the enervating nature of taupe carpet and said finally, on the positive side, if she happened to own fifteen thousand appliances with unusual plugs and ever wanted to use them all at once, she was welcome to run an extension cord over the pretend-cobbled street. Her smile was suddenly gone. She did a little cough and said it was probably good we were just renting and went back to her own house.

I didn't understand why she went to extreme lengths to avoid eye contact with me after that, until I recounted the conversation to Patrick who pointed out that if she owned her house and loved it, she might have been a bit upset to hear an identical one described as soul-crushing.

I found her blog. It was called Living the Cul-De-Sac Life and there was a picture of our house or hers at the top. Since we were not going to be friends, I was disappointed that she was a good writer and that her funny observations were actually funny. I began reading it every day. To begin with, in search of references to myself and then, because she was writing the mirror-image version of my life, the one where my vacuum cleaner cupboard is on the left, and I have boy-girl twins.

*

I got a letter from the library, forwarded by our tenants. It asked me for the Ian McEwan back and £92.90 in compound fines. Because there was no money in Martha's Unexpecteds at the time, I rang up and told them that unfortunately Martha Friel was a registered missing person, but if she was ever found, I would ask her about the book.

*

I started going to the allotment with Patrick sometimes on weekends, on the proviso that I didn't have to help. I said, "aka, she died doing what he loved." He bought a folding chair and a small shed to keep it in so I could sit, reading or watching him, with my feet on a dead tree trunk that demarcated our failing carrots from the thriving carrots of our neighbor. Once, while he was doing something with a hoe that still had the cardboard tag around the handle, I lowered my book and said that I knew it would be expensive if they charged by the word but this is what I would like on my headstone: "It's from Cold Comfort Farm. Someone has just asked the main girl what she likes and she says:

I wasn't quite sure, but on the whole I thought I liked having everything very tidy and calm all around me, and not being bothered to do things, and laughing at the kind of joke other people didn't think at all funny, and going for country walks and not being asked to express opinions about things like love, and isn't so-and-so peculiar."

He said, "Martha, expressing opinions about peculiar people is the only thing you care about. And you never ever need to be asked."

*

In December, I got a part-time job at the Bodleian Library gift shop selling mugs and keyrings and branded tote bags to tourists so that I could spend eight hours sitting on a stool mostly not talking.

A woman wearing a souvenir sweatshirt came in and I watched her put a gift pack of pencils up her sleeve. When she came up to the counter to pay for something else, I asked if she'd like the pencils gift-wrapped as well. I told her it was complimentary. She turned red and said she didn't know what I was talking about. She said she no longer wanted what she had put on the counter. As she turned to walk away I said, "Only five shoplifting days left 'til Christmas," and stayed on my stool.

I told Patrick, who said retail may not be my thing. After Christmas, they replaced me with an older lady who was amenable to standing up.

A short time later I got an email from somebody I didn't know. He said we had crossed over at World of Interiors. "You were really funny. I think you had just got married or you were about to get married? I was doing work experience." Now, he said, he was the editor of Waitrose magazine and he had an idea.

*

I started seeing a psychologist because London wasn't the problem. Being sad is, like writing a funny food column, something I can do anywhere. I found her on findatherapist.co.uk. On the first page of the website there was a button that said What's Worrying You? in white letters on a sky-blue background. Clicking on it produced a drop-down menu. I selected Other.

The title of her listing was Julie, Female. I chose her because she was <5 miles from town center and because I found her headshot compelling. She was wearing a hat. I took a photo of the screen with my phone and texted it to Ingrid. She said, "Headshot hat one hundred percent alarm bells."

Julie, Female and I worked together for months. She said we were doing good work. All that time she was careful never to reveal the particulars of her own life, as though I would be compelled to drive to her house on a non-therapy day and sit outside in my car for long periods if I ever discovered she liked swimming and had an adult son in the military.

Then, one day, in the middle of a session, she said something-something my ex-husband. I looked at her left hand. By that time I knew all Julie's jewelry and mugs and skirts and all her different pointy boots. The nestling ring set was gone from her fourth finger, now noticeably thinner than her other fingers below the knuckle.

Julie, Female's marriage had broken down while we were in her converted spare room doing good work. At the end, I told her that I had just remembered I wasn't going to be able to make it the following week.

Patrick was home when I got back, in the kitchen, wiping something off his elbow with the dish sponge. I told him what had happened.

He said, "You can't just not turn up from now on" and suggested I call her. "You might change your mind and want to start seeing her again."

"I won't," I said. "It's like having a fat personal trainer." He frowned. "Sorry, it is though. I'm not being mean. It's just, clearly you don't understand what I'm trying to achieve."

Patrick put the sponge down, went to the fridge, and took out a beer. Opening it, he said, "Would you write a letter?"

"Probably not."

Now I wish Julie, Female had told me to put £95 in a savings account twice a week and go for a walk.

INGRID HAS NEVER had postnatal depression, but inexplicably after her second baby was born she started getting Botox. Thousands of pounds' worth in her flawless, thirty-two-year-old face.

Hamish asked why, after a session that immobilized the central third of her forehead. She said it was because one, she was tired of looking like someone who had been disinterred, and two, paralyzing her face muscles meant she couldn't, just by looking at him, communicate the depth of anger she felt towards her waste of space husband.

In that case, he wondered if they should have marriage counseling. Ingrid said at best she would consider some sort of one-day thing but would not be doing weekly appointments. She did not need a therapist to excavate their problems while the babysitter's meter ticked up in five-pound increments, since she already knew their issue was having two under fucking two.

The only one-day thing Hamish could find was a group workshop. In the conflict resolution module, the facilitator shared that sometimes, in the middle of an argument, he or his partner might say something along the lines of, "Hey, let's have a time out! Let's go and get burgers!" He said that it worked in almost every instance, especially in conjunction with sticking to I statements, and asked if there were any questions.

Ingrid raised her hand and, without waiting, asked if say, a husband was constantly getting his wife pregnant—with boys—and provided as much help with them as someone with a secret second family, and the best me-time the wife had had in the last fourteen months was during an MRI, and she fantasized all the time about being sent for another one, and they were always fighting, would the burger thing work then?

Hamish turned to self-help audiobooks after that.

*

Ingrid left him when their second son was six months old. The baby was with her, wailing inside his sling, when she knocked on the door of the Executive Home on a Friday night. As soon as she was inside, she dumped her bag and told me that she couldn't do it anymore.

We sat on the sofa and I held the glass of wine she had asked me to pour for myself, so that she could drink most of it but feel like technically she wasn't drinking while breastfeeding. She told me that she had stopped seeing Hamish as a person. Now she only saw him as a source of ironing, and a sex pest because he still wanted to have sex with her. She would love to never have sex again, and if she had to, it wouldn't be with him. I listened and a while later, Ingrid still talking, Patrick came through from the bedroom and said, "I'm not here," and went to work. I told Ingrid she could sleep in our bed with the baby.

She looked at the time on her phone. "Don't worry. I have to go."

"Go where?"

"Home." She sighed in anticipation of standing up.

"But you just walked out."

She emptied the rest of the wine into her mouth then said, "Martha. As if I would actually leave Hamish." She circled her hand above the sling. "As if I could do this by myself."

"But you said you have lost sight of him as a person."

"I know, but it's no reason to ruin the weekend."

I knew she was joking but I didn't laugh.

Really, she said, it was just a question of toughing out the next forty years.

I told her to please be serious. "Are you leaving Hamish or not?"

Ingrid stopped smiling and said, "No. I'm not. You don't just leave your husband, Martha. Not unless there's a proper-proper reason or you're our mother and you don't give a fuck about any-one except yourself."

"But what if you're unhappy?"

"It doesn't matter if you're unhappy. It's not a good enough reason. If you're just bored and it's all a bit hard and you don't feel like you love them anymore, who cares. You made a deal."

She got up and did something to the sling. I followed her to the door and, waiting for me to open it, she said, "I know this won't mean anything to you because you're not having them, but the best thing a mother can do for her children is love their fa-ther."

It didn't sound like something my sister would have thought of and I asked her who said it.

"Me."

"No, but who told it to you?"

"Winsome."

I said, "When were you talking to Winsome?"

We looked at each other, separately incredulous. In general, I spoke to my aunt once in April, when she rang up to talk about arrangements for Christmas, and not again until two weeks before Christmas, when she rang up to reiterate them.

Ingrid said what, and narrowing her eyes, "I speak to her about fifty times a day. That's if she is not already at my house, cleaning and making shepherd's pies and doing all the other things my own mother should do but doesn't because she is too busy making shit out of forks." She sounded so weary.

"But you can't stand her," I said. "You gave birth on her floor for revenge because she offered you a chair with a cushion on it. You've always hated her."

"I hated her because we were supposed to. I never hated her myself, and even if I did, it would be hard to keep hating the only person who's ever helped me without being asked."

"And it really is helpful? Having her around all the time?"

"What? Of course it is."

I had no image of Winsome at my sister's house. The thought of her there, and the two of them forming their own close, separate relationship, Ingrid relying on her instead of me, made me feel peripheral, and jealous of their proximity now that I was in Oxford.

She said, "Don't look like that, Martha. You make me happy but you know you can't actually help me."

For a second she disappeared into some private memory then said, "I didn't know what it was going to be like. I really have to go."

I held the door open and Ingrid walked out ahead of me. She hugged me and then, pausing, said, "That's another reason

I wouldn't leave my husband, Martha. Because I'd have to convince myself first that it was only about us and I didn't owe anything to the people around us." She looked at me in a way that made me feel uncomfortable. "And I would never be able to do that."

I watched her go to the car and put the baby into his seat, just the two of them inside the small cone of light. A minute later she drove away and reconciled with Hamish after their three-and-a-half-hour separation.

*

Not long afterwards they left London because Ingrid said she was sick of playgrounds full of cat shit and condom wrappers. They moved to a village that collectively pretends Swindon isn't right there.

She called me while she was watching their furniture come off the truck and told me she already hated most things about it, in particular the people and everything they stood for, but had decided to endure it because it meant we were only forty minutes apart.

I drove to see her the following day and sat at the island in her kitchen that had been described by the agent as "to die for" instead of, Ingrid said, a future dumping ground for everyone's shit and wallets. I colored in with her son while she put away groceries, breastfeeding the baby at the same time even though he was so big now.

She kicked a block of toilet paper rolls towards the laundry door and said if she had to characterize her stage of life right now, it would be spending two hundred pounds a week on absorbent products—breast pads, paper towels, toilet paper, pull-ups—in such quantity that the cart was full before you put anything else in. I stopped drawing and watched her retrieve a heavy bottle of milk from the floor, open the fridge with her elbow, and swing it into the door without disturbing the baby. "If Sainsbury's had one aisle that was dinner ingredients and things to soak shit up with, I would be in and out in two minutes."

Her son was trying to push a crayon into my hand so I would go back to what we were doing. Ingrid kept talking. I took the crayon and stared down at the page so she couldn't see my face. "I'm legitimately jealous, you only shopping for two," she said. "Oh my gosh. You probably use a basket!"

Later, at the door, she asked if I thought she was going to be able to do it, the house, the village. "You like it, don't you?" Her son was on her hip, trying to make her look at a plastic car he was holding by putting it in front of her face. She kept moving his hand away. "As in, you've made it work. It was the right thing to do, because you've been good, and you and Patrick are good." Her voice went up at the end; they were all questions. She needed me to say yes.

On her son's next attempt, Ingrid took the car from him. He started crying and tried, with his tiny hand, to hit her in the face. She caught his wrist and held it. Her son started writhing and kicking his legs, holding the back of her hair with his free hand. Ingrid continued, undeterred. "So definitely, Oxford is better. Different-better but fundamentally—you like it."

I said yes. "You'll be fine. It was a good idea."

"And you're fine?"

I said totally.

"So no bathroom floor topics." It was another question. Or an instruction, a caution, or my sister's hope.

I said no so that I could leave and Ingrid could convey her son, still flailing, to the bad-choices chair.

*

Was it different-better. Fundamentally. In the car on the way home, I thought about our life in Oxford, with its walks and weekends, its dinners and author talks, minibreaks and exhibitions, Patrick's important work and my very small work. I liked it no more or less than our life in London. It had been nearly two years. In the only way that mattered Oxford wasn't different or better. There were still bathroom floor topics—Ingrid meant, the times I was so scared or leaden or in another way consumed by depression that I couldn't move from whichever corner it had driven me into, until Patrick came, and put his hand out and pulled me up. Then, as always, in a day, a week, however long, I could go into the bathroom and think nothing about the corner where I'd previously trembled, cried, bit my lip, begged, except the whole floor could use a mop.

There was a prescription sticking out of a compartment under the radio. I'd put it there before so I would see it and remember to stop and have it filled on the way home. At a set of lights, I took it out. For some reason, the pharmaceutical company had opted to make their most potent antidepressant a chewable—designed to disintegrate on first contact with the tongues of suffering adults, coating it with a long-lasting taste of pineapple, then collecting as sand-like granules in the pockets of the mouth, ulcerating the gums, before turning into a paste that burned on the way down. I had been taking it for so long. I was taking it before Patrick and I got married. I was taking it when I started throwing things and when I went to the hospital. I was on it now. I wasn't different or better.

That night, I told Patrick I was going to stop taking it because it didn't do anything. I said, "I don't see the point. I'm exactly the same." I was watching him make dinner.

He said, "Do you want me to make you a doctor's appointment so she can tell you how to come off it?"

"No. You just come off it by not taking it."

Patrick stopped his knife halfway through an onion and put it down next to the board.

I said it's fine. "I've done it millions of times. And I don't want to see any more doctors either. I just want to be. I'm so tired, Patrick. I was seventeen." I pressed my eyes so I wouldn't cry. "I'm thirty-four."

He said he got it, it had been quite a while, and came over, letting me stand in his arms for a long time. My face into his shoulder, I said, "I don't even want to take the pill anymore either. I can't swallow another tablet." I don't know why I said please.

Patrick put his hand on the back of my head. He said of course, it was totally fine. He'd rather I came off antidepressants under supervision but he could see how I'd just want to be off everything really, if I didn't think it helped. He said, who knows. "Maybe this is just you."

*

I asked Ingrid what to use instead of the pill. She said the implant thing. If I touched the inside of my arm, I could feel it under my skin.

*

The year that followed was indistinct from any before it. Near the end of it Ingrid called and said, "Literally, why do I always do pregnancy tests in Starbucks toilets?" And this time, she told me, it was a Swindon Starbucks, which made it even worse.

"Are you pregnant?"

"Of course I am."

"Don't you have the implant thing?"

"I didn't get around to it." Her bursting into tears made a noise like static in my ear and then I heard her say, "Three under fucking five, Martha."

HAMISH'S FAMILY HAS a house in Wales. Once she had three under fucking five, Ingrid started making me go there with her whenever Hamish went away for work, even though it depressed us both. There was nothing to do at the house. The nearest town has a Morrisons, a leisure center, and a slag heap.

The baby was a month old the first time we went. Because all three were asleep in the back as we drove into the town, we were not allowed to stop. Ingrid said we would be circumnavigating the slag heap until this lovely micro-holiday was over. "Don't you think"—she put an indicator on—"you can't make a joke about a slag heap that's funnier than just saying slag heap?"

I told her it was the best objective correlative I'd ever heard.

She glanced across from the wheel and looked annoyed. "Can you please not say things that you know I don't understand because my brain is a solid wad of wet wipes at this point."

"Two things that when you put them together in a poem make the reader feel whatever emotion you want them to so you don't have to expressly name it. As in, if you write slag heap it saves you the job of typing morbid existential despair."

"I didn't ask you to explain it but that's fine." She tugged out her ponytail with one hand. "Does Dad know about it though? Maybe that's where the money is." One of the children made a noise and Ingrid lowered her voice. "If you can get the words slag heap into Waitrose magazine, I will give you one thousand pounds."

"Do they have to be next to each other?"

"If they are, I will give you a thousand pounds and a child of your choice. But not the baby because he can't talk and ask me for things."

The eldest one woke up as we were passing the leisure center again and started crying, louder and louder, because he wanted to go swimming. Ingrid started crying because she was too tired to say no a second time. Entering ahead of me, trying to get the pram through the revolving doors, she said, "Breathe through your mouth."

In the changing rooms, three little girls were crouched in the middle of the flooded floor trying to get back into their school uniforms. They could not get their tights on by themselves and were taking turns to point out that they were going to get in so much trouble if they didn't hurry up. I watched them while I was holding things for Ingrid and saw the smallest one give up and drop her head into her hands.

I wanted to go over and help her but Ingrid said talking to a child in the context of a swimming pool changing room was basically asking to be put on the sex offenders' register. "Also, can you please help me? Take this." She handed me some kind of special nappy and told me to put it on the baby.

A moment later, a teacher appeared and stood in the entrance with her hands on her hips. She was incongruously dressed, in a clingy wrap dress and high heels protected from pool water by the supermarket bags she had put on each foot and knotted around her ankles. Ingrid and I both stopped what we were doing when she started shouting. The little girls froze until she was gone, then became more frenzied in their efforts to get dressed, saying we're going to get left behind, we're going to get left behind. The smallest one burst into tears.

I put the baby back in his pram. Ingrid said seriously don't as I went over and, crouching down, asked the girl if she would like me to help her with her laces. She raised her head and nodded slowly. The laces were wet and gray. I told her it was difficult, getting dressed in a hurry and she said, especially because the pool made her legs go sticky. Her ankles were impossibly thin; she seemed too fragile to be in the world. Once I was finished, she sprang up and ran after her friends.

I went back over to Ingrid, who was shoving things under the pram. She said, "I guess you won't be coming to playgrounds with me anymore now you're on the register," but she was smiling. She kicked the brake off. "Gosh they were sweet though."

The sun was sinking on the other side of the slag heap as we drove past it again on the way home. Ingrid, gazing out the window, said, "Boys, no matter what befalls us as a family, I will never let your father move us to Merthyr Tydfil."

*

Later, her children in bed, my sister and I sat on the sofa drinking canned gin and tonic and watching the fire, which had been dying since the second we lit it.

I said, "When you have a baby, do you automatically turn into someone who can cope with seeing a woman with bags on her feet scream at a child who isn't hers? You're suddenly just strong enough to be in a world where that happens?"

Ingrid swallowed and said no. "It makes it worse because as soon as you're a mother, you realize every child was a baby five seconds ago, and how could anyone shout at a baby? But then, you shout at your own and if you can do that, you must be a terrible person. Before you had kids, you got to think you were a good person so then you secretly resent them for making you realize you're actually a monster."

"I already know I'm a monster." I wanted her to tell me I wasn't.

She turned on the television. "I guess you've saved yourself a job then."

It was a movie we had both seen before with an actress who was, in the present scene, trying to force all her shopping bags into the back of a yellow cab. In real life, she had just leapt off a roof. During the advertisements, Ingrid said the thing everybody says. She couldn't understand how anyone could feel so bad they'd want to do that. I was scratching something off my jeans, not really listening, and said without thinking that I obviously could.

"No but like, not that bad, that you'd genuinely want to die."

I laughed, then glanced up to see why she had suddenly turned off the television. Ingrid was just looking at me.

"What?"

"When you're depressed, you don't genuinely want to die. When have you ever felt like that?"

I asked her if she was being serious. "Every time, I feel like that."

Ingrid said, "Martha! You do not!"

I said okay.

"You can't just say okay. Okay what? Okay you don't feel like that?"

"No—okay you don't have to believe me."

She pushed all the cushions that were between us onto the floor and made me shift my legs so she could sit right next to me. She said if that was true, we had to talk about it. I said we didn't.

"But I want to understand what it's like for you. Feeling like that."

I tried to. For the first time, I told her about the night on the balcony at Goldhawk Road. The way I felt when I was standing out there, staring down at the dark garden, then stopped because she looked so upset. Her eyes were enormous and glassy.

I said it's not something you can really explain to someone who hasn't experienced it.

She cried, a single, aching sob, then said sorry and tried to smile. "I suppose it's the ultimate had-to-be-there."

For a while we sat like that, my sister holding my wrist, until I said she needed to go to bed.

*

I heard her get up in the night and went into her room. She was sitting up in bed feeding the baby, beatific in the half-light of a lamp she had dimmed with a towel that was still damp from the leisure center floor.

She said, "Come and keep me awake." I got into bed next to her. "Tell me something funny."

I told her about the time when we were teenagers, that our house—for no reason and as if by some force outside the four of us—began to fill with African tribal art, masks, juju hats, in such quantity that the downstairs of Goldhawk Road started to look like the gift shop at Nairobi international airport. I told her the only piece I could remember exactly was a bronze fertility sculpture that was in the hallway for a while, directly inside the front door, and only because its phallus was so pronounced that, as she said at the time, when it inadvertently got turned ninety degrees it was like a fucking boom gate.

Ingrid said she remembered it as well. "I started hanging my PE bag on it."

Neither of us knew when and how it disappeared. Just that, one day it was all gone. The baby hiccuped. My sister laughed.

I said, "What's the best thing about it?"

Without taking her eyes off her son, Ingrid said, "This. All of it. I mean, it's shit, but all of it. Especially," she yawned, "the time between finding out you are pregnant and telling anyone, including your husband. Even if it's just a week or one minute in my case. No one talks about that part."

She went on to describe a sense of privacy so singular and ecstatic that, as desperate as she felt to tell someone, it was still painful to give up. She said, "You feel the most intense inner superiority because you're walking around or in a Starbucks bathroom and you know there is gold inside you, and everyone else is oblivious." She yawned again and handed me the baby while she put her top back on. "Did you know that's why the Mona Lisa is smiling like that? As in, so smugly. Because she'd just done a test or whatever in the studio loo and got the two lines right before she sat down and he's studying her for ten hours a day and the whole time she's like, he doesn't even know I'm pregnant."

I asked her how they knew that but she said she couldn't remember, something to do with a shadow he put on her neck, to do with some gland that only sticks out when you're pregnant, and I should just google it later.

Cross-legged then, Ingrid spread a muslin square out in front of her and took the baby back, laid him down, and wrapped him in a tight swaddle. She didn't pick him up, instead, gazed down at him and smoothed out a fold in the fabric, then said, "Sometimes, I wish you did want children. I just think it would have been fun, having babies at the same time."

I said maybe I would have but I hated leisure centers and they seemed mandatory to the task.

Ingrid picked the baby up and held him out. "Can you put him back in the thing?"

I got up and carried him against my shoulder. I felt like she was watching me as I set him down on the little mattress and slid my hands out from underneath him.

She said, Martha? "I hope it's not because you really think you're a monster."

I put a blanket over him, tucked both sides, and asked my sister not to talk about it anymore.

*

In the morning I got up and made the older boys breakfast so that she could keep sleeping. The eldest one asked me to make him boiled eggs.

The middle one said, I don't want boiled eggs and started crying. He said he wanted a pancake.

I told him they could have different things.

"No we can't."

I asked him why not.

He said because this isn't a restaurant.

While he was waiting for his pancake, he recounted a dream he had had when he was much younger, about a bad man who was trying to drink him. He said he didn't find it scary anymore. Only sometimes, when he remembered it.

NEAR THE STEPS of St Mark's Basilica, I threw up into a cigarette bin. Patrick and I were in Venice for our fifth wedding anniversary. For the previous two weeks, he'd kept asking me if I wanted to cancel because I was obviously sick. I said, "Refreshingly of body not of mind though, so it's fine."

I was desperate to cancel. But he had bought a Lonely Planet. He had been reading it in bed every night and as ill and scared as I was, I couldn't bear to disappoint someone whose desires were so modest they could be circled in pencil.

Patrick found us somewhere to sit down. He said I should go to the doctor again as soon as we got back to Oxford in case it wasn't just a virus. I said it was and, since it hadn't made me vomit before, clearly that was a separate, psychosomatic reaction to the fact that we looked so much like tourists because of his backpack.

I was pregnant. I had known for two weeks and hadn't told him. The doctor who had confirmed it said no idea to the question of how it had happened with the implant still in my arm. "Nothing's foolproof. Anyway, five weeks, by my calculation."

Patrick stood up and said, "Let's go back to the hotel. You can go to bed and I'll change our flights."

I let him pull me up. "But you wanted to see that bridge. The Ponte de whatever it is."

He said, "It doesn't matter. We'll come back."

The walk to the hotel led us to it anyway. Patrick got out his guidebook and read from a page that had the corner turned down. "Why is the Bridge of Sighs so named?" He said it was funny that I should ask. "In the seventeenth century . . ."

Listening to him read I felt like I was being constricted by sadness. Not because etcetera, etcetera, according to lore, criminals being led to the prison on the other side would sigh at their final view of Venice through the windows of the bridge that are typically baroque in style. Just because of the way Patrick was frowning at the page, the way he looked up intermittently to check if I was listening, the way he said wow, once he'd finished. "That's quite depressing." We flew home the next day.

*

I told him at the allotment. Every day that I'd known, before Venice, in Venice, the week that had passed since, I had set out to tell him but in whatever moment, I found a different reason to defer. He was tired, he was holding his phone, he was wearing a sweater that I did not like. He was too content in what he was doing. That day, a Sunday, I woke up and read the note he had left me. I got dressed and went to find him.

He was sitting on the fallen log, holding something. I did not think I could do it, once I was close enough to see what it was. I could not rupture his existence, reveal my deceit, and bifurcate Patrick's future while he was holding a Thermos.

There was only ever one reason. Once I told him, it would be real and I would have to fix it. There wasn't any time left. I just said it.

In the period of forestalling, I thought I had imagined every reaction Patrick might have, but it was worse than any I could invent myself—my husband asking me how far along I was. It was a phrase too specific to an experience we had not had, or one we were not allowed to use in our version of it.

I said, "Eight weeks."

He didn't ask me how long I had known. It was too obvious. He said, "I don't know how I didn't guess" as if it was his fault and then, sitting forward, his elbows on his knees, looking at the ground, he said, "We're not deciding what to do though."

"No, I'm just telling you."

"So there's not an immediate rush."

"No. But I'm not going to wait for no reason."

He said okay. "That makes sense."

I tipped the tea out and handed him back the cup. "I'm going to go. I'll see you at home."

"Martha?"

"What?"

"Could I have a few days?"

I told him I hadn't booked it yet. There would be that much time anyway.

*

Patrick did not mention it when he got home or in the days that followed but he moved differently around the house. He came home early. He wouldn't let me do anything. He was always there in the morning but whenever I woke up in the night, he was somewhere else. I knew it was the only thing he was thinking about.

Sunday, again, he came into the bathroom while I was in the bath and sat on the end. He said, "So, I'm sorry it's taken me so long. I've just been thinking, you definitely don't want to keep it?"

I said no.

"You don't feel like, if we did—because I honestly think you'd be—"

"Please don't. Patrick."

"Okay. It's just, I don't want it to be something that later we wish we'd thought about."

I pushed the water with my foot. "Patrick!"

"Alright. Sorry." He got up and threw a towel over the wet floor. "I'll get you the referral." His shirt, the leg of his jeans, were soaking.

As he was walking out of the bathroom, I said, "It was an accident, Patrick. It shouldn't have happened." I told him, it was never a thing. But he didn't turn around, just said okay, yip.

I slid down, under the water, as soon as he had closed the door.

*

It was a miscarriage anyway.

It started the morning of the appointment, while I was pushing my bike along a steep bit of the towpath. I knew what it was and kept walking. At home, I called Patrick at work and waited in the bathroom until it was over. It had been so cold outside that I was still wearing my coat when he came in.

He drove me to the hospital and apologized on the way home,

hours later, for not being able to think of the right thing to say. I said it was fine, I didn't want to talk about it then anyway.

I did not tell anyone what had happened and afterwards only cried if Patrick was out—as soon as he left, from the effort of containing it. In short, intense bursts at the recollection of what I had been about to do. For minutes, as I moved around the house, weeping in gratitude that she had let go of me first.

*

Much later—too much later—when Patrick and I talked about what had happened, I said, "to her," he asked me how I knew it was a girl.

I said I just did.

"What would you have called her?"

Flora.

I said, "I don't know."

*

There are things, crimes in a marriage, that are so great you cannot apologize for them. Instead, watching television on the sofa, eating the dinner he made while you showered after the hospital, you say, Patrick?

Yes.

I like this sauce.

*

We said the Cotswolds, a walk or a pub or something, just to get out of Oxford. We said, it will be good. We said, we'll be there in half an hour. Let's just go.

It was ten miles from the Executive Home to the turnoff. Patrick did not take it. It had been wordlessly established by then that neither of us wanted to stop, only drive and keep going until there was so much distance behind us. I looked out my window at the smattering of houses built with their backs to the road. They thickened into the village, thinned again. Fields to the right. We kept to the A road. It narrowed, became woods on both sides. It slowed through other villages, doglegged, widened, and sped up, bypassed a town. Its industrial outskirts became a long section of countryside. Services. Signs for the M6. It said Birmingham, next exit. It stopped being beautiful. On the other side, it was beautiful again. Patrick said how are you going? Good. I'm not hungry, are you? Not really. Do you want music? Do you? Not really.

We passed a sign that said Manchester 40 and we looked at each other and smiled, silently, bulging eyes, like two people in a crowd acknowledging a secret between themselves. Six lanes, a density of cars, drivers on either side became familiar from the slowing and stopping and starting again. They smoked, tapped the wheel. Passengers looked at their phones, ate and drank and put their feet on the dashboard.

Then, we were past Manchester. Countryside but plain, dotted with factories. Silos. At intervals along the road, a suburban house without a suburb.

I said, "How long have we been going for?"

Patrick looked at the time. "We left at nine so, six hours. Five and a half?"

Nothing for a long time except the vague sense of the road curving, and starting to climb. He put the window down, maybe salt in the air but no sight of the ocean. Then winding sharply upwards, until You Are Now Entering an Area of Outstanding Natural Beauty.

It was late in the afternoon. Patrick said I might need to stop for a bit soon. In a mile, there was a sign that said Access with a symbol of a bridge and after the next curve in the road, an un-paved lay-by.

The air was clear and sharp. We stretched and twisted our backs, the same way, in unison. Patrick said one sec, got our jackets, then locked the car. I took his hand and we walked the path that cut through dense wood to a river. It was swift moving but where it curved, in front of us, a pool had formed. It was deep and still and dark green and from the bank we were standing on, a sheer drop of, Patrick said, "nine feet, maybe ten." We looked down into it.

He said okay but I'll go first.

We took our clothes off and hung them over a branch. Patrick said, "I don't see why you get the added warmth of a bra." I took it off and both of us lingered for another minute on the edge, already shivering.

He said, "Aim for the middle" and leapt out. The noise of him hitting the water was like a crack. I followed while he was still below the surface. The water was so cold that, at the instant of entry, it could not be deciphered beyond shock and pressure, then a sharp pain in the heart muscle, lungs like heavy stones, then burning skin. I opened my eyes, a blur of green and swirling silt. I thought, move your arms but they were rigid, above my head. I felt suspended. Then everything was Patrick's grip on my forearm, and the rush of being tugged upwards and the great pull of air. And then we were face to face, speechless, breathing too hard. He still had my arm and swept me forwards to the bank.

I was below the surface for only a second but I thought I was already drowning. I did not think I could swim back but I was only ever feet away from the edge. It was just the pain of the water. And then Patrick was helping me back up the bank, and I was standing, wrapped in my jacket, water running down my bare legs, and it had only been a minute.

We ran back to the car, holding our clothes and shoes. It took a long time to get dressed in the front, hot air roaring out of the vents, talking so fast about what we'd just done.

I said, we are the best.

Patrick said, do you feel like chips, so badly?

We drove out and found a pub. It was empty apart from an old couple sitting at a table on the other side of the room and a woman behind the bar polishing glasses. We ate chips and drank beer on a sofa in front of a fire, and I was so warm and so clean.

"Do you ever think we're the best, Patrick?"

He said no. "But we probably are. No one else would have done that."

I said I know. "Anyone else would have been too scared. We're the only ones."

Patrick said, "Are you super, super conscious of having no underwear on?"

"There's no one here," I said. "We are the only people in the world."

I READ AN article in a Sunday magazine about a newly classified disorder. The journalist, a sufferer himself, described Boarding School Syndrome as a sort of PTSD/attachment disorder hybrid being silently endured by a mass of British men who had been incarcerated since the age of six, at the will of their own parents. Symptoms, he said, included excessive self-reliance, the inability to ask for help, "pride in endurance," an overactive moral compass, and repression of emotions, chiefly negative ones.

Patrick was watching a ball sport on television, next to me. Some time had passed since the miscarriage, not enough that I had stopped counting it in weeks.

I pushed my foot into his thigh and said, "Can I do you a quiz?"

"This only has ten minutes to go."

"I want to see if you have Boarding School Syndrome."

"Ten minutes."

I raised my voice above the commentary and said okay, question one. "Do you struggle to ask for help from others?"

Patrick said no and to the rest as I read each one out, most adamantly to the question of whether he struggled with emotional attachment, on the basis that he had been emotionally attached to me since he was fourteen. I got to the end of the list and pretended I hadn't.

"There's a few more."

"Can I just watch the penalty?"

"Record it."

Patrick sighed and turned it off.

"Do you experience a violent emotional reaction to certain foods, chiefly scrambled eggs with a high water content, vegetables from the brassica family, and/or any liquid that acquires a skin when it is boiled, such as milk or custard?"

Patrick looked at me, sure but not sure I was making it up.

"Aside from at home, do you feel most comfortable eating in the canteen at your work because your food comes on a tray? And, would you agree, or disagree, that it may be because you weren't allowed to pick what you ate until you were eighteen that you are, as an adult, the slowest menu orderer in the world, and sometimes your wife feels like she might die in the yawning expanse of time between the waitress asking you what you would like and you actually being able to say?"

Patrick turned the television back on.

"Until it was pointed out, by her, after you got married, did you know you ate with your head down defending your plate with one arm?" He was turning the volume up. I shouted. "If you answered mostly As, you are the mental one in your relationship, not your wife as everyone has previously supposed."

I thought he was pretending to be irritated by my stupid quiz and only realized he wasn't when he suddenly got up and left the room without turning the television off again. I rose and followed him into the kitchen, apologizing, without a specific sense of what I was apologizing for. He moved from the cupboard to the sink, to the fridge like I wasn't there. It was humiliating. I went upstairs and shut myself in the box room.

For some time, I sat in my chair and snipped off split ends with desk scissors, then turned on my computer, planning to wishlist things on The Outnet. Instead, I went to the magazine's website and read the article again, feeling guilty and then sad, then scared. I closed it, hearing him come upstairs.

Patrick entered but didn't say anything. I turned around, and because he remained mute I said, "I think we should have counseling." I did not mean it. I said it the way I always did—to be wounding, in retaliation for a perceived crime, and was shocked when he said so do I.

"Why?"

"Martha, because."

"Why?"

"Because of the river incident."

I could not look at him then and picked up the scissors again.

He said, Martha. "Can you please stop cutting your hair. Tell me why you think we need counseling."

"Because you have Boarding School Syndrome."

*

He left the house and I went into the bathroom to find the tranquilizers I had been given by an after-hours doctor Patrick took me to at the conclusion of the river incident. I wanted to see when exactly it was that I had got up in the middle of the night and gone outside, walking, then running as fast as I could along the towpath, until Patrick caught up to me at the first narrow footbridge.

I was climbing onto the side of it. He put his arms around my waist and tried to get me down. I fought him and accidentally scratched his face. His energy outlasted mine and he walked me back and drove me to the doctor, while I said sorry over and over and over again.

I picked up the pill bottle and read the date on the label. It seemed wrong. I went to bed, even though there were hours of daylight left because I felt so ashamed, I couldn't bear to be awake.

It was a dream about the baby—the thing that woke me and told me to run along the river, because what if she was there. Two nights before.

*

We had one session with a therapist. She was white but dressed as if she had come directly from a Kwanzaa celebration and said, "Not to worry!" when neither of us could articulate why we'd come.

Patrick could not say, "Because on a recent occasion, my wife behaved like a psychotic, and much older, Anne of Green Gables in the Lady of Shalott episode."

I could not say, "Because I have lately discovered that the pillars of my husband's personality, the qualities for which he is so broadly admired, the exceptional stoicism, emotional equanimity, and never complaining, are actually just symptoms of a newly classified disorder."

"The point is, you have come." The therapist said that was a great sign and directed us to the two chairs that were in the middle of the room, already facing each other and close enough that when we sat down our knees were touching. She told us that because it was very common for partners who'd been together some time to stop looking into each other's eyes, she always started by getting couples to do just that—stare at each other with total concentration and no talking for three minutes. She would simply observe.

Some seconds into the exercise, a quick succession of electronic alerts came from the handbag at her feet. Patrick and I turned at the same time, to see her reach into the bag and feel around for her phone, saying, "I should get that, in case it's my daughter wanting a ride." Once found, she swiped the screen and said without taking her eyes off it, "Ignore me. Keep going. I just need to very quickly reply to this."

Patrick does not hate anything, except swordfish, joke presents, and the iPhone's audible keypad option. As the therapist composed her reply, each letter clicked like Morse code. He looked at me in disbelief, silently mouthed the words "No way" after the therapist leaned forward to put her phone away but levered up again when it beeped twice more in her hand. "Honestly, sorry you two. She's sixteen. They think the world revolves around them at that age."

Patrick got up, announced that he had forgotten to do something and needed to do it straightaway. The therapist looked bewildered as he ushered me out of her office.

We were suddenly outside, running across the road, hand in hand, towards a bar. We drank champagne, then tequila. I told Patrick we were like two people who had decided to turn themselves in but, in the moment of surrender, they had realized that as exhausting as it was to keep running and surviving and not give up, the alternative is worse. I said, "Because the alternative is other people."

Patrick said, "For me, it's being by myself."

Outside, on the curb, he took my hand again. We were looking for a taxi but then he pointed to a shop farther along and said he wanted to pick up some items. We were both drunker than we had ever been together. It was a small convenience store, staffed by a woman with a pinched face who did not find us funny. Patrick put wine gums and a toothbrush on the counter. He said, "Would you like anything, darling?" I picked up a shower cap and said I would like to wear it home, if the woman would be so kind as to scan it and give it back. He put everything on the counter and said, "All this and a packet of the house condoms please."

We kissed in the taxi and went to bed as soon as we got home. It was the first time since the miscarriage. Or, I was too drunk at the time to realize, the first time since I had conceived.

As we were about to finish, Patrick stopped moving and said, "Sorry, keep going. I just need to check my phone in case someone's been in touch about a ride."

"Martha," he said afterwards, lying next to me. "Everything is broken and messed up and completely fine. That is what life is. It's only the ratios that change. Usually on their own. As soon as you think that's it, it's going to be like this forever, they change again."

That is what life was, and how it continued for three years after that. The ratios changing on their own, broken, completely fine, a holiday, a leaking pipe, new sheets, happy birthday, a technician between nine and three, a bird flew into the window, I want to die, please, I can't breathe, I think it's a lunch thing, I love you, I can't do this anymore, both of us thinking it would be like that forever.

A NEW ADMINISTRATOR joined Patrick's hospital last year, in May. She had moved to Oxford for the lifestyle but her husband, a psychiatrist, was commuting back to London because he had just got rooms on Harley Street, which, she said, is a bit of a coup.

I met her at a charity dinner for a cause I can't remember, even though our purpose in going was to have our awareness raised. She asked me what I did and I told her I created content so people could consume it. It was a job I had taken auxiliary to the funny food column, which I didn't mention in case she read Waitrose magazine and realized I was that writer she hated.

I said, "I also consume content, in a private capacity. Not content of my own creation in that instance, obviously. But either way, I am very much a part of the problem."

She laughed and I went on to tell her that whenever I was out and I saw a mother who was on her phone, I worried that it was my content she was consuming instead of looking into her child's eyes.

She said, "It certainly seems like we've lost the ability to not be on our phones, doesn't it?" and sounded wistful.

"But I'm sure at the end of our lives we will all be thinking, if only I'd consumed more content."

She laughed and put her hand on my arm. And for the rest

of the conversation, whenever she imparted some information about herself, emphasized a point, or made some observation, she touched my arm again. And if I said something she thought was funny, she would softly grip it until she had finished laughing. I liked her so much for that reason and because, although she asked me questions beyond what I did, she did not ask me if I had children.

On the way home, I asked Patrick to find out the name of her husband the psychiatrist.

I had not had a doctor for four years; I was not looking for one. But I made an appointment, I think because I wanted to see what kind of person he would be—if, being married to a woman like that meant he would be good. Therefore, unlike any doctor I had seen before.

*

A female receptionist told me that ordinarily I could expect to wait twelve weeks for an appointment but there had been a cancellation—very rare—and the doctor could see me at five o'clock this afternoon if I thought I could get there in time. I could hear her clicking her pen on and off while I held the phone with my shoulder and looked at the train times, then told her I could.

The waiting room was dark and felt too warm because I had run most of the way from Paddington in a coat that was too heavy for May. The same receptionist said that ordinarily I could expect a long wait but the doctor would only be a minute. Also, she said, very rare. I stayed standing and played a game that my father invented for me at the beginning: how would I improve this room, if I was only allowed to remove one thing? I chose the visible price tag on the cyclamen, then turned at the sound of a heavy door opening across thick carpet. A man wearing corduroy trousers, a white shirt, and knitted tie came out and said, "Hello Martha, I'm Robert." He shook my hand, firmly, as though he hadn't presumed it would be limp.

In his office he told me to sit wherever I liked, establishing himself in an ergonomic chair that had a wider armrest on one side to accommodate his notebook, open to a page that was empty except for my name. I sat and waited while he underlined it. Then with the other hand he smoothed his tie and I saw that his index finger was bandaged. He held it straight, separate from his other fingers to exempt it from use.

He looked up and asked me to start from the beginning. Why had I come to see him? And to my reply, which felt uninteresting as I delivered it, could I remember the first time I felt like this?

Cyclonic, becoming rough or very rough. Occasionally good.

I started with the day of my last A level, and I stopped at half past nine that morning, when I had gone outside with a bag of kitchen scraps and a woman walking past holding the hands of two toddlers smiled at me and said I looked as tired as she felt. I stood still until she had gone, then went back inside with the bag and flung it down the hallway. It hit the wall and burst. I told him that Patrick would be the one to find it because I was here, and he would just clean it up, the spaghetti and the eggshells and still, after so much time, pretend that was a normal thing that wives did.

Robert asked me if I threw things a lot or did anything else that I wouldn't consider, "in your word, normal."

I told him about the time I had lifted a terra-cotta pot and shattered it against the garden wall. I told him about smashing my phone so many times against the kitchen tiles that pieces of glass got in my hand, about throwing the hairdryer at Patrick, the bruise it left, about driving my car on purpose into a metal guard rail in a car park, about standing with my back to the wall and banging my head over and over because it felt better than I did, about the days I could not get up, the nights I couldn't go to sleep, the books I'd ripped up and clothes I had torn apart by their seams. With the exception of the hairdryer, none were unrecent.

I apologized to him and said it was completely fine if he couldn't think of anything, in terms of helping me. As an afterthought I said, "The funny thing, not funny ha-ha but as in funny terrible, is that once it finishes and I feel normal, I see the leftovers, smashed bits of plate in the bin or whatever, and I think, who did that? I truly can't believe it was me." I told him about Ingrid's fashion crises. That he continued to take notes was peculiarly affecting to me, his acting as though everything I said was worthy of writing down.

He turned the page in his notebook and asked me what diagnoses I'd been given by previous doctors. I said, "Glandular fever, clinical depression, then—this is in order—" and proceeded to list them, one after the other until I was being boring and did a little laugh. "Most of the index of the DSM, really."

I looked around for the dictionary of mental illnesses that was always somewhere on display in the office of the kind of doctors I saw. It had become a dismal kind of Where's Waldo—trying to pick its blood-red spine out of the shelves of psychiatric textbooks with titles that seemed intentionally menacing. But it wasn't any-where. I felt another surge of gratitude as I turned back and saw that he was waiting for me.

"What I'm most interested to know is what diagnosis you've given yourself, Martha."

I paused as if I had to think about it. "That I'm not good at being a person. I seem to find it more difficult to be alive than other people."

He said that was interesting. "But based on the fact you've come here today, you must also think there's a medical explanation."

I nodded.

"What would you say it was, in that case?"

I said, "Depression probably, except it's not constant. It just starts for no reason or a reason that seems too small." I braced myself for him to take the laminated list out of his drawer, turn it towards me, and make me do my Always, Sometimes, Seldom, Nevers.

Toujours, parfois, rarement, jamais.

Instead, he took a moment to recap his pen, laid it on the note-book, and said, "Perhaps you can tell me what it feels like when you suddenly find yourself in the trenches, as it were."

I described it in the ways I had to Patrick, after his first expo-sure to it—that day in summer when we weren't yet together—and so many times since. I said, "It's like going into the cinema when it's light and when you come out you're shocked because you didn't expect it to be dark, but it is.

"It's like being on a bus and strangers on either side of you suddenly start screaming at each other, fighting over your head and you can't get out.

"You are standing still and then you're falling down a flight of stairs, but you don't know who pushed you. There is no one behind you.

"It's like when you go down into the Tube and the sky is blue, and when you come out, it's pouring with rain."

For a moment he waited as though there might have been more, then thanked me for those descriptions, which he said were very helpful.

I bit my thumbnail, then looked down at it for a second and peeled off a part that hadn't torn completely. "Mainly, it's like weather. Even if you see it coming, you can't do anything about it. It's going to come either way."

"Brain weather, as it were?"

"I suppose. Yes."

Robert said, "I'm very sorry for you. It sounds like it has been hard for a long time." I nodded, biting my nail again. "I wonder, has anyone ever mentioned ____ to you, Martha?"

I moved my hand and said no, thank goodness. "It's the only one I haven't got, or been told I have. Although actually," I recalled as I spoke, "when I was maybe eighteen, one did say, a Scottish doctor said he couldn't rule it out but my mother told him she could, because the only thing it made me do was cry all the time; that I wasn't a complete nutcase who thinks she's Boudicca and that God talks to her through her orthodontia."

"No, of course. But may I say," he paused briefly, "the sort of symptoms your mother described, in such vivid terms, only exist in the popular imagination. Actual symptoms might include—" Robert named a dozen.

I had been starting to feel uncomfortably hot and now my

throat felt like someone had stuffed a rag down it. I swallowed. "I don't really want ____ though," I said and felt stupid, then rude.

He said, "I quite understand. As a condition ____ is not well understood and undeniably, within the general public, it carries somewhat of a—"

"Why do you think it's that?"

"Because typically it begins with—" a little bomb going off in your brain when you're seventeen. "And you will have been given—" Robert listed every medication I had ever taken, all the familiar and long-forgotten names, then told me the clinical reasons why they would not have worked, worked poorly, or made me much worse.

I swallowed again as the tears that had been an ache behind my eyes since he said it sounds like it has been hard for a long time began to spill down my face. Robert picked up a box of tissues and because it turned out to be empty, he took out his own handkerchief and passed it across the distance of carpet between us. I wiped my face and wondered who ironed this man's handkerchiefs for him.

I asked him why no one else had thought of it, apart from the Scottish doctor who wasn't even sure.

"I would say it's because you've been managing it so well, for many years."

I could not stop crying because the only thing I thought I had managed well was being a difficult, too-sensitive person. Robert got up and poured me a glass of water. I made myself sit up straight and say thank you. I drank half of it, then said ____ out loud to see what it felt like, applying that word to myself.

He returned to his chair, smoothed out his tie, and said, "That's my sense, yes."

"Well." I breathed in slowly and out again. "Hopefully it's just the twenty-four-hour kind."

Robert smiled. "I hear it's been going around. Would you be interested to try what I generally prescribe for that, Martha? It tends to be very effective."

I said alright and quietly looked out the window at the Victorian buildings on the other side of Harley Street while he began my prescription. They were so beautiful. I did not know if they had been built for sick people. I didn't think so much trouble would have been taken if they had been. I turned back to Robert saying, "You'll have to pardon the speed of my typing. I had a contretemps with a tomato." I asked him if he'd needed stitches. As he loaded the printer, he said a half a dozen in fact.

At the end, we came together at the door and Robert said he would look forward to seeing me again in six weeks. I wanted to say something more than thank you but all I said was, "You are a nice person" in a way that embarrassed us both, and after shaking hands again, I turned and walked quickly back to the waiting room.

The receptionist took my payment and said, "That turned into a double appointment but it seems the doctor has put it through as a single."

I asked her if that was rare. She said very.

*

Outside, I put on my coat against a wet mist and walked slowly towards the chemist on Wigmore Street. Partway, I stopped and got out my phone. A man coming towards me on a scooter had to swerve out of the way. He said fuckssake watch it. I stepped back into the doorway of a closed-down restaurant and googled ——, clicking on an American medical website that presents all its information in quiz format, or as articles with headings that read like a supermarket women's magazine if you imagine them with exclamation marks. Ingrid used it before Hamish blocked it on her browser because, she told me, literally whatever symptoms you put in, you always have cancer.

I sat down on the step and scrolled down.

——: Symptoms, Treatments and More!

——: Myths and Facts!

Living with ——? Nine Foods to Avoid!

I wished my sister was with me, to take my phone and pretend to read on. Easy Weeknight Meals for People with ——! Five Weeks to a Flat Stomach for —— Havers. Think You've Got ——? It's Probably Just Cancer!

I scrolled past —— and Pregnancy because I already knew what it would say and clicked on —— Symptoms: How Many Can You Name? I could name them all. If it were a game show, I would have a chance at the car.

*

I walked out of the chemist and realized when I reached the station that I did not want to go home. I decided to walk to Notting Hill instead. I had no reason for going there, except it would take a long time. It was starting to get dark when I got to the edge of the park. I walked along the cycle path, waiting to cry. The pill bottle rattled inside my bag with every step. I didn't cry. I just looked up at the trees, their black branches dripping rain, and held Robert's dry handkerchief inside my pocket.

At the top of the Broad Walk, I thought about Patrick accidently hitting Ingrid in the chest when we were teenagers, and now, at the Executive Home, cleaning up the mess I had left, waiting for me to get back from wherever I was.

I got my phone out as I walked. Contacts, Favorites, Patrick as HUSBAND. I did not know what he was going to say or what I hoped he would say. Continuing ahead I imagined him hugging me, asking me if I was okay. Being shocked, contesting Robert's diagnosis, saying obviously we need a second opinion. Or "now I think about it, that makes sense." I put my phone away and left the park at the next gate.

Dark then, I went up Pembridge Road to Ladbroke Grove, then onto Westbourne Terrace. The organic supermarket where Nicholas and I worked had become a clinic offering laser hair removal and cosmetic injectables. The shops and bar on either side of it were still open but I was too wet to go inside. I just stood there for a minute, hearing my cousin. "Ideally, Martha, you want to figure out the reason why you keep burning your own house down." I turned and walked back down Pembridge Road to the station, letting myself get trapped behind slow-walking tourists because I still didn't want to go home.

*

On the train back to Oxford, I called Goldhawk Road, expecting to hear my father's voice. I had already tried to call Ingrid at Paddington to tell her about the appointment. Her autoreply said I Can't Talk At The Moment. Now, exhausted, I just wanted to listen to my father talk about something uninteresting, knowing he would continue for some time as long as I said really at intervals.

My mother answered and said immediately, "He's gone to the library. Ring back later."

As a source of solace, I had always considered my mother many rungs below last resort. It is funny to me now, the line that spoke itself to me just then: Oh well. Port in a storm.

I said, "You and I could chat."

My mother exaggerated her shock. "Could we? I'm not sure I even know how. Do I ask what you've been up to?"

It is funny, now, because she was the storm. Just about to break over my head. I told her I was on my way back from London where I had seen a psychiatrist.

"Why?"

"I'm not sure."

"Well I hope you didn't believe a word he said. I've never known a psychiatrist who wasn't full of shit. They want us all to be mad. It's very much in their interest."

She knew. My grip on the phone was so instantly rigid, it sent a little shock up my arm.

My mother said, "Are you still there?"

"Do you remember that time when I was eighteen"—saliva was flooding my mouth in the way that precedes vomiting—"you took me to a doctor who said I had ____?" My right thigh started shaking. I tried to stop it with my hand.

"I do not."

"He was Scottish. You knocked over his coat stand on the way out on purpose and refused to pay. His receptionist chased us to the car."

My mother said, "What about it if I do remember?"

"Why did you get so angry?"

There was a silence and I checked my screen to see if she had hung up. But the timer was ticking on and I put the phone back to my ear.

Finally she said, "Because he was trying to put some awful label on you."

"He was right though. Wasn't he?"

"How do you know." It wasn't a question. She said it like a child in a sibling argument. How do you know.

I told her it didn't matter. "You knew he was right. You have known the whole time and you didn't say anything. Why would you do that to me?"

Both of my legs were trembling then.

"I didn't do anything to you. I told you, I didn't want you to have to go through your life with that terrible label attached to you. If anything, I did it for you."

"But the thing about labels is, they're very useful when they're right because," I carried on through her attempt at interruption, "because then you don't give yourself wrong ones, like difficult or insane, or psychotic or a bad wife." That was when I started crying for the first time since Robert's office. I put my head down so my hair fell and hid my face but my voice was getting louder and louder. "My whole adult life I've been trying to work out what is wrong with me. Why didn't you tell me? I don't believe you it was about labels. I don't believe you." A man across the aisle got up and ushered his son and daughter to seats farther away. "You were perfectly happy for it to be other things. You let me think it was depression and everything else doctors told me. Why not this? Why didn't you—"

She cut in then. "I didn't want it to be true. ____'s a hateful disease. Our family has been ravaged by it. My family and your father's. I've seen what it does, believe me, and I couldn't bear the idea of it being you as well. I couldn't. If that makes me a bad mother—"

"Who?"

"What do you mean?"

"Who in our family?"

My mother exhaled and began speaking in the weary tone of someone commencing a list they know is long. "Your father's mother, his sister who you never met. One or likely both of my aunts. And my mother, who you may as well know now did not die of cancer. She walked into the sea in the middle of February."

She stopped and then, sounding exhausted, said, "And probably—"

"You."

She said yes. "Me."

"Not probably though."

"No. Not probably."

Out the window, the outskirts of London had been giving way to countryside. The train slowed down and stopped on a section of floodlit track. A dense flock of birds rose off a bare tree. I watched them until finally my mother said, "What do you want me to do?"

The flock separated into two, looped upwards, and came

back together. "You can stop drinking." I hung up, assuming my mother had already done the same.

I felt ragged. For the rest of the journey, my mind ranged through periods of illness. The memories came out of order. I tried to locate my mother in each of them but she was never anywhere. Coming into the station, I sent her a text message, telling her not to say anything to Ingrid or my father. She didn't reply.

*

I let myself in to the Executive Home and went into the kitchen. Patrick and some number of colleagues were sitting around the table. There were bottles of beer in front of them. Someone had supplied Pringles and supermarket dip.

Patrick said hi Martha and got up, making a gesture out of their view, as he came over, to indicate that he'd definitely told me about what was presently happening but I'd evidently forgotten. I moved my head away from his attempt to kiss me and, with an uncertain look, he sat back down.

One of the doctors, opening himself another beer, told me I was allowed to come and join them. Another one said it was a good idea, since they were just chilling. All the other doctors signaled their agreement, all the other useless, useless fucking, fucking doctors, with their doctorly confidence and doctorly way of owning a room and the air in it, telling me what I was allowed to do and deciding for me what was a good idea. I said no thank you and ran upstairs, leaving them alone to talk to each other with surety about what they knew, although no doctor I had ever met, except one, knew a fucking thing. Not even Patrick. My own husband, a doctor, had not worked out what was wrong with me. In all this time.

I had a shower. Afterwards I stood in the middle of the bathroom, dripping without a towel, looking at the plants and the £60 candle, the bottles of things. None of it was mine. All of it had been chosen by a woman who as far as she knew did not have ____, a woman who just thought she wasn't good at being a person.

I pretended to be asleep when Patrick came up later. The next morning, once he left, I took one of the new tablets out of the bottle still in my bag. It was tiny and pale pink. In the kitchen I filled my hand with tap water, Me Cookie, and then went for a walk.

All the way, I thought about my diagnosis. The fact that, in receiving it, the mystery of my existence had been solved. ____ had determined the course of my life. It had been looked for and never found, guessed about, never correctly, suspected and disqualified. But it had always existed. It had informed every decision I had ever made. It made me act the way I did. It was the cause of my crying. When I screamed at Patrick, it put the words in my mouth; when I threw things, it was ____ that raised my arm. I'd had no choice. And every time in the last two decades that I'd observed myself and seen a stranger, I had been right. It was never me.

I could not understand, now, how it had been missed. Less and less as I kept walking. It is not uncommon. Its symptoms aren't hidden. They can't be disguised by the afflicted person in its throes. It should have been obvious to Patrick, the observing person, all along.

*

He came home that night and apologized that I hadn't remembered about the thing last night. I was standing at the sink, filling a glass. I looked over my shoulder and saw him hovering in the doorway, holding a plastic bag with something in it. He asked me how my day was. I said fine and turned the tap off. He appeared to me, then, with his plastic bag, unintelligent. An uncertain person, unquestioning. I asked him to move and he stepped aside. He said sorry when my elbow knocked into him on the way past and I was filled with disdain for a man who was so kind, and obedient, and oblivious.

MY FATHER RANG and asked if I could come into town and have lunch with him. I assumed he wanted to talk about what my mother had told him and our argument on the train because he mentioned straightaway that she wasn't going to be home, as though he knew I'd say no if she was.

I had thought about her constantly in the week that had passed since my appointment, enacting conversations with her in my mind, phone calls, scratching out letters listing every one of her crimes, all the ways she had hurt my sister, and me, and my father, as far back as I could remember. Pages about her dereliction of duty as a mother—her choosing to make ugly statues out of rubbish instead of caring for us. About her drinking and falling down, her stupid cruelty towards Winsome, her being fat and unimportant, the embarrassment of my life and now I never wanted to see her again.

Patrick kept asking me if I was alright. He kept telling me I seemed a bit preoccupied. A bit stressed. He wondered if something had happened. But my anger at my mother left no room for Patrick—his failure to notice there was something wrong with me was so much less than her effort to pretend there wasn't, her decades-long devotion to not noticing.

I told him to stop asking and he did, leaving me free to think about my mother to the exclusion of everything else, awake and in dreaming. Patrick and telling Patrick and Patrick's possible reaction to my ___ had become irrelevant to me. All I wanted was to hate my mother, and punish her and expose what she'd done. I said yes to lunch.

*

My father was in the kitchen buttering sandwiches when I arrived. We took them up to his study and sat on the sofa under the window, with our plates on our laps. He asked me what I'd been reading. I had been reading nothing and said Jane Eyre. He told me he ought to pick it up again as well, then after a brief hesitation, "Do you know, your mother hasn't had anything to drink this week. Nearly six days."

Tensing, I said, "Really. Well, did you also know she—" and then I stopped. His face was so open. He looked so certain that I would be gladdened by the fact. That he even thought it was worth reporting. "Did you know she—"

He waited and in another moment, my reply still half-said, he picked up his sandwich. A little piece of cucumber slid out. He said whoops. It was unbearable. I did not want to hurt him, I wanted to hurt her. In some direct way, not through him. I just said, "It isn't the first time though, is it? And six days isn't even her personal best."

My father peeled back a corner of bread and put the cucumber back in. "I suppose not, no."

"Do you want to talk about the ___ though?"

"The what?"

"My diagnosis. The new doctor."

He apologized. He said he was drawing a bit of a blank.

My mother hadn't told him. I assumed, for a second, in deference to my text asking her not to. But then, of course not. I felt so tired.

My father said, "You'll have to give me a bit of a clue."

I began to tell him what Robert had said.

The interest on his face became concern and then total grief as I kept going. He said goodness. "Goodness me." Over and over. I could tell he wanted to believe me when I said, as some sort of conclusion, that it is good because it means I'm not insane.

He said yes, okay. "I can see that and, supposedly, it does favor the brilliant. In fact"—he put his plate aside and stood up, going over to his computer, which was enormous and old, purchased with the money from Jonathan's engagement ring—"let's have a look."

He poked at the keyboard with his index fingers, saying slowly out loud, "Famous . . . people . . . with . . . ____." He pressed one more key and looked up at the screen, squinting at the slideshow he was being offered. I watched him try, with some effort, to guide the mouse towards its target. And I felt happy, unaccountably, except that I was with him, in this room where we had spent so much time and where I had always felt alright, if it was just us.

He clicked and said, "Look, here we go. Right off the bat," reading out the name of the famous artist who appeared first. I looked at his black and white photograph and said it was a curious choice—the artist sitting on the edge of a bed, holding a rifle. "Didn't he shoot himself in the head?"

My father seized the mouse. Another dead artist appeared, then a dead composer and two dead writers as he kept clicking, faster and faster, in search of a better example. A dead politician and a dead television presenter. I watched, aware that I should have been upset by an online roster of suicides, but I wasn't. For everything it had done to me, I had outrun it. More brilliant people, famous and unknown, had not been able to although they would have done so much to save themselves and I had done so little. I did not deserve to be alive instead of them. They had suffered, and lost. I had been told by a doctor that I had managed very well. I should not have been so lucky.

After a series of dead actors, my father glanced over his shoulder and in a desperate voice said, "Who is that?"

"He is a comedian who used to be addicted to painkillers. But he is still alive so that's good."

"Yes." My father smiled feebly before turning back to the screen and skipping past a picture of a pop star he didn't recognize either, until finally he dropped back in his chair. He pronounced the name of an American poet, who was dead but of natural causes. Exhausted, but gratified. He said, "Well, I did not know that."

I laughed and said, "Amazing."

"It is amazing. My daughter and the architect of postmodernism!"

I asked him if he thought we should go and make coffee and he leapt out of his chair and went ahead of me to the kitchen.

*

Late in the afternoon, at the front door about to leave, I hugged my father and with my cheek still pressed into his chest, the familiar feel and wool smell of his cardigan, I said, "Please don't tell anyone about the ____. Ingrid or anyone. I haven't told Patrick yet."

He stepped back. "Why not?"

I looked down and smoothed out a kink in the carpet runner with my foot.

"Martha?"

"Because. I have been busy."

"Even so, even if you have"—my father paused, trying to think of a kinder way to say don't lie, you are never busy—"whatever the case, this is more important than anything else. It's the most important thing. I'm surprised, if I'm quite honest."

I had committed so many crimes as his daughter and never, once, had my father been angry with me. He was angry at me now, for a crime of someone else's.

"Well," I said, "if I'm quite honest"—my father flinched at my tone—"I haven't had time to talk to Patrick because I've been trying to process the fact that your wife had this information all along and decided just to keep it under her hat. I mean yes, my daughter has been unwell on and off for most of her life and can be a touch on the suicidal side, but why burden her as to the reason. I'm sure it will all come out in the wash." I could not tell if it was still shock at the way I was speaking on my father's face, or incredulity, or upset because he knew it was true. He only said Martha, Martha as I shoved past him and left, shutting the door with too much force. That I had not told Patrick did not seem wrong, until then. It had not made me feel guilty. But I walked to the station, heavy with conviction, hating my mother for that as well.

*

As the Tube passed out of a tunnel to a section of overland track, my phone rang inside my bag. I answered it and Robert's receptionist told me Doctor wished to speak to me if I would kindly hold.

I waited, listening to an unnerving section of Handel's Messiah, until there was a click and then Robert saying hello Martha. He hoped he hadn't caught me at a bad moment but he had realized this morning, reviewing my notes, that he'd failed to ask me one of the standard questions before giving a prescription— it was an oversight for which he was very sorry, although not a dangerous one in this instance.

The Tube was coming into the next station and I could only just hear him over the recorded announcement. I apologized and asked him if he could say it again.

He said of course. "You're not pregnant or trying to be? I neglected to ask during our appointment."

I said no.

Robert said marvelous and told me no change was required, as to the medication, he simply needed to check for his records, and now he could let me go.

Over the loud beeping of the doors, I said sorry. "Just quickly, would it matter if I was?"

He said beg your pardon.

A group of teenage boys were trying to get into the carriage too late. One forced the doors and held them open while the others ducked under his arms. I wasn't conscious of getting up but heard him call me bitch as I pushed him out of the way so I could get off.

On the platform, I asked Robert again if it would matter if I was pregnant on this medication.

"Not in the least, no."

The Tube tore away and in the total silence that fell then, I heard him say, "Any medication in this category and certainly the versions you've been prescribed in the past are all perfectly safe."

I asked him if he would mind waiting a moment while I found somewhere to sit down. Instead, I leaned over a rubbish bin and spat into it, holding my phone as far away as I could. Nothing came out even though a thick, vomitous feeling had appeared at the back of my mouth.

Robert asked me if something was wrong. There was a row of seats next to the bin. I went to sit down but missed the edge and dropped onto my tailbone. The platform was empty now. I stayed there on the dirty ground. "No. Sorry. I'm fine."

He said good. "But should you find yourself becoming concerned later, I can assure you it's perfectly safe, for mother and baby. Both pre- or postnatally. Thus, if this medication works and you decide to become pregnant, at a later point, you would not need to discontinue it."

It was like a dream where you try to stand up but you can't, you need to run away from something but your legs won't move. I tried to answer him but there were no words. After a time, Robert asked me if I was still there.

I said I don't want a baby. "I would be a bad mother."

I do not remember how his reply began, only that it ended by him saying, "If that belief is connected to a sense that you're perhaps unstable or might present some risk to a child, I would only say that ____ does not disqualify you from having children.

I have many patients who are mothers and do very well. I have no doubt you'd be a wonderful mother, if it's something you wanted. Really ___ is not a reason to forgo motherhood."

I told him I could not think of anything worse and laughed merrily as my hand went into a fist. I hit myself in the head. It didn't hurt enough. I did it again. There was a spark of white behind my left eye.

Robert said indeed, indeed. "I am here, should you ever change your mind."

Another train was coming. I watched its progress towards me. A minute later I was standing up in a crowded carriage, staring at nothing, letting myself be thrown back and forwards as it jolted over the tracks and tore through the total darkness of the tunnel.

*

There was an airport car parked in front of the Executive Home. Patrick was standing beside it, trying to help the driver put his suitcase into the back.

He saw me and let the driver take it, then jogged towards me looking unusually irritated. "I thought I wasn't going to see you before I left. Did you see my calls?"

I said no and made up some reason why not, but Patrick's attention had shifted to whatever it was he'd just noticed on the side of my head.

"What happened to your face?"

"I don't know."

He reached out to touch it. I batted his hand away and started laughing.

"Martha, what is happening?" In frustration, he said for goodness' sake, which made me laugh more.

"Stop it. Martha, seriously. Stop. I've had enough."

"Of what? Of me?"

"No. Damn it."

That was very funny as well.

He was angry then and he said, "I'm going away, I'm not going to see you for two weeks. Why can't you just be normal?"

I was overtaken with laughter then. I said, "I don't know, Patrick. I don't know! Do you know? I don't know. It's a mystery. A complete mystery!" and I walked into the house, sufficiently enlarged by the exchange that I could hate my mother and my husband at the same time as I did, from then on. Intentionally and unintentionally, they had both ruined my life.

That night, I took my pink pill even though it didn't really matter if I got better anymore.

PATRICK WAS GONE for ten days. He texted. I did not reply except to tell him I was going to stay with Ingrid for the week, to which he said, "Great, have fun."

I said to her, a few days. I said, to help you out. And she was too desperate for help to query it. And she was perpetually tired, often in tears because of the children, otherwise shouting at Hamish. The house was untidy and always loud with appliances and television and her friends and their children coming and going all day, the crying and door-slamming in the night, and I was perfectly invisible. Even when I could not contain my grief to my room, nobody noticed. I did not go home after a few days. I was still there when Patrick got back. He texted me. I said Ingrid wanted me to stay another week.

Only once, in what became two weeks and then three, did my sister ask me how I was, and she did not query it either when I said I was amazing, or request information beyond that. I said nothing about Robert or Patrick. I told her I was not speaking to our mother and she was not interested in the specifics of why since she had been not-speaking to our mother at so many points, for so many reasons, in her own life.

By the time he drove to the house, it had been a month since Patrick and I had seen each other. He walked in the open front door and came to the kitchen. Ingrid and I were at the table, helping the boys with their tea.

He said, "It's time to come home, Martha."

I did not intend to go with him but Ingrid leapt up and said yes, yes definitely, and started making a lap of the kitchen, collecting up anything that was mine. I put down the fork I was holding, a little ring of sausage on the end of it that I had been trying to coax into her middle son's mouth. I thought I had been very helpful. My sister's relief was so plain and she was so insistent that I could just go now and Hamish could bring all my stuff later that I stood up and followed Patrick out to our car, both of us carrying the various possessions she'd put in our arms.

*

My anger towards him did not diminish in the weeks after that. When I was with him, it was acute, fed by the way he drank from a cup, his teeth-brushing, his work bag, his ringtone, his laundry at the bottom of the basket, the hair on the back of his neck, his effort to be normal, his buying batteries and shaving cream, saying you seem unhappy, Martha. It made me mean and baiting in conversation, dismissive or contemptuous. I was ashamed afterwards, but I could not resist my anger in the moment. Even when I resolved to be better, to talk to him, a sentence that started well ended hatefully. And that was why, mostly, I avoided being in the same room, or home at all if he was there.

Alone, I felt grief. It was intense but not constant, and in between I felt an unnatural serenity that I had not experienced before. It was, I decided, the serenity of a cancer patient who has been fighting for so long, they are relieved by the discovery it is terminal, because they can stop now and just do what they like until the end.

The only thing Patrick said in reference to the new way of things was that it had occurred to him, the other day, that it had been a long time since he had seen me cry. He said, "I guess you've finally worn out the mechanism" and "ha-ha," the words not the sound.

That was his way of asking me to tell him what had happened. I said, "Can you start sleeping in a different room?"

*

My editor sent me an email about a column I had written. It was a Monday afternoon. I counted later, in my diary, six weeks since I saw Robert.

The subject was Feedback. My stomach didn't plummet when I read it, or the first sentence of his many mistyped paragraphs. "Hey, apols it's taken me ages to get back to you." Things, he said, had been insane. "Anywya," he went on, "some pretty gnarly issues with this one, think you've missed the mark, over all too harsh/judgy." He wanted me to start again. "Something funnier & more first person. Taek your time."

I looked out the window, at the leaves of the plane tree, enormous and iridescent under the sun. On their passage back to the screen, my eyes stopped at a pattern of deep triangular dents in the wall above my computer. I wondered how the last email my editor had sent me like this had made me feel so humiliated and scared and hot and nauseated that I had risen out of the chair I was sitting in now, crossed to the cupboard and returned with the iron and, holding it over my head, driven it nose first into the wall over and over and over. This time I just felt very still. I said oh. That was when I knew I was better, the pills Robert gave me had worked.

I turned back to the window and looked at the tree for a while, then rewrote the column, about the time I lost my eco-cup and had to drink takeaway coffee out of a cocktail shaker because I had said so many judgmental things to my barista about people still using disposable cups and it was the only substitute I could find.

That I was able to return to it at all, to put his email out of my mind and work until I was finished, was extraordinary to me. I could not send it then, because my editor would know it had only taken forty minutes to produce six hundred funnier & more first-person words. I saved it and started writing an email to Robert.

I wanted to tell him what had just happened. I wanted to say it was the first time I had been able to decide how to react to something bad, even such a small thing, instead of coming to consciousness in the middle of already reacting. I said I hadn't known you could choose how to feel instead of being overpowered by an emotion from outside yourself. I said I couldn't explain it properly. I didn't feel like a different person, I felt like myself. As though I had been found.

I deleted it all and sent one line to say I was feeling better and grateful and I was sorry for emailing him. Then I put his name into Google.

*

No matter what private morsel she could have inadvertently divulged in our countless hours together, I never would have parked outside Julie, Female's house in the hope of acquiring another precious fact about her life. But I thought about Robert constantly for days after that. I Google Image–searched him and clicked on photographs taken at conferences. I read journal articles he had written and watched a long presentation he had given to an audience of psychiatrists, on YouTube.

I imagined going back to London, to Harley Street, at a time when he might emerge from his rooms and knew that if I saw him pause on the curb, appraise the evening while doing up a raincoat, I would step back and watch him, wondering where he was going and who was waiting for him and whether on the train he would think backwards through his day, reconsidering each patient with his newspaper unread in front of him.

I was consumed by the desire to know what Robert thought of me; whether, after I came to see him, he had told the wife I had met and liked so much about a new patient, a woman he'd diagnosed with ＿＿. It began to matter to me so much that Robert would have found me intelligent and amusing and original and that he'd recall me that way now, even though I hadn't been any of those things in the hour I had been in his rooms.

As I was sending my column on Friday morning, he replied. My heart did a single thud when I saw his name. After a week of thinking about him in imagined terms, having the certain knowledge of what he'd been doing seconds ago was so exquisite, I screen-shotted my inbox and then the email after I read it. It said, "Wonderful, glad to hear it. Sent From My iPhone." Then I deleted them both, cleared my history, and went downstairs. Robert's name and his single line of reply should not feel so precious to me that I needed to preserve them. What I had been doing for so many days until then was the occupation of the mad, and I was not mad; I knew Robert was just a person.

But if I had been found out, I would have said it was because he had saved my life, and the only thing I really knew about him was that he once cut his hand slicing a tomato.

I canceled my follow-up appointment because I didn't have anything else to say.

Supposedly, my column was spot on.

*

Everything was normal after that. I was normal and I lived hyperaware of it. I broke something, accidentally, and responded the way a normal person would, with frustration that only lasted as long as it took to clean up. I burned myself and felt a normal level of pain, and inconvenienced not enraged when I could not find the stuff to put on it. The house and objects in it were just objects, not imbued with menace or intent. Going out, I felt so normal I wondered if it was obvious to other people. I had conversations in shops. I asked a man if I could pat his dog. I said to a pregnant woman, "Not long to go," and she laughed and said, "I'm only five months."

And I felt normal grief, commensurate with the discoveries

I had made and the consequences of making them when I had. On which basis, my behavior towards Patrick was also normal. Anyone party to it would have to admit that under the circumstances, a wife acting as if she hated her husband, it was all very normal.

*

On a day in November, Patrick came into the box room while I was writing the deadline my editor had given for my next column into my calendar. At my desk, my back was to him. I sensed him walk up and stand behind me, looking over my shoulder.

I said, "Can you not?"

He pointed out that the deadline was a day before my birthday. He wondered why I hadn't written it in.

"Do adults usually write My Birthday in their diaries? Why did you come in?"

He said no reason and I thought he would leave then but instead, he retreated to a cane chair in the corner. It cracked when he sat down. Without turning around, I told him it wasn't really a chair for sitting on.

"Do you want to have a party?"

I said no.

"Why not?"

"I'm not in the right place, re celebrating."

"It's your fortieth though," he said. "We have to attack the day."

"Do we."

"Fine. Don't then." The chair cracked again with his getting up. "But I'm going to organize something because otherwise we will get to the actual day with nothing planned and you will punish me for it."

"Right. So," I turned around and looked at him for the first time since he'd come in, "the party is more a hedge against me being upset than you wanting to celebrate your lovely wife who you love so much."

Patrick put both hands on his head, elbows out. "I can't win. I seriously can't. I love you, that is why I am trying to do this thing. To make you happy."

"It won't. But do what you need to do."

I put my back to him again and he left, saying as he went out, "Sometimes I wonder if you actually like being like this."

He sent me an invitation by email, the same one he sent everyone else.

*

The next conversation Patrick and I had, of length, was in the car driving home from the party, when I told him that his pointing at people, the gun fingers he did while offering them drinks, made me want to shoot him.

He'd said I know what, Martha, how about we don't talk until we get home.

I said, "How about we don't talk once we're home either," and turned on the heater, as high as it would go.

*

Always, when I see Ingrid's eldest son he says, "Can you say about how I was born on the floor?" He tells me his mother is too tired to and his father only saw the end part. He says his brothers don't believe babies can happen on the floor—meaning, they will need to hear it again too, but separately, after him. On my lap, he puts one hand on each side of my face and tells me I have to do the funny version.

The last line is his. The last line is, "But my mum didn't like it and that's why sometimes everyone calls me Not Patrick."

Before he slides off my lap, he needs me to explain one more time how Patrick wasn't his uncle then and a bit later, he was. The fact is astonishing to him. It seems to confirm his belief that the very nature of things pivots on his existence, but he cannot fully enjoy it until he has my assurance that things can't go back the other way. That Patrick will always be his uncle.

THE MORNING AFTER the party, Ingrid called to post-mortem it, she said "as is my wont." I was still on the sofa where Patrick had left me to go and buy a newspaper, believing he was and would be back soon. She told me she was in the bathroom hiding from her children, and would have to hang up if they found her. Over the sound of slopping bathwater, she rated the outfits the women wore in ascending order from worst to okayish, then talked for a while about Oliver's new girlfriend who had got spectacularly drunk and flirted with Rowland. At the end of the night, Ingrid had seen her mine-sweeping the room for abandoned glasses, and later, being broken up with outside. It was so weird, she said, that it wasn't our mother doing the mine-sweeping, insisting when she could no longer stand up that someone had spiked her drink, Ingrid would say, with ten other drinks. At the party, my sister hadn't asked me why our mother wasn't there and didn't then. Her not appearing at an event thrown in celebration of someone else was not extraordinary.

"Did you have fun?"

I thought she meant it as a real question and said no.

"Yes. That was obvious."

I felt accused and told her I tried.

"Did you? Really? Was that when you locked yourself in the

toilet or when you were looking at your phone during my stupid speech?"

"Can you please remember that I didn't even want a party," I said. "The whole thing was Patrick's idea. But whatever. I'm sorry."

I heard the loud suction of water, my sister getting out of the bath. She told me to hang on for a second, then sighed heavily into the phone before she began talking again. "I know you and Patrick have been having a shit time for reasons I can't work out but I wish I could understand why you can't just backburner it for one night, and be like fuck it, it's my birthday, my husband's done all this, everyone is here, I'll just have a champagne and a fucking olive and get back to my marriage problems tomorrow."

I could not explain to Ingrid why I behaved like I hated Patrick without revealing why, by that time, I truly did. And I was so exhausted—all of a sudden—so exhausted by being the bad one, the disappointing one, the ruiner of everything again, again, again, that when I replied I was almost shouting. "Because it's all false, Ingrid. All those speeches and laughing and oh Martha, you look lovely, happy birthday, the big four-oh. They're not my friends. None of them know the first thing about me, why I am the way I am. And it's my fault because I am a fuck-up and a liar. You don't even know me."

"Literally what are you talking about?"

I moved the phone to my other hand. "I have ____."

"Who said that?"

"A new doctor."

As though I'd complained that I was fat, Ingrid said, "Well that's stupid. He's obviously wrong."

"No he isn't."

"What? Really?"

I said yes.

"You have actual ___? Fuck." She was quiet for a second. "I'm so sorry."

"Don't be. I'm fine with it. He gave me something that worked. I've been a new man for six months."

"Why didn't you tell me?"

I said, "I haven't told anyone except our parents."

"Why not? If you're fine with it, why wouldn't you just tell everyone?"

"Because it's still fucking embarrassing."

"I wouldn't have judged you. Nobody would have. They shouldn't anyway." Then, sounding so completely unlike herself I worried I was going to laugh, my sister said, "We as a society have to break down the stigma around mental illness."

"Oh my gosh, Ingrid. I'd rather we as a society built it up a bit so we could talk about something else."

"That's not funny."

"Okay."

"What does Patrick think?"

"Ingrid, I just said."

"What?"

"He doesn't know."

"What? Oh my God, Martha. Why the fuck would you decide to tell our parents instead of your own husband?"

"I didn't decide. I told our father by accident. Our mother, it transpired, did not need to be told."

"What? Why not?"

I asked if we could talk about her later.

"Fine. But—" Someone screamed Mum and started banging

on the bathroom door. Ingrid ignored it. "I still don't understand why you don't want him to know. You're having a horrible time and apart from the fact that it would probably help if he had this fundamental information about his wife, secrecy is extremely shitty married-person behavior."

"He should have known."

"Why? You didn't."

"I am not a doctor."

"And Patrick's not a psychiatrist. And you know now so does it still matter?"

"Yes."

"Why?"

There was another loud noise in the background, the door being flung open too hard and hitting the wall, followed by the voices of her children. Ingrid told me to wait. I heard her say, "Out, out, out," but they wouldn't go and by the time she came back, she had forgotten her question.

"Martha, you need to tell him. You can't just keep going indefinitely, thinking you can be happy on any level, ever, if you're not telling him this giant thing."

"I don't think we can be happy on any level." Ever—it was the first time I had heard myself say it, plainly, aloud.

"Martha, seriously." Ingrid was worn. "Where is he now?"

I told her he had gone to get the paper. From where I was sitting, I could see into the kitchen, the clock on the oven. We had been talking for two hours. I had no idea where Patrick really was.

"Please promise that you'll tell him as soon as he gets back. Or even, I don't know, write him a letter. You're good at that."

I said I would and that I had to go because my phone was on four percent. I did not know if either was true.

*

I sat there for a bit longer, until my guilt became annoyance or the other way around. Either way, a feeling powerful enough to compel me off the sofa and upstairs. I had a shower and dried the floor with my dress, still there from the night before. I went downstairs to the kitchen and tipped Patrick's coffee out, peeled a banana and did not eat it, and by the time I had done all those small, stupid things, I didn't care about anything. I got a pen out of a drawer and wrote the letter, standing up, the paper pressed against the wall until the ink ran out and I decided to go to London.

*

The oil light came on as I started the car, and so I walked to the station. On the platform, I got a text from Ingrid. I read it, with no instinct to throw my phone against something or grind it into the ground with my heel, then got on the train, not sure where in London I was going.

In my seat, I put my bag against the window and leaned my head on it. Someone had scratched the word Wrekt into the glass. I went to sleep wondering why they had chosen that word, spelt that way, and where they were now.

When I opened my eyes, the train was coming into Paddington. My sister's message said, "I meant to tell you on the phone. I'm having another baby. sorry x 100000000."

I GOT A Tube to Hoxton, to a place I'd gone to a year before when Ingrid had decided to get her sons' names tattooed on the inside of her wrist by a man she found on Instagram. She said he had 100,000 followers.

A girl behind the desk said the studio didn't do walk-ins, playing with her septum piercing as she spoke. "But he's got a gap in five minutes and could do you something small, i.e. not this," referring me to her exposed clavicles, tattooed with a pattern of leaves and vines. I said it was very impressive. "Yeah, I know. You can wait over there if you want."

I pretended to study the menu of terrifying body art options on the wall until the man with all the followers came and took me out the back, directing me to a reclining chair, drawing up next to me on his saddle stool. I showed him a picture on my phone.

I said, "Not colored in. Just the outline of it. As small as possible."

He took the phone and made the picture bigger. "What is it?"

I told him it was a barometric map of the Hebrides. I wanted it on my hand, I didn't care where.

He said cool, picked up my hand, and rubbed his thumb over the fine cross-hatched forty-year-old skin of mine. "Yeah, I reckon just below the nail." He let go and pulled a cart towards him, picking things out of its small drawers.

"Is that where you're from or what?"

I said no and then nothing for a second, unsure whether to tell him the reason. I wanted to, but worried that it would be as incomprehensible, then as quickly boring, as someone's explanation of a dream, a revelation had in therapy or a description of what their wedding dress was going to look like.

Then I remembered I didn't care about anything anymore.

He had picked up my hand again and was washing alcohol over my palm with cotton. I said, "The weather there is generally just cyclones and torrential storms and hurricanes that are unpredictable and devastating, which, I assume, makes it hard to live a normal life. It's how I feel. I have ____."

He swiveled, and tossed the cotton in a waste bin and said, "Who doesn't, love?"

It made no sense and felt like the most intense kindness—that this man with a crucifix and a snake and a dead rose and a knife with blood dripping off it tattooed on his neck, and the name Lorna, which, based on the date of birth underneath it, might belong to his mother, was so unperturbed by my revelation that he didn't look up or ask me anything else until he'd finished drawing on my thumb with pen.

"But you're alright now, are you? You don't seem like a mentalist."

"Yes, I'm fine now."

"So why do you still want your weather on you?"

"I think," I said, maybe "a memorial. I lost things."

He had been about to start. The point of the needle was against my skin but he took it away again and did meet my eye then as he said, "Like what? Friends?"

I opened my mouth and said, "No, when—"

When I was a teenager, a doctor gave me some pills and told me not to get pregnant. The next doctor gave me something else, but said the same thing. Another doctor and then another one and another, diagnosing and prescribing and insisting their predecessor had been wrong, but always issuing the same caution.

I took everything they gave me, imagining the pills dissolving into my stomach, whatever was inside them spreading through my body like black dye or poison, making it toxic to the fetus I was told strenuously and repeatedly not to conceive.

I was seventeen and nineteen and twenty-two and I was still a child who didn't think doctors could be wrong, or I did not suspect they might warn me against pregnancy, not because the medication was dangerous but because in their minds I was dangerous. To myself, to a baby, to my parents, to their excellent and unblemished professional records. Not a single unplanned baby born to a mentally ill girl on their watch.

And so I did as I was told and I made sure I did not get pregnant and I never stopped being scared, until I met Jonathan. Briefly, with him, I was allowed to think I was a different person. If I stopped it all, I could have a baby.

But I couldn't stop it all. My body could not live without the black dye flowing through it. And then Jonathan saw who I was, someone with tendencies, and he said thank God. And I said yes, thank God that I did not manage to get pregnant.

Because even if a baby survived inside me and even if it was born and I could care for its body, one day a little bomb would go off in its brain and all the pain and sadness it would feel in life from then on would be from me, and my guilt at what I had given it would make me hate it like my mother hated me. I accepted it. A biblical genealogy.

Depressed seaside mother begat Celia.

Celia begat Martha.

Martha should not beget anyone.

And then, a doctor said I'd got it wrong. Robert said, "___ is not a reason to forgo motherhood." He has many patients who are mothers. They do very well. He has no doubt I would be a wonderful mother. If that is something I want.

Listening to him, sitting on the dirty platform, is when I realized that what I had always believed to be true was the understanding of a sick child. I had never thought to question it when I became an adult. Instead, I put evidence to it and stoked it, all those beads on the one long string. I imagined more than what I'd been told and whenever I imagined my damaged baby, a child damaged by the kind of mother I would be, I felt fear and worse shame, and that was why I had been lying.

All the time. To anyone. Strangers, people at parties, my parents. To my sister as we gazed down at her swaddled baby in the soft darkness. To myself, looking out the window on a 94 bus. I lied to Robert. He said, "if you decide to become pregnant," and I told him I couldn't think of anything worse. And I lied to Patrick, before we were married and every day afterwards.

My husband does not know that a child is the only thing I have ever wanted. He doesn't know that seeing my sister become a mother, a lovely good mother, was like being cut open, and her conceiving so easily and having more babies than she wanted made it too wide to ever close. And I have hated her sunmoonstarsgreatloveofmylife for complaining about all of it, her ruined body, the newborns who exhaust her with their crying, the toddlers and their constant touching and constant need, the cost, washing washing washing always washing, and muddy shoes, the end of sex, their fingerprints on all the windows, lice again!, the night terrors, sudden fevers and fighting, the endless noise, and they make her completely useless because God, these perfect perfect perfect beautiful boys. The best thing she has ever done. But you are so lucky—you probably use a basket—you probably didn't even know they sell toilet paper in forty-eight packs!

There is nothing inside me except want for a child. It is every breath in and every breath out. The baby I lost that day by the river, I wanted her so desperately I thought I would stop being at the same time as her. I have cried for her every day since then.

And I am still lying because I wrote you a note this morning, Patrick, and I did not leave it for you. It is here in my bag. I am looking down at its folded pages. I am leaning forward and retrieving it, and the man with the tattooed neck is saying no problem and throwing it away for me.

I didn't give it to you because you do not deserve to know these things about me, about my desire for a baby or even about my diagnosis. Those things are mine. I have been carrying them by myself and it is like having gold inside me. I have been walking around, knowing I am better than you. That is why I smile at you like the Mona Lisa, Patrick, while you study me so closely and remain oblivious. You didn't see it. You were not looking for it. And none of it matters anyway. If I tell you or not. It is too late.

I said, "No when—well, just different opportunities I guess. Things I wanted to do and didn't."

The man said, "Yeah, right. Life. What a bucket of shit. Let's get you done."

I thought it would hurt but it didn't and I reached into my bag again with the hand he wasn't holding and got out my phone. Over the sound of the needle, he said he'd never had a client scrolling Instagram at the same time as getting inked.

He was finished in a few minutes and as he wrapped my thumb I asked him if he remembered my sister, the woman who had to stop before he had finished the first letter of her eldest son's name because she was going to pass out, so instead of their three names, she has a tattoo of a very short line.

"If she was the one who said I should be in jail for not offering my clients epidurals, then threw up all over the floor, then yeah."

We stood up at the same time and as I was leaving he said he'd usually suggest a couple of ibuprofens or whatever but clearly, I was pretty fucking down with pain.

*

It was late, after ten, when I got back to the Executive Home. I had been caught in the rain. My hair was dripping down my back. I wiped under my eyes and my fingertips were black with mascara. Patrick was in the living room. He had ordered take-away, enough for one person, and was watching the news.

He did not ask where I had been. I wasn't planning to tell him or, before that moment, speak to him at all when I got home but the fury caused by coming in and finding Patrick engaged in normal activity was so intense it felt like heat and whiteness in front of my eyes. He was not entitled to the ordinary evening he had created for himself or any content in domestic life from now on, its basic rituals and small, common pleasures. Because of what he had done, I had gone without it and I would never acquire it in however much time was still to serve out.

I went over and stood between him and the television and told him I'd been in London, getting a tattoo. He didn't look up. Instead, he moved his fork around in his plastic container, searching through the rice for a chunk of something to stab with it. When I asked him if he would like to know what it was of, Patrick said up to you and kept going with the fork.

"It's a map of the Hebrides. Would you like to know why I got that?" I said, okay then, I'll tell you. "It's a reference to the Shipping Forecast, Patrick. Cyclonic, occasionally good etcetera. That funny joke I made once, remember? About it being a metaphor for my mental state. You're wondering, why now? It's because I saw a new doctor who gave me an explanation for that state." I said, mid-May, before you ask. "So yes, seven months."

"I know."

"Know what?"

"That you went and saw a psychiatrist."

I said, "What? How?"

"You paid with my card. Robert's name was on the statement."

The next wave of fury originated from so many sources I could only grasp one: how much I hated Patrick referring to him by his first name.

"If you didn't want me to know, you probably should have paid Robert with cash."

"Don't call him that. He's not your friend. You've never even met him."

"Fine. But you have ____, is that what you're about to say?"

I said oh my God. "How do you know that? Did you call him?" I told Patrick—I shouted—that he was not allowed to do that even though, in the unflooded part of my mind, I knew he hadn't and even if he had, Robert could not have shared my diagnosis.

And Patrick, who was never sarcastic, said, "Really? I didn't realize that. Is there like a doctor patient confidentiality thing?"

Like a child, I stamped my foot and told him to shut up. "Tell me how you know."

"I know the drug."

"What drug?"

"The one you're on." He dropped his fork into the container and put it on the coffee table.

"I didn't tell you I was on anything. Did you go through my stuff?"

Patrick asked if I was serious. "You leave it lying around, Martha. You don't even throw the empty packets away. You just shove them in a drawer or leave them on the floor somewhere for me to pick up. I mean, I assume they're for me to pick up since that's what we do, isn't it? You make a mess and I clean up after you, like it's my job."

My hands were in fists, so tight they seemed to be throbbing. "If you knew everything, why didn't you tell me?"

"I was waiting for you to tell me but you didn't. And then after a while it seemed like you weren't going to and I had no idea why. It's clearly right," he said. "You clearly have ____."

As I spoke back, I felt the muscles around my mouth contorting and making me ugly. "Do I, Patrick? Clearly? If that is so fucking clearly right, why didn't you work it out before? Is it a competence issue? As in, does a person need to be physically bleeding for you to comprehend that they're not well? Or is it, as a husband, you're not interested in your wife's well-being? Or is it just total passivity? Your absolute, blanket acceptance of how things are."

He said okay. "This conversation isn't going anywhere."

"Don't! Don't walk out." I moved as if I would block him from leaving.

Patrick didn't stand up, leaned back in the sofa instead. "I can't talk to you when you're like this."

I said, "I'm only like this because of you. I'm well. I've been well for months. But you make me feel insane. Wasn't that clear too? Didn't you wonder why instead of being better to you, I've been worse?"

"Yes. No. I don't know. Your behavior's always been"—he paused—"all over the place."

"Fuck you, Patrick. Do you know why? You don't. It's because I've always wanted a baby. This whole time, my whole life, I've wanted to have a baby but everyone told me it would be dangerous."

Very slowly, Patrick said, "Do you really think I wasn't aware of that either? I'm not stupid, Martha. Even if it's always, how annoying they are and how much you can't stand them and how tedious motherhood is, babies are the only thing you ever talk about. You won't let us sit near anyone with a baby in a restaurant, then you'll be staring at them all night. Or if we pass a pregnant woman or someone with a child, you go completely silent and whenever we go to something, you're so incredibly rude to anyone who dares to mention their children. We've had to leave things early so many times, just because someone asked you if you have kids." Patrick stood up then. "And you're obsessed with Ingrid's boys. Obsessed with them, and you pretend you're not jealous of her but it's so obvious that you are, especially when she's pregnant. You're not a good liar, Martha. A chronic one, but not a good one."

I went around the coffee table, grabbed the front of his shirt with both hands and wrenched it and twisted it and said guess what, Patrick, guess what. "Robert said it would be fine." I tried to push him. "He said it would have been fine." I tried to hit his face. "It wouldn't be dangerous but you knew that too, you knew that too." Patrick got my wrists and would not let go until I stopped struggling against his grip. Although, then, he ordered me to sit down, I went back to the coffee table, put my heel to the edge, and pushed it over. The takeaway container was upended, the liquid left in it spilled across the carpet. Patrick said for God's sake, Martha, and went out to the kitchen.

I didn't follow him. Every cell in my body felt individually paralyzed except for my heart, beating hard and too fast. A moment later, he returned with a tea towel, dropped it over the liquid that had soaked into the carpet, and stamped on it. I couldn't do anything except watch, until I stopped feeling my heart. And then I told him to stop it. "Just leave it. Listen to me."

"I am listening."

"Well stop cleaning up then."

He said fine.

"Why didn't you say? Why did you just let me lie. If you had said something since the appointment, I could be pregnant now. You always wanted children, Patrick—I could be pregnant now. Why would you do that?"

"Because—you just said—you should have been better. You got your diagnosis finally, you got the right meds, and you weren't any better to me. I couldn't work it out but then I realized." He shifted the tea towel with his foot. The liquid had settled darkly into the carpet, a stain that would never be got out. "This is who you are. It has nothing to do with ——. And," he said, "I don't think you should be a mother."

I opened my mouth. It wasn't speech or screaming that came out. It was primal sound, coming from somewhere, my stomach, the bottom of my throat. Patrick went out and left me there. I sank to my knees, then my face was to the floor. I was gripping handfuls of my hair.

There is a gap after that, a blackout in my memory until, a few hours later, I am standing at one corner of the bed, dragging the sheets off it while Patrick puts things in a suitcase that is open on the floor. Sun is coming through the window. I'm compelled to the bathroom to throw up.

When I came back, Patrick had closed the suitcase and was carrying it out of the room. I called something after him, but he did not hear me. A moment later, I heard the car start and I went over to the window. He was backing out of the driveway. I tried to bring the blind down, pulled too sharply and it broke. For a long time, I just stood there with its slack cord in my hand, staring unfocused at the house on the other side where another woman had lived my life in mirror image.

Then Patrick was turning back into the driveway. I didn't

know why he had come back. I watched him park the car and get out. He had a bottle in his hand and once he had raised the hood he emptied it into the engine, closed the hood again, and walked away, in the direction of the station.

Patrick is a man who puts oil in the car as his final act before leaving his wife. I put my hand on my chest but felt nothing.

I SPENT THE day and first night without him on the stripped bed; after he left there did not seem to be a reason to remake it. Life, a life involving sheets and dishes and letters from the bank did not exist anymore.

Between sleeping and waking and sleeping again, I googled Robert. Then I googled Jonathan. His wife is a social media influencer. Her Instagram is a mixture of holiday photos, sponsored posts about a brand of collagen drink, and photos of what she is wearing shot in the mirror of the elevator that I used to take down to the street to breathe. She gets the most likes when she posts pictures of her little tribe, #thestronggirls, all of whom have blonde hair and names that are also common nouns. Objects and fruit. I scrolled all the way back to her wedding to Jonathan on a rooftop in Ibiza. I wondered how much he had told her about me, how much @mother_of_strong_girls knows about her husband's forty-three-day starter marriage.

*

Ingrid texted me in the morning. She said she had spoken to Patrick. She said, "Are you okay?"

I sent her the bathtub emoji, the three-pin plug, and the coffin.

She asked me if I wanted her to come and get me. I said I didn't know.

I was still in bed—on bed—half dressed, in the underwear and tights I had worn to London and surrounded by mugs that were empty or had become receptacles for tissues and dried-up curls of orange peel when I heard Ingrid let herself into the Executive Home. She went straight to the living room, trailed by smaller, quicker footsteps, and turned the television on to some sort of cartoon before coming upstairs.

I thought she would come and lie with me on the bed and stroke my hair or my arms as she usually did. I thought she would say, it's going to be alright and can you try and stand up now, can you get all the way to the shower? Instead, she threw the door open, looked around and said, "This is quite the visual and olfactory cocktail. Wow Martha."

*

At my party, I hadn't noticed her stomach. Now I saw how already round it was. Ingrid crossed both sides of her cardigan over it as she entered and went to the window. Once she had wrenched it open, she turned back and pointed at the sheets. "How long have they been on the floor?"

I said I meant to deal with them but ending my marriage and trying to get a fitted sheet on by myself felt like too much at the same time. She stood at the end of the bed, stone-faced, and pushed the fingertips of one hand into the place where her ribs met the top of her stomach, as though she was in pain. "If you're coming, come. It's four thirty. The boys are downstairs and I'm not getting stuck in traffic with them hungry."

I took too long to get up. I took too long finding something to wear, a bag to put things in. My sister's rising impatience slowed me down even more. I gave up and lay back down on the bed, facing away from her.

Ingrid said, "Do you know what? Fine. I can't do this anymore either. It's so boring, Martha." She left the room and called out from the stairs. "Ring your husband."

I heard her summon her children from the front door and a moment later, the door slamming shut. The television was left on.

It was the first time she had refused to do her job. I wanted her sympathy and she wouldn't give it to me. I wanted her to make me feel like I was good, and right to make Patrick go. I was angry and then, at the sound of her car starting, lonelier than I was before she came.

I did not ring my husband. I could not call my father, who would be stricken and unable to hide it. I picked up my phone and dialed my mother.

I had not spoken to her since the day of my appointment and I did not want to speak to her then. I wanted her to answer and say, "Well isn't this a turn-up for the books" so that I could fight with her and she would hang up on me and then I could feel aggrieved and tell Ingrid and she would agree that it was classic her. Literally, so typical.

I had not forgiven my mother for what she had done. I hadn't attempted to, or had to try and stay angry. Hating someone who was capable of seeing their daughter in pain and saying nothing, compounding it instead by drinking, was effortless.

It rang once. She picked up and said, "Martha, oh, I've been hoping and hoping you would ring."

It was not her ordinary voice. It was from before, before I became the teenager who really brought out her bitchlike tendencies, her resident critic. The voice she used to call me Hum. She asked me how I was feeling and said, "Awful probably" when I answered with a sound instead of words.

She continued on that way for ten minutes, asking questions and answering them herself—correctly. As I would have.

After we hung up, I went downstairs, found two open bottles of wine and took them back to my bedroom. I would not have called her again except her final question was, "Will you ring me back later? Anytime. Even if it's the middle of the night," and her answer to it was "Okay good. I will speak to you soon then."

*

I was drunk when I called the second time, before dawn. I told her I didn't know what to do, I begged her to tell me. She began to say something general. I said, "No, right now, what do I do? I don't know what to do." She asked me where I was and then said, "You are going to stand up, and then you are going to go downstairs and put your shoes and coat on." She waited as I did each thing. "Now, you are going to go for a walk and I will stay on the phone."

I walked slowly and felt sober by the time I got to the end of the towpath. She said, "Right, turn around and walk fast enough that you can feel your heart beating." I don't know why she said that but I did.

It was light by the time I reached Port Meadow again. Fog was thinning on the far side, gradually revealing the line of spires. She said, as I got home, "Have a bath." Then, "Call me in twenty minutes. I will be here."

*

I began to ring my mother every day.

People describe things as "the only way I can get out of bed" but usually they do not mean literally. But I meant it that way—I rang her in the morning, the moment I woke up. I could not move, or eat or walk through the house, open windows or wash my hair unless she was talking to me and telling me what to do.

In the afternoons, I sat in the front window of the Executive Home, looking out at the street. The house on the opposite side was for rent. We talked until the side of my face was hot from the phone or I couldn't turn my head because I had been holding it with my shoulder, or I noticed it was nighttime. We talked only about small things. Something she had heard on the radio, a dream one of us had.

We did not talk about Patrick but I wondered if she was talking to him too. I wondered if she knew where he was. We did not talk about Ingrid; my mother must have known we were not speaking. She must have known my father and his grief were best kept away from me for the time being because he did not call and I was grateful.

One morning I called her and announced, like a child, "Guess what? I'm already up" and she said, "Are you! Well done."

She said, "What was that bang?"

I told her I was getting a cup out of the cupboard because I was making tea and she said, "That's very good."

Her voice was the only thing I ever heard from her end, no noise in the background. If I asked her what she was doing, she would say just sitting. I apologized once and said she must have to go, she must have work to do. She said her public would just have to wait for boundary-pushing installations. I had never heard her joke about her work before.

She never asked me why I had rung on that occasion or this one—she knew I called in panic, in boredom, in loneliness, when the silence of the house became unbearable. I did not notice for a long time that no matter what time it was, my mother never sounded drunk.

In between, I walked until I could feel my heart beating. Mostly the towpath, across Port Meadow or, early enough that it would be empty of students and tourists, through the park of Magdalen College. The deer grazed and ignored me.

Then, although she did not ask, I began to tell my mother what had happened, about my marriage, and children, and Patrick. She told me to say what I liked; nothing could shock her. She said, "I'll see the most poisonous thing you've ever said to him and raise you something much worse I've said to your father."

I told her that, to begin with, I was angry because he hadn't noticed there was something wrong with me. That is what I thought. But he could not have missed it. It must have occurred to him at some stage, or he had known from the beginning. In either case, he didn't do anything because he liked it that way. That was so obvious now—me being the problem, Patrick getting to be the hero. Everyone thinking he was so amazing for putting up with such a difficult wife. Saves lives all day at work, comes home and keeps going. Everyone thinking, what a busman's holiday that marriage must be.

I said that he should never have accepted the way I treated him but he did because the only thing he cared about was having me, the thing he'd always wanted. He just accepted everything and always let it be my version of the story, believing that way he wouldn't lose me. I said, not me—a version of me he made up when he was fourteen. I said he should have grown out of it like everyone else does, instead of marrying his own invention.

He gave up his own chance to be a father. He shouldn't have let me take that from him. He shouldn't have made me responsible for that.

I told her it was Patrick's fault I am not a mother. I lied, but so did he.

For a long time I went on that way. Mostly my mother listened without saying anything. She never seemed shocked, even by the things I could barely bring myself to say aloud. She just said of course, of course. I'm not surprised. Who wouldn't feel like that?

Finally, I exhausted myself. I said Patrick and I should never have been together. We had broken each other. Our marriage never made sense. And then I was quiet.

It had been nearly a month, hours and hours of every day, and as though it was now her turn my mother said, "Martha, no marriage makes sense. Especially not to the outside world. A marriage is its own world."

I asked her to please not get philosophical.

Her thin laugh annoyed me. She said, "Alright but Maya Angelou—"

I cut her off. "Please don't Maya Angelou me either. I know I'm right. We were dysfunctional. We made each other dysfunctional. I had to be the one to end it but I know it's what he wanted too. He was just too passive to do it. Of course it's sad, obviously. But it is best for everyone. Not just us."

"Yes—well." My mother sighed. "What time will you get there tomorrow?" She had seemed about to say something else.

I asked her what tomorrow was.

"Christmas Day."

I was quiet for a minute, trying to imagine it, driving by myself to London, seeing my father, facing Ingrid, the chaos of her children, Rowland's excruciating conversation, the endless, pointless friction between Winsome and my mother. Her drinking. "I don't think I can. I think it's too many people."

"It's only going be Winsome and Rowland, me and your father. Sorry, I thought I told you that. Your cousins are elsewhere. Ingrid and Hamish have taken the boys to Disneyland. I have no idea why. And for ten days—you could do every room in the Louvre twice in that time."

She waited for me to ask where Patrick was, then after a moment of silence said, "He's gone to Hong Kong. It will be a difficult day. I know. But will you come?"

I said no. "I don't think so. Sorry."

My mother sighed again. "Well I can't make you. But please think about whether you need to make yourself more miserable than you already are. Spending Christmas alone, Martha, I'm not sure. It will be very bleak. And if I can say so, I would just like to see you myself."

As soon as we hung up, I went for a walk. The thought of the towpath, doing it again, exhausted me and I went another way towards town.

*

Broad Street was crowded. I felt dazed by the concentration of people with plastic bags, coming in and out of shops, buying shoes and mobile phones and things from Accessorize. Babies cried in their prams, hungry and overheated. Children lagged behind their parents or strained ahead on safety reins.

Mothers were shopping with teenage daughters who walked with their heads down, texting. A girl stormed out of a Body Shop, letting the door spring back on her mother who was trying to keep up.

The girl didn't ask to be born, her mother could just fuck off. She got out her phone and the mother, who was beside her then, said that was it, Bethany, she'd had enough. They walked off in opposite directions. I was in the mother's way and she stopped in front of me, close enough that I could see her earrings were tiny candy canes. For a second we were face to face, looking directly into each other's eyes, but I do not think she saw me. I went to step aside but she wheeled around and began chasing after her daughter, holding her purse above her head and waving it like a white flag.

I walked on slowly, staring at the faces of people coming towards me, jostling past on both sides, wondering if any of them had burned their own houses down and if they had, how long it was before they could come out and walk around and want things from Accessorize.

I went into a Costa and bought a muffin. I was not hungry and, back outside, I tried to give it to a homeless man sitting under an ATM. He asked me what flavor it was and when I told him he said that he didn't like raisins.

I kept walking to the covered market. Standing outside a sweet shop, I called my mother. There was a child sitting at a high table in the window with his grandmother. He was eating ice cream. Even though he was holding it with mittened hands, and still wearing his parka and woolly hat, his lips were violet.

She picked up and asked me if everything was okay.

"If I come tomorrow, will you not drink?"

There was no pause. She said, "Martha. You asked me to stop. The day you called me from the train."

"I know."

"Well I stopped," my mother said. "I haven't had anything to drink since then. After you hung up, I tipped it all down the sink. In the language of group"—she said the word as though it had a capital—"it has been two hundred and eighteen days since my last drink."

We had never—Ingrid, my father, Winsome, Hamish, or Patrick—none of us had ever asked her to stop. Out of loyalty, or sensing the futility, we had never even discussed doing so among ourselves.

I had not noticed I was smiling at the boy with the violet lips. He stuck his tongue out at me.

My mother said, "Are you laughing?"

I said no. "I mean, yes. But not about you. Something I've just seen." I said it's good. "That's good."

*

It was midafternoon, already beginning to get dark, when I arrived at Belgravia. I had woken up not intending to go and spent the morning on the sofa watching television with the lights off, trying to convince myself that I did not feel guilty about disappointing my mother, that the sick feeling and tightness in my forehead was the first symptom of a migraine, and that I had not sunk so far into despair that by the time Mary Berry's Absolute Christmas Favorites came on at noon I wondered if I would stop breathing.

Winsome opened the door and looked ecstatic to see me, her unshowered niece who was wearing a T-shirt and sweatpants under her coat and holding a hostess present she had purchased at a convenience store on the way in. She fussed excessively over my coat and expressed too much gratitude for the present, then ushered me into the formal living room.

I had not come with the expectation of feeling better. I had come because I did not think I could feel worse but when I entered the room I felt an instant and perverse nostalgia for those hours of cloistered misery at the Executive Home. Seeing Rowland and my mother and father sitting in the overwhelmingly empty-looking room, each opening a very small present, I felt indescribably worse. I had done this. I was the reason Ingrid and my cousins had chosen to be elsewhere. The room hummed with their absence. There was a separate undercurrent of sadness that was so palpable, a stranger coming in would have inferred a recent bereavement. It was Patrick's not being there. I had accomplished that too. And like my aunt, my parents and my uncle were absolutely thrilled to see me.

My father came over and hugged me, patting me on the back at the same time like I had done something praiseworthy in turning up at Belgravia, late, unannounced, and disrespectfully dressed, on the most important day of the year for my aunt. And she had set aside lunch for me—on the off chance, Winsome said, hope against hope!—that I would surprise them all. And Rowland, who always went to such great lengths to avoid acts of service, told me to sit down and he'd go and get it.

My mother waited until last and held me for as long as my father had but afterwards, instead of releasing me completely she held me at arm's distance, her hands just below my shoulders, and said she had forgotten how beautiful I was. She was not drunk.

And I shook her off. And when Rowland came back I said I wasn't hungry. And when my father quoted me a line from the novel he was reading at the time, claiming to find it both hilarious and apposite, I just shrugged and when Winsome came over to me with a present that she'd had under the tree—hope against hope etcetera—I opened it and said I already had a vase and could not, anyway, foresee a time when I would receive flowers. And then I said I was leaving, and declined to take it, then and for a second time at the front door.

*

The line from my father's book was hilarious and apposite. "The cremation was no worse than a family Christmas."

*

I called my mother early the next morning while I was getting dressed. As soon as she answered, I started talking about yesterday, how horrible it was without the others. Not Patrick obviously. I was glad he wasn't there. Repetitiously I said, "It's best for him as well. He wanted—"

She said, "No. Stop." Her patience was expended. Her voice wavered. "You don't get to decide what is best for other people, Martha. Not even for your own husband—especially not your own husband. Because, incidentally, you have no idea what Patrick wants." I wanted to say something to stop her but my mouth had gone dry, and she continued. "From what I can tell, you've never made an effort to find out. Sometimes I wonder if you thought it was going to be easier just to blow everything up. Tip, tip, tip, kerosene everywhere, match over the shoulder as you walk away. Incinerate the lot."

She stopped and waited. I said, "Why are you saying this? You are supposed to be on my side. You have to be nice to me."

"I am on your side. But I was ashamed of you yesterday. You embarrassed yourself, and everyone else. You acted like a child. Not even taking the vase—"

I shouted at her. I told her she was not allowed to tell me off.

"No actually, I will. Somebody needs to. You think all this has happened to you and only you. That's what I saw yesterday. It's your terrible personal tragedy, so you're the only one who's allowed to be in pain. But," she said, my girl, "this has happened to all of us. Do you not see that? Not even yesterday? This is everyone's tragedy. And if he'd been there, you would have seen it's most of all Patrick's. This has been his life every bit as much as it's been yours."

I told her she was wrong. "He's never felt the way I have. He has no idea what it's like."

"Maybe so but he's had to watch you. He's had to hear his wife say she wants to die, see her in agony and not know how to help her. Imagine that, Martha. And you thinking he liked it that way! He stayed with you through it all, no matter the cost to himself, and in the end he is hated for it and told to go."

"I don't hate him."

"Pardon?"

"I never said I hated him."

"Even if that were true, for everything else you've said, let me tell you, anyone except Patrick would have left you a long time ago, without needing to be asked. You lied first, Martha. He didn't make you. Nobody did."

I felt sick. My mother exhaled heavily, then kept going. "I am not saying you haven't suffered, Martha. But I am saying, grow up. You're not the only one."

She stopped and waited until I said, "How do I do that?"

"What? I can't hear you when you're whispering."

I said, slowly, "How do I do that? Mum, I don't know what to do."

"I would ask your husband for forgiveness and," she said, "consider yourself very lucky if he gives it to you."

I DIDN'T CALL her again. At the end of the week I got a letter.

It said, Martha. You know as I do that the conversation we've had over these weeks is finished. What happens next is your choice but I hope you'll consider the following in making whatever decision you do.

All my life I've believed that things happened to me. The awful things—childhood, my mad/dead mother, disappearing father. That because she had to raise me, I lost Winsome as a sister. Your father not succeeding, this house, living somewhere I can't stand, my drinking, my becoming a drunk. On and on it goes, all of it happening to me.

And then—you. My beautiful daughter, breaking when she was still a child. Even though you were the one in pain, even though I chose not to help you, in my own mind it was the worst thing that ever happened to me.

I was the victim, and victims of course are allowed to behave however they like. Nobody can be held to account as long as they're suffering and I made you my unassailable excuse for not growing up.

But then I did grow up—age 68—because you made me.

I know it hasn't been that long but this is what I have been able to see since then: things do happen. Terrible things. The only thing any of us get to do is decide whether they happen to us or if, at least in part, they happen for us.

I always thought your illness happened to me. Now I choose to believe that it happened for me because it was why finally I stopped drinking. I did not start drinking because of you and your illness, as I'm sure I let you believe, but you are the reason I stopped.

Perhaps what I think is wrong. Perhaps I'm not entitled to think of your pain that way, but it is the only way I can think of to give any of it a purpose. And I wonder, is there any way you could come to see that what you've been through is for something?

Is it why you feel everything and love harder and fight more ferociously than anyone else? Is it why you are the love of your sister's life? Why you'll be a writer of much more, one day, than a small supermarket column? How you can be my fiercest bloody critic, and someone with so much compassion she'll buy glasses she doesn't need because the man fell off his stool. Martha, when you are in a room, nobody wants to talk to anybody else. Why is that, if not for the life you have lived, as someone who has been refined by fire?

And you have been loved for all your adult life by one man. That is a gift not many people get, and his stubborn, persistent love isn't in spite of you and your pain. It is because of who you are, which is, in part, a product of your pain.

You do not have to believe me about that but I know—I do know, Martha—that your pain has made you brave enough to carry on. If you want to, you can put all of this right. Start with your sister.

*

I put the letter in a drawer and picked up my phone. There was a text message from Ingrid. They had been back for days but we hadn't spoken since she drove to Oxford. I had texted but she hadn't replied. Her message said, "Get drain unblocker stuff on the way home because the bath isn't emptying. sorry for sexting you while you're at work." Eggplant emoji, lipstick mouth.

While I was still looking at it, the gray dots appeared and disappeared and appeared again.

"That wasn't for you obviously."

I sent her the rosary, a cigarette, and the black heart. I started another one, the road and the running girl, and didn't send it, because if she knew I was coming, she would be gone by the time I arrived.

*

She was in the front garden, sitting on a neglected outdoor table, legs dangling, watching her sons ride their bikes into each other on purpose. In spite of how cold it was, all three of them were wearing shorts, and T-shirts from Disneyland. She turned around when they called out to me, but showed no reaction as I walked over waving stupidly until I was all the way there.

"Hello Martha." It felt like being stung, my sister greeting me as though I was a friend, or no one. "Why are you here?"

"To give you this." I handed her a plastic bag with the drain unblocker stuff in it. "And also to say sorry."

Ingrid looked in the bag and said nothing. Then, "Excuse me," leaning sideways to see past me to where her sons had started skidding their bikes on purpose, which they knew they weren't allowed to do—she started shouting at them—because they knew it wrecked the grass.

There was no grass, it had been wrecked since the afternoon they moved in and, although they ignored her, she repeated her warning to them at the same volume every time I thought she had finished and tried to say something.

The rain that had been falling all morning had stopped as I was getting out of the car, but the sky was still dark and each small gust of wind shook water from the trees. I waited.

Ingrid gave up and said, "Go then."

"I wanted to say—"

"Hang on." My sister got off the table and retrieved a Matchbox car from a puddle, took out her phone, and sent a series of messages before she came back and started drying a different section of table with a tissue she took a long time to locate in her pocket.

"Ingrid?"

"What? Go. I said go." She didn't sit on the table again, just perched on its edge.

I apologized. It was a version of what I'd composed in the car, except circuitous and halting, with endless repetitions and false starts, more and more excruciating as I labored on. I felt like a child at a piano lesson, stumbling over a piece I had played perfectly at home.

My sister became visibly more irritated the longer I went on. Except for saying, "I already know all this" as I returned again to the section about wanting children, before my anticlimactic finish. "So that's it probably."

She said right and pressed her fingers into a rib on one side.

The thing was, she told me, staring ahead, I had worn her out. I had worn everybody out. It had all got to be too much. She couldn't care for me anymore as well as her children. She said that she was going to forgive me at some point but it wasn't now.

I said okay, and thought to go, but Ingrid shifted along and asked me if I was going to sit down or not. For a minute we watched her sons who were by then trying to make a ramp from planks of wood and a brick. Then I said, "They're so amazing." Ingrid shrugged. "No really. They're amazing."

"What are you basing that on?"

"Because they were babies five minutes ago and now look at what they're doing."

"I guess. Riding bikes."

I said no. "I mean repurposing the shit out of found objects."

Ingrid covered her face with her hands and shook her head as if she was crying.

I waited. A minute later she said, "Okay fine" and took her hands away. "I have forgiven you." Her eyes were red, and rimmed with tears but she was laughing. "You are still the worst. Literally, you are the worst person there is."

I told her I knew that.

"Why," she said, with sudden sadness in her voice, "why did you lie to me about not wanting children? Why couldn't you trust me?"

"I could trust you. I couldn't trust myself."

She said why not.

"Because you could have talked me into it. Like Jonathan. If you had told me I would be a good mother, I would have let myself believe you."

Ingrid leaned against me so our arms were touching.

"I never would have said that."

"You did say it. You told me all the time I should have a baby."

"No, I never would have said you'd be a good mother. You'd be shit at it."

She kicked my foot and said God, Martha. "I love you so much it actually hurts my body. Can you get me that?" She pointed to the plastic bag. I picked it up off the ground and Ingrid said, looking into it, "This is the expensive kind. Thank you" and for a minute I felt like we were together inside our force field.

Then, shouting. A fight had broken out over the brick.

Ingrid said well this is over and told me I was welcome to go and sort it out, she needed to go inside and make their tea.

We both got up and I went over to the boys, all now holding sticks.

She was nearly at the house when she called my name and I turned around and saw her, walking backwards over the last bit of lawn, and I just remember as she reached her arms up to tighten her ponytail, a cloud crossed quickly in front of the sun so the light was flickering on her face and on her hair as she shouted, ecstatically, to all of us, "My famous pasta-with-nothing-on-it."

*

Later, while they were in the bath, we sat outside the door, leaning against the wall. We were talking about something else when Ingrid said, "If you have been better since June or whatever, why are you still behaving like you used to? I mean, to Patrick. I'm not judging. It's just that, if you're feeling more rational, why isn't it necessarily, you know, manifesting outwardly." She winced like someone anticipating an explosion.

"Because I don't know how else to be with him." I said I know it's not an excuse.

"No, I get it. However many years versus seven months. But you need to figure it out."

I told her I didn't feel ready to do that, to see him, and I knew that I would not be able to forgive him anyway.

"Do you know where he is?"

"London."

"Do you know where though?"

"No. He's probably got the flat back."

"He's getting it back but for now he's at Winsome and Rowland's." Ingrid looked grave.

I asked her why that mattered. "Winsome and Rowland are in the country."

"But Jessamine's there."

I laughed and said if there was one thing I had never worried about, it was Patrick being with someone who wasn't his wife.

Even though I had made him leave, and punished him relentlessly for months so that he would, and I had told him that I did not love him anymore—calling it out after him as he walked out of our bedroom for the last time—I felt as if I had been shoved when Ingrid said, "But Martha, as far as Patrick is concerned you're not his wife."

INGRID MADE ME wait while she searched in a drawer for her key to Belgravia. "In case, in case."

I had already accepted a muesli bar and a bottle of water and a three-disc self-help audio book that she'd turned up in the drawer first. In twenty-one days, I could master the art of self-forgiveness.

I told her I didn't need the key. "If he isn't there, I'll just go home. There's no other reason to go in."

"Yes there is. You might need the bathroom or something."

She found it and held it out. When I wouldn't take it, she grabbed my hand and tried to close my fingers around it.

"What the fuck is that?" She was holding my thumb.

"The Hebrides."

"Right. Of course it is. Please can you just put this in your bag?"

I took the key so she would stop talking about it.

*

Patrick wasn't there. I knocked and waited on the steps outside my aunt's house until my face ached and my hands went numb inside my pockets. I went back to the car and sat, with my coat on, for an hour. The square was deserted. Nobody came and went. It had only been six weeks since Patrick left but, within days, time had acquired an unreal quality and my loneliness became so total that now—sitting in the car—it seemed to challenge the existence of things.

Another hour passed. Still nobody came. I began to feel delirious. There was only cold. I googled "hypothermia in car" but while my fingers were trying to find each key, my phone died and that was why, I told myself, I needed to go inside. But it was a compulsion to see, if not Patrick, then something of his. After weeks alone, culminating in these two hours in the car, seeing nothing out the window except darkness and an absence of human beings, even he no longer seemed real.

*

Everything was wrong inside. For a moment, I stood in the foyer with Ingrid's key in my hand, unnerved.

It was Winsome's rule that personal effects were not allowed in public areas, but Jessamine's things were everywhere, her shoes kicked into all corners of the foyer, clothes in piles down the length of the hall. I took my coat off and went into the formal living room. There was a wine bottle and two glasses, empty except for brown sediment in the bottom, sitting directly on a walnut end table.

One year, drunk on Christmas Day, my mother told everyone that when Winsome died, her ghost would return to haunt the formal living room terrorizing us all with cries of "Wet on wood! Wet on wood!" and invisibly shifting coasters through the air. I went over and picked up the glasses to take down to the kitchen, collecting other things as I moved through the room, last of all a phone charger and a pink plastic bottle of nail polish remover. That my cousin would put a cosmetic solvent on the lacquered lid of her mother's piano felt like the totality of her nature. I wanted to leave. But nothing I'd collected in there or as I progressed towards the kitchen stairs belonged to Patrick. I left it all heaped at the entrance and went back to the main stairs.

His suitcase and things he must have acquired since leaving were in boxes, stacked outside Oliver's room, the boxes taped shut and numbered, I knew, to correlate with a spreadsheet that would describe the contents of each. I didn't open them. The numbers were handwritten. That was enough.

On the way back to the stairs, I went into Jessamine's room to use her bathroom. Patrick's watch was on her bedside table beside a water glass and a purple hair elastic with blonde hairs stuck in the metal bit. I went over and picked it up. I felt sick, not because it was there. Only because of its intrinsic familiarity, the weight of it as I turned it over in my hand and the recollection that came with it, of the particular way he put it on, the first time I'd seen him do it. I did not feel entitled to the memory. Patrick wasn't mine. I put the watch down and went into the bathroom.

In front of the mirror, I wiped my face with tissues, the floor where he had delivered my sister's baby in reflection behind me. A wastebasket overflowing with Jessamine's cosmetic debris was beside the toilet. I went over and dropped the tissues into it. They fell on top of a foil sheet, shaped for a single tablet. That was the other one thing I never worried about: Patrick being sent out to buy the morning-after pill for someone who wasn't his wife.

At some point, driving out of London, I realized I had forgotten my coat in the rush to leave and became less certain, as I kept going, that I had closed the front door.

*

For the week after that, I packed the Executive Home, moving through the house filling boxes that, had I labeled them, would have said: Loose cutlery tipped in from the drawer. Can of sardines in oil/birth certificates. A cushion, a hairdryer, a gravy boat wrapped in a duvet cover.

I fed myself blue Gatorade and water crackers from the emptying pantry and slept on the sofa in my clothes.

It snowed the day I left. In the morning, two men arrived in a truck to meet all my moving and storage needs, per the promise painted on its flank. They began loading it while I was still finishing our bedroom. Except for one suitcase, Patrick had left everything behind.

I packed his wardrobe and dresser, then opened the drawer of his bedside table. On top of other things was a book my father had given him for Christmas a year ago, which Patrick had persisted in reading, in spite of it being about poetry, not even actual poetry. I picked it up and opened it to a section marked by some index cards, their exposed edges bent and soft.

He had been going to say, "No doubt my wife will correct me later and insist it was just for the open bar, but we are all here for the love of this uncommon, beautiful, maddening woman— who does not, in my opinion, look a day over thirty-nine and twelve months." He was going to say, "I wish it wasn't the case, but everyone knows Martha is the only thing I've ever wanted in my life . . ." I couldn't read anymore. I slid them back into the book and returned it to the drawer, and instead of packing all its contents, I went around the entire cabinet with tape. The men came to the door and I told them I was finished, they could take everything now.

They left and I walked through the house, holding the address they had given me for a storage facility somewhere in London. I knew each dent in the skirting boards, each chip in the doors, all the places on the living room walls where we had once tried to paint over marks left by a previous tenant. Patrick bought paint in the wrong finish and still now, they stood out like a solar system of high-gloss patches in a vast matte universe. The taupe carpet bore the impressions of our furniture, dust sat like strips of gray felt along the top of each non-standard socket, their uses never determined. For seven years, the Executive Home had exuded a sort of psychic hostility, perceptible only to me. I do not know why, in my last hour there, it offered me a sense of home. I went upstairs again to see the box room.

Outside its small window, snow was settling into the boughs of the plane tree's leafless branches. I opened it halfway and went back to the doorway, remaining for a moment. A small flurry of flakes blew in, drifted to the floor, and melted into the carpet.

*

The agent had let himself into the house and was downstairs in the kitchen with a couple, younger than Patrick and me. He was saying something about quality appliances. I glanced in, unnoticed as I passed on my way to the door, and saw the wife open the oven, screw up her nose, and say, "Babe, look." I closed the door behind me, put my key through the mailbox, and drove away.

*

Past the gates of the Executive Development, I pulled over and parked next to a break in the tall border hedge. I went through it, coming out to the broad expanse of field carved into allotments. It was deserted, the earth was bare and ugly and sodden underfoot. I did not know why I wanted to stop and go in; I had never come by myself before. Without Patrick I couldn't find the garden that belonged to us, except by running up and down the paths between them, eyes streaming when I went against the wind, hair wrapping around my face when it was behind me.

When I saw our shed, I ran toward it, cutting across other people's gardens to get to ours—a square of black mud, and orange leaves submerged in the water that had pooled in the furrows Patrick had dug. Apart from those, and tendrils of old potato plants flattened by rain, there was nothing to show of his work. Winter had erased the hours he had spent here, by himself, or with me sitting and watching him push the spade in with his foot, pull out weeds, things that had gone to seed.

The door of the shed was unlatched and banging in the wind. People had carried off his tools, and the chair he'd bought me. The only thing they'd left, because it couldn't be moved, was the fallen tree.

I went to sit down but remembering caused me to kneel in front of it in the dirt. And then, to fold my arms over it, to sink my head, breathing in the wet wood, hearing Patrick say how far along are you? Could I have a few days? I said I'm not going to wait for no reason, Patrick. I will see you at home.

Soon I was so cold I had to get up. I could not bear to leave. I had been pregnant once. I had been pregnant, here, and that made it sacred, this square of black mud that I would be abandoning to the elements. Leaving something that belonged to us unprotected from anyone who wanted it and thought it was no one's anyway—there was nothing here except for a dead log. I picked up a twig and pushed it into the ground, and made myself walk back to the car, leaning into the wind.

In the immediate quiet of closing the door, I remembered Patrick telling me, as we drove to the Executive Home for the first time, that soon we would be self-sufficient, in the area of lettuce. I laughed, and I was still crying. Briefly, that first summer in Oxford, it had been true.

*

A mile on, I put the address into Google Maps, even though I had lived at Goldhawk Road since I was ten, bar the interruption of two short marriages. As I joined the motorway, the map lady said, in fifty-four miles take the left exit and when I missed it, make a U-turn as soon as possible.

THE FRONT DOOR of my parents' house was ajar. I went in and found Ingrid on the sofa in my father's study, sitting, with her feet on the ground, not lying the length of it with her feet extended in some way up the wall. And her eyes were fixed on my father, who was standing in the center of the room, preparing to read something from a book open in his hands like a hymnal. And my mother was with them, holding a small feather duster— the likes of which I had never seen in the house—aloft over some object on the mantelpiece.

The impression they gave was of actors in a play, waiting for the curtain to open on them but too slow off their mark, so that just for a second the audience sees them that way—frozen in naturalistic positions—before they snap to action.

The mother starts waving the duster, the father begins reading from the middle of a sentence, the character of the sister leans forward like she is listening. That she is getting her phone out is obvious to those on the other side of the fourth wall. The father looks up and stops reading because another actor—clearly, the complicating character—is coming in, managing many bags. He invites her to sit down and the mother goes out saying something about coffee, and having inquired about her drive down, the father says, "Now where was I up to? Yes, here we go" and starts again. One sister gives up the pretense of paying attention and looks openly at her phone.

The other one stands where she is, does not put down her bags but listens, giving the audience time to wonder about her backstory, why she has come, what she wants, what obstacles are ahead of her and how they will be resolved in ninety minutes. Whether there will be an intermission. If the parking machine takes cards.

"The great revelation perhaps never did come. Instead there were little daily miracles, matches struck unexpectedly in the dark; here was one." He finishes. "Isn't that brilliant, girls? It's—"

"Virginia Woolf."

Ingrid said it without taking her eyes off her phone but then, anticipating his inquiry, lifted her head and said, "It was on Instagram."

He said, "What is the Instagram?"

"Here." She thumbed the screen and held the phone out to my father who took it and did a primitive imitation of scrolling that involved all the fingers on his right hand and a palsied flicking action with his wrist. "You can put any nonsense you like on it, even poetry, and someone will like it. One finger. Dad. Go up from the bottom."

He mastered it and minutes later, my father declared @author_quotes_daily a repository of genius and then asked how much it cost to join. Ingrid told him his only outlay would be buying a mobile that didn't have an antenna, which she said she would do for him online, to the expression of uncertainty that formed on his face at the mention of a retail interaction.

I said I needed to unpack. Ingrid offered to help me and got up.

Outside the door I told her I did not need help.

"By help, I mean I'll sit and watch you do it."

She followed me to the stairs.

"Where are the boys?"

"Hamish took them to get their haircuts fixed. I thought I could do it but, turns out, it's quite hard." She was puffing before we were halfway up the first flight and required small breaks on the second. "I was going to open a salon called Mum Cuts—but—obviously that can be read two—ways depending—on—I need to sit down for sec—your mental state."

Outside my door, Ingrid told me to move so she could open it for me. Looking in and reversing straight out she said, "Why don't you take my room instead?" Mine had been pressed into service as a box room for sculptures that, my mother explained when we inquired later, "were not there yet conceptually."

We went next door and I pushed the bags in the bottom of Ingrid's empty wardrobe, then went and sat with her on the futon that had come with the birch table and the brown sofa, and borne the brunt of her teenage smoking.

She talked for a while about the particular occasion of each burn mark, her room, things she had written and drawn on the wall, many of which remained, including, she showed me behind the curtain, the words I HATE MUM. And then, times she remembered me coming in and getting her when there had been A Leaving. Idly she had picked up my hand and noticing it, rubbed her thumb over my tattoo as if it might come off. "Do you ever regret getting this?"

"Yes."

"When?"

"When I see it."

"I would judge you, except—" She turned her wrist up and showed me the very short line. She said anyway. "What are you going to do now? Do you have a plan? Because you could—" Her tone indicated the start of a list but nothing came after her preparatory inward breath, except an outward one. She looked sorry.

"I know, don't worry."

"I will think of something."

I told her it was fine. "It isn't your job. I have one anyway or not—it's not a plan-plan. It's more—" I paused. "I need to figure out what kind of life is available to a woman my—"

"Don't say my age."

"A woman who was born at roughly the same time as me, who is single and doesn't have children or any particular ambition, and a CV that," I wanted to say "is shit" but there was so much concern on my sister's face, I said, "that lacks an obvious through-line."

"It doesn't have to be miserable though. Like, don't automatically assume it has to be—"

I said, "I'm not. I want it not to be miserable. I just don't know what non-miserable options exist if you don't like animals or helping people. If you've wanted the things women are supposed to want, babies, husband, friends, house—"

"Successful Etsy business."

"Successful Etsy business, fulfillment, whatever, and you didn't get them, what are you supposed to want instead? I don't know how to want something that isn't a baby. I can't just think of something else and decide to want that instead."

Ingrid said yes you can. "Even the women who get those

things lose them again. Husbands die and children grow up and marry someone you hate and use the law degree you bought them to start an Etsy business. Everything goes away eventually, and women are always the last ones standing so we just make up something else to want."

"I don't want it to be an invented thing."

"Everything is invented. Life is invented. Everything you see anyone doing is something they made up. I invented Swindon for fuck's sake, and made myself want it and now I do."

"Do you really?"

"Well, I don't not want it."

"How did you?"

"I don't know," she said. "Just by focusing on—or doing practical things and pretending to enjoy them until I sort of do enjoy them or can't remember what I enjoyed before."

I bit my lip and she went on. "Like, maybe sort your clothes out or do stupid yoga, and it will probably come to you or you'll come up with it. You're so clever, Martha, the most creative person I know." She hit me because I rolled my eyes. "You are, and I need to go home so can you please pull me up?"

I did and my sister kept hold of my hands for a second, standing in the middle of her bedroom, and said, "Little daily miracles, illuminations, something-something, Woolf matches. Do that. Do what Virginia says."

I went downstairs with her and promised, because she made me, that I would do something practical, but not a gratitude journal because, she said, it would freak her out.

"Or like, a vision board. Unless it is just pictures of an over-forty Kate Moss on a superyacht."

"Bikini askew."

"Always."

"I love you Ingrid."

She said I know and went home.

*

My father had left the study light on and the book open and face-down on his desk. I went in and picked it up but couldn't find the bit he had read. Trying to wedge it into a nonexistent space on his shelves, I thought of him saying once—the summer I spent in this room—"all of life on one wall Martha. Every kind of life, real or made up."

I stayed there and read so many spines, then one by one I started taking books off, building a pile in my left arm. My selection criteria was threefold. Books by women or suitably sensitive/depressive men who had made up their own lives. Any book I had lied about reading, except Proust because even with everything I had done I did not deserve to suffer that much. Books with promising titles, that I could reach without having to stand on a chair.

They were old. The covers made my fingers feel chalky, and the pages smelled like the boredom of waiting for my father to finish in a secondhand shop when I was young. But they would tell me how to be or what to want and they would save me from a gratitude journal and it was the only thing I could think of.

I STARTED WITH Woolf, her entire back catalogue, reading all day, in a room of my parents' own, and sometimes when I began to worry I was going mad from so much time doing only that and conceived the thought in Woolfian language, I went out and read somewhere else. At night I read until I fell asleep and wherever I was, every time somebody in a book wanted something, I wrote down what it was. Once I had finished them all, I had so many torn-off bits of paper, collected in a jar on Ingrid's dresser. But they all said, a person, a family, a home, money, to not be alone. That is all anybody wants.

*

I tried to go running. It is as awful as it looks. At the shopping center, 0.7 miles from my parents' house, I gave up and went in to buy water. Because it was a Monday morning, shortly after nine, and I was a woman over forty wearing athletic clothing, I did not arouse attention as I made circuits of the ground floor trying to find somewhere.

There was a WH Smiths. The only route from the front door to the fridge cabinet was an aisle with a sign above it that said Gifts/Inspiration/Assorted Planners and yet it was, solely, row on row of gratitude journals. I stopped and looked at them in search of the worst one to buy and send to my sister. Although there were so many individual injunctions on their mint and glittery lilac and butter yellow covers—to live and love and laugh and shine and thrive and breathe—considered together, it seemed like humanity's highest imperative is to follow its dreams.

I chose one that was inexplicably thick, with twice as many pages as its shelf mates, because it said, on the cover, You Should Just Go For It. It was meant to sound carefree and motivating but for want of an exclamation mark, it came across as weary and resigned. You Should Just Go For It. Everyone Is Sick Of Hearing You Talk About It. Follow Your Dreams. The Stakes Could Not Be Lower.

It was my day, the woman on the till told me. "Free pen with every journal." She was so old to be working there and breathed heavily from the exertion of crouching down to retrieve the box from under the counter. "Whichever one you want." The pens were also inspirational. I took one that had a phrase on it misappropriated from third-wave feminism, thanked her, and walked to a café kiosk in the center of the mall that was pumping synthetic bread fragrance into the air.

I ordered toast. It took a long time to come and I reached the bottom of my Instagram feed while I was still waiting for it. The final post was a picture of F. Scott Fitzgerald, @author_quotes_daily. The caption said, "What people are ashamed of usually makes a good story."

My toast had still not appeared. I slid Ingrid's journal out of the bag and wrote the caption out on the first page, then glanced quickly over my shoulder in case I had been seen. But I was the only person who would judge a woman who was sitting by herself in a shopping center bakery on a weekday morning, when her running clothes and her gratitude journal testified to an effort to improve herself on two fronts. I shifted in my chair. It was in a spirit of repentance probably that I turned to another page, somewhere near the middle because I did not know where to start. I just did. You Should Just Go For It. Seriously, Nobody Cares.

IT WAS THE first week of March. I was sitting on the back door-step of my parents' house, barefoot, tugging weeds out of cracks in the concrete, noticing how bright amber my tea looked with the cold sun on it, talking to Ingrid's eldest son on the phone. They had started ringing me again.

He was explaining the chapter series he was reading, with un-sparing detail and, intermittently, a full mouth.

I asked him what he was eating.

"Grapes and a slavery roll."

I heard Ingrid ask him for the phone.

"He means savory. Sorry, God, there are seven million of those books. I swear they've got children writing them in a sweatshop somewhere. How are you?"

I told her about the job I had got. A guidance and careers counselor at a girls' school. She did not find it ironic that I'd been offered the position, as I did. "You've literally had all the jobs." She said shit. She had to go. "Someone's playing with doors."

I went to hang up and saw a text from Patrick. We had not spoken since he left.

It said, "Hi Martha, I'm moving back into the flat tomorrow and need some of our furniture etc. Where is the storage place?"

I hesitated over it for a moment, trying to assimilate the new and extraordinary pain of a message that begins with hi and your name, when it comes from somebody you used to be married to. I rubbed my eye and under my nose and then replied, asking if we could do it tomorrow instead.

He said he couldn't. He was working.

I replied with the address of the storage unit, wondering as I typed it if Patrick realized it was our wedding anniversary. And then, as I sent it, if you have given up on being married, whether it isn't your wedding anniversary anymore.

Patrick wrote back, asking if I could meet him there in two hours. My desire not to was so acute that I could barely induce myself to get up and go inside, after I replied to say yes.

*

He was going to be late. I was already there when he texted to say so, waiting outside the locker, at the very end of a corridor so dark and desolate it felt post-apocalyptic.

Probably, he was still an hour away—he said sorry and something to do with a truck and a road closure. I could go if I needed to. I said I didn't mind and got the journal out of my bag. It was stained, coming apart, now ludicrously thick from getting wet and being dried on the radiator so many times.

I sat down on the floor and wrote for a long time until I realized, turning over, that I had reached the last page. I did not know how to finish it. When, after minutes of thought, no suitable ending had presented itself, I went back to the beginning and started reading. I hadn't until then, knowing that whatever

I'd find in my writing—self-fascination, banality, descriptions of things—would make me go outside and set it on fire.

It wasn't that or, at least, I saw shame and hope and grief, guilt and love, sorrow and bliss, kitchens, sisters and mothers, joy, fear, rain, Christmas, gardens, sex and sleep and presence and absence, the parties. Patrick's goodness. My striking unlikeability and attention-seeking punctuation.

I could see what I'd had now. Everything people want in books, a home, money, to not be alone, all there in the shadow of the one thing I didn't have. Even the person, a man who wrote speeches about me, and gave things up for me, who sat beside the bed for hours while I was crying or unconscious, who said he'd never change his mind about me and stayed even after he knew I was lying to him, who only hurt me as much as I deserved, who put oil in the car and would never have left me if I hadn't told him to.

It wasn't my final revelation. That I desperately wanted him back wasn't a revelation at all by the time I reached the last page. It was the small, awful reason why I had lost him. It wasn't my illness; it was nothing I had said or done. I wrote it down and closed the journal, finished, although most of the page was still blank because the reason our marriage had ended didn't fill a whole line.

At the far end of the corridor, the elevator opened.

I got up off the ground and put the journal on top of my bag.

Patrick walked towards me, so slowly, or it was such a long way, that before he was halfway I could not remember how people stand. When someone you know beyond all being, who you have loved and hated and have not seen for months, is coming towards you, avoiding your eye until the last minute, then smiling at you like he's not sure when or if you've met, what are you meant to do with your hands?

*

Our conversation was two minutes long, a confusion of sorrys and hellos and thank yous, unnecessary questions and even more unnecessary instructions about locks and how they're opened. It seemed like a joke. A game to see who could last the longest pretending to be other people. Neither of us gave in and the conversation ended with a slew of okay greats. Patrick took the key and I left.

My bag was too light but I did not become conscious of it until two stops remained of the long journey home. I looked inside, as though it could possibly be in there when the bag felt empty on my shoulder. It was not on the seat beside me. It had not slipped out onto the floor. I made a scene. I tried to wrench the carriage doors open before the train had come to a full stop at the next station, then shouldered through the packed crowd on the platform and forced my way into the carriage of a train about to leave on the other side. It would have been too full with half the number of people already in it. A man shook his head at me. I didn't care.

On the way back, it kept being held in the tunnel—I stayed standing, as if doing so would make the journey faster, imagining the journal lying on the ground somewhere between the station and the storage facility, a passer-by picking it up, checking for a name inside, seeing there wasn't one, walking off with it anyway, tossing it in the first bin they came to. Or taking it home. The idea was so much worse—what felt like my singular possession being put next to the pile of takeaway menus and mail to be dealt with in their kitchen, it being read in front of the television, "another funny bit" out loud to an uninterested husband during the advertisements.

*

I was told by a station attendant when I finally arrived that nothing like a diary had been handed in but if I wanted an umbrella
I could take my pick. I went out and walked back to the storage
center the way I had come, crossing in the same places I had an
hour and a half earlier, still empty-handed at the end of it.

As I entered, the clerk pointed out that I was back again.
Evidently I couldn't get enough of the place. He was sitting behind his desk, as before, leaning back with hands laced behind
his head, watching his CCTV screens like there was more to see
than deserted corridors from a host of angles. I signed his stupid
entry book again and as I got into the elevator I heard him saying, "Your boyfriend is still up there. He's going to regret pulling
the lot out at once."

*

All our furniture was in the corridor, removed a piece at a time
by Patrick and arranged by accident in the simulacrum of a
room. An armchair, a television, a floor lamp. He was sitting on
our sofa. His elbow on the armrest, reading.

He glanced up and seeing me said hi like I'd just got home,
then went back to his book. There was no point in asking for it
back. If he'd read from the beginning, he was now almost finished. I sat on the sofa, at the opposite end, and waited.

Patrick turned a page. Had it been anyone else—if it had been
Jonathan, it would have been an act of rare and ingenious cruelty,
reading my diary in front of me. Jonathan would have pretended

he was too deep in concentration to brook an interruption—he would have put one finger up if I'd tried to speak, shifting his expression from sadness to amusement, intrigue, a little shock, devastation, in the course of a single page, and making intermittent comments on my portrayal of things.

But it was Patrick. He was concentrating. His expression was earnest and his reactions were slight, a small frown, an occasional almost imperceptible smile. He didn't say anything until the end. And then, only, "I can't read your writing. I never what?"

"Oh." I looked upside down at the last thing I had written. "It says I never asked what it was like for him."

He said, "The ____?"

"No, all of it. Our marriage. Being my husband. I never asked you what any of it was like for you."

"Right." He closed the journal.

"It's the thing I'm most ashamed of now, I think." I stood up and put my hand out for it. "Out of, obviously, an array of options."

Instead of getting up, Patrick stayed seated and briefly scratched the back of his head. I waited. He kept the book in his hand. "Do you want to know?"

I said no and forced myself to sit down again, "I don't." I was not as brave as that. "What was it like for you, Patrick?" My bag was on my shoulder. I didn't take it off.

He said, "It was fucking awful."

Ingrid said fucking car alarm, fucking pantry moths, an actual fucking raisin in my bra, and it was unshocking. But I had never heard Patrick swear, not once in our lives, and said by him, the force and violence of the word made me recoil.

He said sorry.

"No. I'm sorry. Keep going. I want to know."

"You know already. It's everything your mother told you." He put the journal aside. "Just that it was always about you. I know you were sick but I was the one who had to absorb all your pain and have your rage directed at me, just because I was there. It took over everything. I feel like my entire life has been subsumed by your sadness. I tried, God Martha, I tried, but it didn't matter what I did. A lot of the time it seemed like you actively wanted to be miserable but you still expected constant support. Sometimes I just wanted to go to a restaurant based on the food not on whether the manager looked depressed or the color of the walls reminded you of something bad that had happened to you once. Sometimes I just wanted us to be normal."

He paused, clearly uncertain whether to articulate his next thought. He did. "You threw stuff at me."

I looked down. I thought, perceiving myself from outside, I am hanging my head. I am bowed by shame.

"I can't describe what that was like, Martha. I really can't, and you expected me to just get over it. You would say you wanted to talk about things but you didn't. You decided that because I don't provide a continuous emotional commentary and describe every single feeling I have as it's occurring that I don't feel anything. You told me I was blank. Do you remember? You said I was just the outline of where a husband should be."

I said I didn't remember. I did. It was in a department store. We were buying a mattress. I kept asking for his opinion. He kept saying he didn't mind either way, until I stormed out and did not come home for so many hours without telling him where

I was that by the time I got back he had called everyone he could think of to see if they had heard from me. "I mean yes, sorry. I do. I'm sorry."

"You constantly accused me of being passive and not wanting anything but I wasn't allowed to want anything. That's how it worked. Accepting whatever I got was the only way to keep the peace. And even"—Patrick felt the back of his neck, pressing his fingers into a muscle, looking as if he'd located some source of pain—"you've known me this long but you think the first thing I'd do after I left you is go and sleep with your cousin."

"No I—" I did.

"It belonged to one of her Rorys. He had the same watch as me. But you didn't even question if there could be another explanation or consider you could be wrong. What's the point, if that's who you think I am?"

I said I am so sorry. "I'm the worst person in the world."

"No you're not." Patrick's hand came down in a fist and he hit the arm of the sofa. "You're not the best person in the world either, which is what you really think. You're the same as everybody else. But that's harder for you, isn't it. You'd rather be one or the other. The idea you might be ordinary is unbearable."

I did not dispute him. Only said, I'm sorry it was fucking awful.

"Some of the time." He sighed and picked up the journal again and let it fall open anywhere. "Most of the time it was amazing. You made me so happy, Martha. You have no idea. You have no idea how good it was. That's the part I'm finding hardest to deal with. That you were oblivious to everything that was good about it. You couldn't see it."

I told Patrick I could now.

"I know."

I watched him turn back, in search of some particular page, scan it silently for a second and then he started reading aloud: "At a wedding shortly after our own, I followed Patrick through the dense crowd at the reception to a woman who was standing by herself."

I touched one of my ears and felt very hot.

"He said instead of looking at her every five minutes and feeling sad I should just go over and compliment her hat." Patrick looked up. "Did I?"

"Yes."

"I don't remember that. I just remember"—he smiled vaguely—"at the time thinking you were so, I mean who would care so much about some woman who can't get an hors d'oeuvre in her mouth, but you were beside yourself. You looked like you were in physical pain. You just talked and talked and talked until she was okay. That's what I, that's the kind of thing . . ." He trailed off, and turned somewhere else in the journal and said, "This is brilliant. Really Martha."

I asked him if he had known today was our wedding anniversary when he texted about meeting.

"Yes, sorry. It wasn't on purpose. I just needed to get things done."

I said, "Anyway, I should go." He handed me the journal.

We both stood up.

"Okay, well."

"Yes, great."

I said goodbye and it wasn't enough, one word, too quotidian to contain the end of the world. But it was all there was. I started walking towards the elevator.

Patrick said Martha, wait.

"What?"

"You were right. I did know there was something wrong. Not to start with but the last few years." He looked, suddenly, ill. "I knew it wasn't you. I knew there was something wrong but I was just trying to keep going. I felt like I couldn't face the whole process. Or I was scared that we'd find out and it would be something we couldn't deal with and it would be the end. And sometimes, you're right as well, I didn't mind everyone thinking I was this incredible husband, because I felt useless, most of the time. But the thing—" He broke off and then, with uncut anguish, Patrick said, "The thing I am most ashamed of is saying, telling you you shouldn't be a mother. It's not true. I was so angry." It was just the worst thing he could think of.

I asked him to stop talking but he didn't. "I can't ask you to forgive me. It's beyond apology. I just want you to know that I understand what I did, and that whatever we both end up doing, I have to rebuild my life with that reality in it, that I was intentionally cruel, to my own wife."

There was a noise from another aisle. Something being dropped on a metal floor, someone shouting. After it echoed out I said, "I should have told you I wanted her. At the time. I should have told you then."

"How do you know it was a her?"

"I just did."

"What would you have called her?"

I said, "I don't know."

But her name was written down, so many times in the book.

Patrick spoke it aloud. He said, yes. It would have been good.

I looked at the ceiling and pushed my hands upwards over my face to get rid of more tears from what seemed like a special well of them reserved for her and apparently, fathomless. "You must think I'm despicable."

"I don't," Patrick said. "You thought it was the right thing to do. You thought it was best for her, even though you wanted her so much. That's how I know," he said, sorry, maybe this is a bad thing to say, "but that's how I know you were supposed to be a mother. You put her above yourself. That's what mothers do, isn't it?" He said obviously, I'm only guessing.

I could not keep standing up. Patrick moved aside and I took steps back to the sofa. And he sat next to me, and let me lie with my head on his lap, and put his arm over me, it felt like a weight, and I cried and cried and cried, from the bottom of myself, and when I finally sat up again, I saw tears in his eyes too—Patrick, who once told me that he hadn't cried, properly, since his first day of boarding school when his father shook his hand and said goodbye then drove out the school gates while his seven-year-old son ran after the car. I pulled my sleeve over my hand and wiped his face then mine. I couldn't think of what to say. Just, eventually, "This is all such a big pity."

I meant it seriously. I asked him why he was laughing.

He said he wasn't. "You're actually not like the rest of us. That's all."

"Neither are you, Patrick."

Then it was over and we stood up and said goodbye again. It was something else, the whole world was in it.

I was a distance along the corridor when Patrick called out. "It makes a good story, Martha. The way you wrote it."

I glanced back and said okay.

"Someone—they should make it into a movie."

There was more noise from the other aisle, I turned and walked backwards, shouting. "I don't think in a movie, the denouement—I don't think the final parting can take place at EasyStore Brent Cross."

Patrick said, "You're probably—" I spun back to the elevator and ran. I didn't want to hear the rest.

*

The man behind the desk pointed out that I was off again. Presumably I'd be back later. I pushed through the doors without acknowledging him. The light outside was so bright I walked into it with my hand shielding my eyes.

*

I was on the platform waiting for the next train, with my bag on my lap, holding my phone. If I believed that the universe communicated with human beings through signs and wonders and social media I would have thought when I opened Instagram, that the first, minute-old post on my feed was a supernatural message, channelled through @author_quotes_daily, meant solely for me.

A headlight appeared in the tunnel. I screen-shotted it—I would write it down once I was on the train, in letters large enough so that all the empty space on the last page of the journal would be filled. But the train stopped and I got on and there were no seats. I never wrote it down. I can't remember where it came from. But it plays all the time in my head, repeating itself like a phrase of music, the recurring line of a poem. "You were done being hopeless."

You were done, you were done, you were done being hopeless.

LAST NIGHT PATRICK came in while I was watching a movie Ingrid recommended, as a shit remake of a movie that was shit to begin with. I told him we could turn it off.

He sat down and said because it was based on a true story, I obviously wanted to watch the entire thing, just for the words that come up afterwards. Someone-someone died at eighty-three. The painting was never found.

He said, "How things end is your favorite part. Also I'm too tired to talk." I started talking. He said, "Genuinely, Martha. I'm too tired to talk" and closed his eyes.

*

This is how it ends.

*

A few weeks ago I took my father to a bookshop in Marylebone to see the display in the window. For a long time he stood on the curb and stared at it with the expression of someone who cannot work out what they're looking at.

He is the Instagram poet, Fergus Russell. He has one million followers.

The book, which occupied the window by itself, is the anthology of his most liked poems. Reading an early review, my mother said, "Finally, Fergus, you've got your definite article." He said there should be a verb form of the adjective forthcoming. "For when an anthology that's been forthcoming for fifty-one years forthcomes."

It began to rain while we were still outside the shop, harder and harder, but my father seemed not to notice. When I saw that water, overspilling the gutter, was running over the tops of his shoes, I made him come inside with me so I could find the manager.

They shook hands and my father asked if he could sign a small number of copies but it was fine if they would rather he didn't. He offered to show his driver's licence to prove he really was Fergus Russell. The manager patted his pockets for a pen and said it was fine; there was a picture of him on the back cover. He told my father it was their fastest seller since the bottom fell out of the adult coloring-book market.

A week after publication, my father's editor had called and said, according to early data, on its first day it moved 334 units—unheard of in poetry—and that was just in bookshops in central London.

Winsome put on a dinner for him at Belgravia. Everyone came back. It was the first time we had all been together since Patrick and I had separated. Our family treated us like we had just got engaged. Ingrid said we should make the most of it and set up a registry at Peter Jones.

As the others were sitting down, Winsome sent me into Rowland's study to get something. The door of an immense armoire behind his desk was ajar. Stacked inside were dozens of copies of my father's book, some unwrapped, others still in the plastic and paper bags of bookshops in central London. I opened other cupboards. They were full of the same thing. I closed them quietly and left the room, despising Rowland for buying 334 copies of my father's book as a private joke against him.

Back in the dining room, Rowland was berating Oliver for the profligate amount of gravy on his plate. My uncle hated waste and spending money so much that once, at this table, we had all agreed that his shower soap was a theoretical construct. Recalling it now, I realized it could only be from kindness that he would have driven the Twatmobile from bookshop to bookshop, buying every copy of my father's book. As I edged behind his chair Rowland turned to my father on his other side and said loudly that as far as he was concerned, it wasn't poetry unless it rhymed so there was one sale he could bloody well forget. I patted his shoulder. He ignored me.

I didn't tell anyone, except Patrick later, about what I'd seen. Once the book began selling in the thousands, I knew it couldn't only be to Rowland anymore.

It took my father half an hour to sign the window copies and the pile on the front table. The manager put Autographed First Edition stickers on their covers before stacking them back, then took his phone out to take a photo. As he arranged the shot, my father stepped to the side. The manager signaled for him to move back. "Oh right, right," my father said. "With me in it," then, sheepishly, "Could you also get one of me and my daughter?"

Afterwards we walked down Marylebone High Street towards Oxford Street, sharing my father's umbrella. He asked me if I had any plans and when I said I didn't, he told me he would like to buy me an ice cream. Because the sight of an adult eating ice cream in public has always filled me with inexplicable grief and still does, I said I would let him as long as the event could take place inside.

Farther down, we found a café and sat in the window. The waiter came and put metal bowls of gelato in front of us and left again. My father said, "This is one of the ice creams I couldn't pay for myself when you were growing up" and then moved on to the topic of what it had been like to see his own book in a shop because I couldn't reply.

He said at the end, "Of course, it will be your turn next. Your book in a shop window."

My ice cream had melted and dripped off the spoon when I picked it up. I made a track through the puddle with my finger and said, "The Collected Funny Food Columns of Martha Russell Friel."

My father said I was very funny, and wrong on that score.

"Why did you stay with her?" I hadn't meant to ask but while he was signing, I had stood and read the poems again. They were all about my mother. I didn't understand how his passion for her, woven into each line, had survived their marriage. Her stifling of him, The Leavings. "Or," I said, "why did you always come back?"

He gave a small shrug. "I loved her unfortunately."

We said goodbye outside. My father was going the other way and made me take the umbrella. It broke as I put it up and I was attempting to shove the tangle of bent spokes into a bin when I saw Robert come out of a shop a few feet away from where I was standing. He had a newspaper in one hand and held it above his head while he dashed over the crossing towards a taxi stopped on that side.

He saw me as he was opening the door and paused as if, in another moment, he would be able to place the woman on the other side of the street who looked like she was going to wave, then didn't. He was still holding up the newspaper and made a friendly gesture with it before ducking to get in. I do not know if he recognized me, or if he acknowledged me to be on the safe side.

The taxi drove away and I kept walking. Nostos, algos. I never went back after the first appointment. I booked dozens in the months afterwards and always canceled them the day before. The last time I rang his rooms, the receptionist told me I had so many late cancellation fees against my file, this was one of the very rare occasions that she couldn't let me make another appointment unless I paid them.

I still long to see him sometimes but I know that I won't because there is nothing else to say. And there will never be £540.50 in Martha's Unexpecteds—even if there was, I worry that as an expert in the human mind, he would be able to discern from my body language that of the 820 views his 2017 address to the World Psychiatric Association has racked up on YouTube, 59 of them were me.

He spoke on the subject of ——. The conference took place a short time after we met. When I first found it I hoped but now

I just wonder if I am the articulate young woman with classic symptoms who he will refer to throughout as "Patient M."

*

Ingrid had her baby. It was two weeks late and enormous and came out facing the wrong way. Patrick and I went with my parents to see her the afternoon it was born. The delivery required forceps and, she told us, that toilet plunger thing and a fucking episiotomy by a doctor who was seriously trying to shut the barn door after the horse had bolted. She suspected him of doing a bad job with the stitches and, as such, she'd decided to just disassociate from the whole area, which she described then, and has since, as her Baginasaurus Wrecked.

Winsome was already there when we arrived—by herself because Rowland was on a quest to find unmetered parking, from which, she felt, he was unlikely to return. She stood rinsing a bag of green grapes under a high tap over the sink, pretending that she couldn't hear anything my sister was saying. Afterwards Hamish asked Patrick how common it was, these days, for a sonographer to misread the baby's sex. Ingrid had told everyone it was a boy. Patrick said it wasn't common, especially not across multiple scans.

"I didn't have multiple scans." She looked up from whatever adjustment she was trying to make to the strap of her bra and said, "The magic isn't there when you have three boys in the room with you breaking the equipment."

Patrick said, "Even so—"

"And they didn't tell me it was another boy." Ingrid said, "I didn't ask. I just assumed."

Hamish made no reaction, except to say ah. Then, regrouping, he said, "Either way we should settle on a name for her while we're all present."

Ingrid looked over to Winsome who was by then snipping the large bunch of grapes into many small ones and arranging them in a cut-glass bowl she had brought from home. "I would like to call her Winnie." And to Hamish, "Is that fine?"

He recited his daughter's full name. My mother was by the crib, smoothing out wrinkles in the blanket. Hamish said, "What do you think, Celia?"

She said the name was perfect. "We need as many Winnies as we can get in this life."

I glanced at my aunt and saw her produce a tissue from her sleeve, putting her back to the room to privately dab her eyes.

"Actually," Ingrid said, "Winnie Martha sounds weird. Let's just not have a middle name." And to me, "I love you though."

*

I apologized to Winsome about the vase. I called her first, after reading my mother's letter and triaging my crimes, letting myself address the smallest or one of the smaller ones first. I asked if I could come and see her and on the day, she invited me out to the garden where a table was preset for afternoon tea.

Even though, on Christmas Day, she had looked on the verge of tears when I'd said in the foyer that I didn't want the vase,

Winsome told me she had no memory of the incident whatsoever, and patted my arm. I asked if she would forgive me anyway.

"Forgotten is forgiven, Martha. I can't remember who said that or where I read it but if I had a motto, that would be it. Forgotten is forgiven."

I told her it was F. Scott Fitzgerald. The curator of @author_quotes_daily had been on a jag.

Winsome offered me a biscuit and asked me if I had any holidays planned.

"How did you put up with my mother for so long?"

She said oh. Indeed. And then, "I suppose because I've always been able to remember what she was like before our mother died and I loved her enough to last."

"Were you ever tempted just to give up on her?"

"Daily, I suppose. But you forget, Martha, I was an adult then and she was a child. I knew who she was meant to be. That is, who she would have been had our mother not died or perhaps, if we had had a different mother entirely. I would like to say I did my best, but I was not an adequate substitute."

I accepted another cup of tea. Watching her pour, I told her I could not imagine how hard it must have been. Winsome said well, nevermind and I decided one day I would ask her about it, but not then because there was more sadness in the way she said those two words than could be managed by either of us, sitting at her garden table, having afternoon tea.

"Forgotten is forgiven." For whatever reason, Winsome said it again.

I repeated it after her. "Forgotten is forgiven."

"That's right. Difficult but possible. Unless you want it, Martha, I might have this last biscuit."

*

Even with four under fucking nine, Ingrid is still Ingrid. Attached to every text she has sent since Winnie was born is a GIF called Sad Will Ferrell. He is sitting in a leather recliner that is vibrating at its highest setting, trying to drink wine and crying as it bounces out of the glass and runs down his chin. It is figuratively her though. It has never stopped being funny.

*

Patrick and I left the hospital after Oliver arrived with Jessamine and the Rory she is about to marry. Nicholas is in America now, working on a special farm.

· My parents wanted us to go back with them, to Goldhawk Road, for dinner. Arriving, my mother asked me to come out to her studio because she had a thing she wanted to show me beforehand.

I said, "Am I allowed to? Nothing is on fire."

She flicked her hand, refusing to be mocked, and once we were across the garden, she held the door open and ushered me in. The sensation of being somewhere I had been vigorously discouraged from entering for most of my life was still strange. I sat on a crate in the corner. It was crusted with globs of something white.

In the middle of the room, hidden under a dirty sheet, was some object that at its highest point touched the ceiling. My mother went over and stood beside it, crossing her arms and cupping her elbows with opposite hands in a way that made her look nervous.

She coughed and said, "Martha. I know you and your sister tease me for the repurposing but all I've been trying to do, all these years, is take rubbish and turn it into something beautiful and much stronger than it was before. I'm sorry if that's a bloody metaphor for everything." She turned and dragged off the sheet. "You don't have to like it."

My lungs went hard. It was a hollow figure, woven like a cage from wire and what looked like bits of old telephone. My mother had melted and poured copper over the head and shoulders. It had dripped down, into the torso, running over a heart that was suspended somehow in empty space and glowed dully under the lights. She had made me eight feet tall, beautiful, and stronger than I was before. I told her I was fine with the metaphor. And in the shed, before we went out, I told her she was right—the things she had said on the phone and in her letter. I have been loved every day of my adult life. I have been unbearable but I have never been unloved. I have felt alone but I have never been alone and I've been forgiven for the unforgiveable things I have done.

I can't say I have forgiven the things that were done to me—not because I haven't. Just because, Ingrid says and it is true, people who talk about how they've forgiven others sound so arseholey.

*

My mother's sculpture is too big to be in a house. Supposedly, I am being sniffed by the Tate lot.

*

Patrick and I are not living together.

The same day we'd said goodbye to each other in a corridor surrounded by our own furniture, Patrick turned up at Goldhawk Road and said, both of us standing outside the house, that he wanted me to move back into the flat.

I rushed forward, expecting that he would hug me but he didn't and I withdrew my arms.

He said sorry. "I meant, and I will live somewhere else."

I asked him what he was proposing in that case, if he wanted me as a tenant.

"No, Martha. I'm just saying if we're going to do this, I feel like we have to be careful. Two people who have ruined each other's lives shouldn't get a second go at it. But while we're trying to—"

"Please don't say trying to make things work."

"Fine. Whatever we're trying to do, while we're doing it, I don't want you to have to live with your parents."

I told him his idea was weird. "But okay."

I went inside, got my things, and Patrick drove me home.

Winsome invited him to stay at Belgravia but he rented a studio. It is non-depressing, and most of the time he is here. We talk about various things: if the hinge on the dishwasher door can be fixed or not; how two people who have ruined each other's lives can be together again.

When people discover that you and your husband were separated for a time but have since reconciled, they put their head on the side and say, "Clearly you never stopped loving him deep down." But I did. I know I did. It is easier to say yes, you're so right, because it is too much work to explain to them that you can stop and start again from nothing, that you can love the same person twice.

*

Patrick woke up when the shit remake had finished and started looking for his shoes. I did not want him to go. I said, "Do you want to watch Bake Off with me?"

We watched the episode with the Baked Alaska. He hadn't seen it.

At the end, I told him that Ingrid still thinks the saboteur took it out of the fridge on purpose. Patrick said there was no way. He said, "She just made a mistake because the pressure is so extreme." I smiled at him—a man who can work all day in intensive care, then characterize the pressure on a contestant in Dessert Week as extreme. He asked me what I thought. I told him I had been on the fence but now I could see it was no one's fault.

We said goodbye to each other in the hall, he kissed the top of my head, and told me he would come back tomorrow. I went to bed. I still think it is weird. There are days when I cannot bear it, days when he says it feels like nothing has changed, and days when it feels to both of us like so much has been lost it is beyond repair. But we are together in, Patrick says, injury time—time we are not entitled to—and so we are grateful. He has started referring to the studio as the Hotel Olympia.

I don't have a baby. There is no Flora Friel. I am forty-one. Maybe there never will be, but I have hope, and either way, Patrick is always just there.

A Note on the Text

.

The medical symptoms described in the novel are not consistent with a genuine mental illness. The portrayal of treatment, medication, and doctors' advice is wholly fictional.

Acknowledgments

Catherine. And James. Libby, Belinda, and the staff, and free-lancers, of HarperCollins. Ceri, Clare, and Ben. Fiona, Angie, Kate, the Huebscher family, Laurel, and Victoria. Clementine and Beatrix. Andrew. Thank you.

And my aunt Jenny, who was all my Christmases growing up.

About the Author

MEG MASON is a journalist who began her career at *The Times* and has since written for *The New Yorker, GQ,* and *The Sunday Telegraph*. Her work appears regularly in *Vogue, Stellar, ELLE,* and *Marie Claire.*